Faith

in the

Floodwaters

My Name Will Never Fade

–Book 2–

MICHAEL WINSTELL

Faith in the Floodwaters
My Name Will Never Fade–Book 2

© 2023 by Michael Winstell
www.michaelwinstell.com

All photography by Jennifer Conti
www.jennyvphotography.com
Cover model: Savannah Martin
Photographs used by permission.

Set in EB Garamond 12.

This book is a work of fiction.
All people, places, events, and situations are products of the author's imagination or are used in a satirical or non-literal manner. Any resemblance to persons, living or dead, or actual events or locales is purely coincidental.

For my mother, Linda.

Praise God for your faith.

Books by Michael Winstell

He Calls Me by Name

Serenity Hope

Chastity Grace

Charity Joy

Amy (A Short Story)

My Name Will Never Fade

Destiny in the Dust Storms

Faith in the Floodwaters

Patience in the Plague (coming soon)

Chapter One

July 1888
Johnstown, Pennsylvania

"ALLAN CHARLES SHELTON! If you run me into a wall, I swear before heaven that you'll sleep on the floor for a week!"

Allan kept his hands over her eyes. "Dear wife, would I ever do such a thing to you?"

Faith Shelton groped the air with her hands, unable to hold back her smile. "You bumped my head on the threshold after our wedding, remember?"

"I do. Just a few more steps."

"I feel like a fool!"

"That's what all these people watching you must think."

"What?" Faith tried to wriggle out of her husband's grasp to look around but he kept his hands in place.

"I'm joking!" he laughed, turning her head forward again. "There's no one watching. Please, just two more steps."

Faith pursed her lips.

If this isn't the best surprise of my life, he's going to be on the floor for a month!

Her foot struck a stone step.

"Up we go," Allan said.

Faith walked up the step, noticing that the surface beneath her feet felt different– textured, alternating between hard and soft. Grass and stone. Her heart was racing now and she trembled with excitement.

I want to look!

"Keep your eyes closed," Allan said as he slowly pulled his hands away.

Faith bit her lip and squeezed her eyes shut.

Say it say it say it say it...

"Okay," Allan whispered in her ear. "Look now."

Faith opened her eyes and gasped.

It was the most beautiful house she had ever seen, a tall red-brick Victorian masterpiece. A stone walkway led up to a massive front porch with columns supporting a balcony on the second floor. The roof was peaked at the center, flanked by two regal towers. Large windows bordered by elaborate shutters spanned the structure and delicately carved flourishes adorned the eaves. Large bushes bursting with flowers surrounded the house and broad-leafed trees shaded the lush carpet of grass. A wrought-iron fence topped with *fleur-de-lis* encircled the property.

Faith turned around. Allan was grinning ear-to-ear.

"What do you think?" he asked, spreading his arms wide.

"It's...it's amazing! Is it really ours?"

Allan nodded.

"Can we go inside?" she asked.

"Of course! It's our house."

Faith clasped her hands together and hurried up the walkway. Her hard-soled shoes clicked on the stone steps leading up to the wraparound porch. She ran her hand over the columns and envisioned herself on a warm Sunday afternoon in a cushioned rocking chair, sipping on a glass of fresh-squeezed fruit juice and enjoying the blossoming garden. Curling her arm around one of the columns, she swung herself around to look at her darling husband, who still stood out on the walkway.

She beckoned him with a grin and he ascended the steps. His strong hands gripped her waist and pulled her close to him. Faith wrapped her arms around his neck and stared into his eyes, mesmerized by their gray-green hue.

"I'm in love with this place," she whispered, "and I haven't even been inside yet."

Allan's eyes sparkled as he rushed over to the door. Faith studied the ornate woodwork, noting the intricate patterns carved into the heavy double doors inlaid with stained glass. She leaned forward to get a better look and spotted the decorative "S" half-hidden in the fragmented glass panes.

"Your home awaits, my lady," Allan said as he turned the door handle.

Faith took a deep breath to calm her nerves. She gave Allan a giddy smile and walked through the front door.

For the second time, her breath was taken away.

A spectacular chandelier hung in the two-story front hall and a river of marble flooring swept into the house, terminating at the foot of a bifurcated staircase that spread out like a ballgown. The walls were stained wooden panels and the windows let in a great deal of light, making the space feel open and airy. There weren't any furnishings and the walls were bare, but Faith could already imagine hosting fancy parties with elegant guests reclining on fashionable furniture and admiring the tapestries, window dressings, and artwork.

She stood in the center of the house and spun around, twirling her silk skirts.

This is unbelievable!

"Quite a place, isn't it?" Allan asked, stepping into the house and shutting the door.

"It's like a dream," Faith said, craning her neck to look at the soaring ceiling. Then she gave him a pouting expression. "Pittsburgh is going to feel so dreary after this."

Allan laughed. "Pittsburgh was always dreary. That's why we are moving to Johnstown."

"Darling," Faith said, fixing him with her eyes, "tell me the truth: are we moving to Johnstown just for me?"

"What do you mean?" Allan asked.

"Your business is in Pittsburgh. Your father is there. Your life."

"You are my life."

A warm blush spread across Faith's cheeks. "But I will be with you wherever we live."

"I know you don't want to stay in Pittsburgh. And frankly, neither do I. Look at this place! Would you rather keep on living in the seventh floor of a fifty-year-old building overlooking a dirty river, or would you want to live here in the shadow of green mountains?"

"I want to live here," Faith whispered, moving close. "With you. My husband."

A sly grin crossed Allan's face.

"Would you like to see upstairs?"

"What's upstairs?"

"Oh, the usual...closets, bath chamber, sitting room. And yours and my bedchambers, of course."

"Bedchambers, you say?" Faith raised an eyebrow. "I suppose we must go and have a look."

Allan took her hand and they walked up the grand staircase together, their footfalls echoing throughout the empty house.

****

The sun was starting its downward trek to the horizon as they walked through the garden behind the house. Scents of gardenias and jasmine drifted through the air, intoxicating Faith's senses, which were still reeling from the beauty of the house itself. She had been especially delighted to discover that her bedchamber was a grand space flooded with sunlight, with an adjoining boudoir. Allan also had a bedroom, though hers was more inviting, which suited her fine because she hated sleeping alone. There were two other bedrooms on the second floor and one more in the attic for servants' quarters. The parlor, dining room, and drawing room were spacious and elegant, perfect for entertaining large numbers of guests. Faith didn't yet know anyone in Johnstown but she planned to change that very soon.

She looked over at her husband walking beside her. Allan Shelton, Jr. was the picture of the modern American businessman in her estimation: dignified, intelligent, strong features, well-dressed, but still exuding a rugged personality, as if he could at any moment fling aside his top hat and waistcoat and jump on a horse and ride off into the sunset like those barely-civilized cowboys she had heard about out West. Perhaps it was her country upbringing, but she wasn't attracted to dainty men like those pink-skinned European types lounging about and spending their family's royal money.

Allan was still plenty sophisticated, though. His father had seen to that, securing a place for him at Princeton and then in the family metalworks business, which had recently been absorbed by Andrew Carnegie's Iron and Steel Works. Faith often wondered what her husband was like before she had met him at that banquet three years ago. She'd heard tales of the wild Princeton parties and she didn't delude herself with the notion that her husband had remained a chaste and studious young man. Allan never shared any intimate details of his collegiate days with her, though at social events, she would often find him among his old friends, laughing the sort of laughter that usually accompanies lewd tales.

None of that mattered, though. He was all hers now. No doubt many women had tried to catch his favor and some may have succeeded for a time, but when it came to marriage, he chose her — a poor girl from the northern Allegheny Mountains who had found her way into the upper echelons of society.

Of course, she had a few secrets of her own about how she got there in the first place...

A gentle summer breeze followed them along a half-hidden walkway to a small gazebo tucked beneath a cluster of poplar trees. Allan took her hand and sat down beside her. She stared into his eyes, absolutely in love with him and feeling absolutely foolish about it.

They had only been married for eight months, and she was happy to discover that his fondness for her grew deeper and stronger with each passing day. Sometimes she wondered if she was really in a dream, and the thought of waking up terrified her.

He brushed a strand of hair away from her eyes. She touched his hand and pressed it against her cheek.

"I don't deserve you," she said.

"You're right," he answered. "You deserve so much more."

Faith smiled.

"I'm still speechless," she said. "Is this really our home?"

"Yes, my love. When we get back to Pittsburgh, I will have the movers start packing up the apartment. We'll need a lot of new furniture, so while I am getting all the paperwork taken care of at the office, you can do some shopping."

"Can we afford all this?"

Allan rested his hand over hers.

"There is no price on your happiness. And I know how much you dislike Pittsburgh. Honestly, I could do with a change of scenery myself. I will have to make frequent trips back, but I will spend every moment I can here with you."

"What about your father?"

"What about him?"

"How does he feel about you moving away?"

Allan's eyes fell. Faith's eyes widened.

"You haven't told him yet?" she exclaimed.

"I...I..."

Allan's words faltered. He paused for a moment and looked up at the gazebo roof.

"I know what he would say if I had asked him beforehand. And it wasn't easy, believe me. I still feel plenty guilty, and I know he'll want to tan my hide when I get around to telling him. I also haven't told him about my new position at Cambria Iron Company, but seeing as Mr. Morrell gave me the job personally, I don't think Father will be able to raise too much of a fuss."

"The important thing is that you're making your own decisions. You can't live in your father's shadow forever."

"He'd like it if I did. I don't know if I'll ever grow big enough to make it on my own."

"Allan." Faith touched his face with a gentle hand. "You are a good man. I love you. We are going to make a happy life together. Everything else doesn't matter much."

He nodded slowly, his eyes gazing off into the unfocused distance. Then he rose to his feet, pulling her up with him.

"Do you like the house?"

"I've already told you a dozen times I do!"

Allan ran his finger over her nose. She loved it when he did that.

"I'm so relieved," he said. "Honestly, I've been terrified all day.

17

The only person I'm more afraid of disappointing than my father is you."

Faith embraced his shoulders and lay her head against his chest. "You could never disappoint me, Allan Shelton."

He put his arms around her and they held each other in silence for a couple of minutes, surrounded by lush flowers and fluttering butterflies. Faith could hear his heartbeat, deep and rhythmic. He seemed invincible to her. His father was a stout and commanding man but the son was destined for even greater things. She knew that Allan was going to leave a lasting legacy and she was thrilled to be a part of it.

Then she did something she didn't do all that often. She prayed.

Thank You Lord for this wonderful man, my husband. Please bless our life together, and please give him peace.

She looked up into his eyes and thought he looked a little more relaxed than just a moment ago. Had God really answered her prayer that quickly?

"How do you feel?" she asked.

Allan kissed her forehead. "When I'm with you, I feel at peace."

"You said that even after we move here, you will still have to travel back to Pittsburgh."

"Yes, but only when it is absolutely necessary. The telegraph is a remarkable invention. Besides, I am confident that you will turn this place into a palace of comfort and tranquility."

A piercing whistle shrieked in the distance, vaporizing the romance in the air.

"That's the one-hour whistle," Allan groaned. "We need to start heading back to the station."

Faith nodded, casting one last yearning glance around the garden. "I can hardly stand the thought of going back to Pittsburgh after seeing all this."

"All the more reason to hasten the move. I suspect that we will be residents of Johnstown in a matter of weeks."

Arm-in-arm, they strolled out of the garden back to the front gate where the carriage was waiting for them in the same spot when it had brought them to the house a couple of hours earlier, though the driver was now different. The coachman hopped down from his perch and opened the door when they approached.

"Train station, sir?"

"Straight away," Allan replied as he helped Faith into her seat and sat down on the opposite bench. The coachman closed the door, climbed back into the driver's seat, and gave the reins a gentle tug. The horse obediently plodded forward, its shod hooves clopping loudly on the cobblestone street.

Faith settled onto the bench and stared out the window at the beautiful house that would soon be their home. Watching it disappear down the street was like leaving a new friend she had just met. To keep from feeling glum, she turned her attention to the small yet bustling community of Johnstown. When she and her husband had arrived this

19

morning, they had taken a carriage through the town and seen a few of the prominent landmarks, such as City Hall and St. John's Church and Central Park on Main Street. Before heading to their new house, they had stopped for lunch at a quaint little cafe, and it was there that Faith found herself falling in love with the town. It was so green compared to Pittsburgh, which was choked with smoke billowing from countless steel factory smokestacks. Of course, Johnstown had plenty of factories and smelters and boilers, but those were concentrated in the upper region of the town, leaving the downtown district relatively smoke-free and pleasant.

Faith had also been taking stock of the townspeople. Few were opulently dressed, at least compared to the Pittsburgh crowd, but there was an ease about them that was absent from their big-city counterparts. It took her a few minutes to realize the difference: people in Johnstown actually smiled.

As the carriage bumped and jostled its way down the street, Faith studied the faces of the people once more. She felt a strange kinship with them, and part of her wanted to stick her head out the window and declare, *"I'm one of you now! I have a house up the street!"*

No one would have cared, of course, and many probably wouldn't have understood her. She was surprised to discover that a sizable portion of Johnstown residents were first-generation immigrants from Denmark and Germany, and the Irish might as well have been speaking a foreign language too. Pittsburgh was also a cultural melting pot but somehow that city seemed to absorb its residents into its collective identity. Yet here in Johnstown, cultural distinctions seemed to thrive, as evidenced by the variety of languages on storefront windows and the delicious aromas of unfamiliar food. Pittsburgh was a giant American industrial machine, while Johnstown exuded a romantic European flourish.

Perhaps Johnstown is where I will finally feel at home...

Her head rested against the seat back as she watched the life outside the carriage window. This place was wonderful, but she knew she would have to make an effort to convince Allan to feel the same. Despite his kind words, she knew that Pittsburgh was in his blood. She looked over at him sitting across from her, his nose buried in the *Pittsburgh Gazette.* No doubt checking on his holdings in oil, coal, and of course, steel.

Faith smiled to herself and rested her chin on her hand. That was Allan, always thinking about business. He was happy to spoil her, which she didn't mind at all. And he was also a surprisingly romantic and tender person, contrary to the personalities of most businessmen she had come across. His mother had died when he was a child and she could only imagine what kind of woman could tolerate a man like Allan Shelton, Sr., her father-in-law. That man didn't have a gentle bone in his boulder-sized body.

The thought of the inevitable confrontation between father and son about this move to Johnstown worried her. Her husband was

21

head-strong and confident, but Shelton Sr. was a force of nature.

A knot tightened in her stomach. She wished she had asked Allan if their new house was fully paid for or if it was being financed. Her gaze turned toward the window again and the fear multiplied. What if Allan's father refused to let them leave? What if she found herself imprisoned in Pittsburgh forever? What if this was all taken away from her?

"Dear, are you all right?"

She looked at Allan, covering her startled expression with one of calmness. She had always been very good at masking her true feelings.

"Of course," she answered, smoothing a wrinkle in her skirt. "Why?"

Allan folded his newspaper on his lap and narrowed his eyes. "You had that look you get sometimes."

"What look?"

"Like your mind is racing faster than a locomotive."

Maybe her masks weren't as good as she thought...

"I'm just taking it all in," she said, gesturing toward the window. "Thinking about our new life here." After a nearly imperceptible pause, she added, "I hope you didn't have to sell too many stocks to pay for our new home."

Allan laughed. "Don't you fret none about that," he said. He held up the newspaper and pointed to an article. "Besides, when the new factory opens in Conemaugh, I'll have enough this time next year to buy us another home."

"Another home? But why?"

"Why not? And I don't mean a true home; maybe a summer house. Or a winter house. I'm quite tired of snow, to be honest. I hear Savannah, Georgia is lovely in the winter."

Faith reached out and put her hand on his knee.

"One thing at a time."

Allan grinned. "Quite right. As always."

A train whistle shrieked and Allan knocked on the carriage wall.

"Faster," he commanded.

The driver snapped the reins and the horse sped up to a canter. The carriage bounced and rocked, tossing Faith around her seat. Allan chuckled and squeezed in next to her, folding her in his arms. Paying no mind to her hat or hair, she rested her head on his chest.

Please, she prayed, *don't ever let this go away.*

Chapter Two

THE TRAIN LURCHED forward, jolting Faith awake. She looked around the first-class car, which was about half-full with passengers. Allan was seated across from her, reading the *Philadelphia Herald.*

Faith blinked and rubbed her eyes. She didn't realize that she had dozed off in the short span of time between boarding and departure for Pittsburgh. As the train began picking up speed, she looked out the window, which afforded an elevated view of Johnstown since the tracks were built into the hillside. From this higher vantage point, she could get a better sense of the city's layout. When she and Allan had arrived this morning, the valley was blanketed in fog, so this was her first chance to get a clear view.

Johnstown was definitely a work in progress. There were some regions that were well-maintained and manicured, such as the area where their new home was located, about half a mile from the riverbank. On the other side of the river was the industrial part of town, a smattering of clapboard houses and factories with gushing smoke-stacks. The wind seemed to be continuously blowing roughly north-east, carrying the smoke away from the wealthier areas.

Just think, she told herself. *Soon you won't have breathe that foul Pittsburgh air anymore!*

She raised her eyes to look at the hills across the valley. They weren't particularly high, but they made a sort of hedge all around the community, like it was its own little world. That was another thing that she wasn't too fond of about Pittsburgh – it was constantly build-ing, changing, and growing, always too quickly.

She really couldn't complain, though. Making the journey to Pittsburgh when she was just eighteen had been the best decision she had ever made. She had realized at a young age that she didn't want to spend her life in the highlands of northwestern Pennsylvania, and she realized soon after that she had been blessed with beauty, which meant that she could make men do what she wanted. Nearly every boy in her little village tried his hand at courting her but Faith wasn't going to let herself get tied down to a small farm on a mountainside somewhere.

And when Mama died, there wasn't any reason to stay.

"Tea, madam?"

Faith flinched with surprise and the concierge recoiled, though his hand was steady enough to keep the teacup from spilling.

"I'm sorry," Faith stammered. "Just...admiring the view."

The concierge smiled. "Quite all right, madam. Tea? We also

26

have juice, tonic, water, bran – "

"Tea is fine."

Faith took the cup and saucer and set it on the small table next to her chair. The concierge offered a bowl with sugar cubes and Faith took two. She waved away the milk.

"Anything else, madam? Sandwiches, cheese, fruit?"

"No, thank you," Faith answered, watching the sugar dissolve into her tea.

"Very good, madam. And for you sir?"

"Coffee," Allan said without looking up from his paper.

"Right away, sir."

The concierge hurried off. Faith continued to stir her tea and Allan folded his paper down.

"Everything all right, dear?" he asked.

Faith gave him a fleeting smile. "Yes. I'm fine. I was just..."

"Just what?"

Faith sighed. "Thinking of my mama. I don't know why."

Allan crossed his legs and settled back in his chair. "Do you miss her?"

"I suppose. Sometimes she'll just pop into my head, or something will remind me of her. It's been more than four years since she died. I don't doubt that she would have hated life in Pittsburgh, but now we've got this beautiful house in a new town with lovely green hills and a peaceful river...I just wish she could see me now so I could ask her – "

"If she's proud of you?"

"Yes."

"I'm sure she'd be proud of you. What mother wouldn't? You have everything that a woman could want."

Faith touched his hand. "Almost everything."

Their fingers toyed with each other. Faith could feel warmth spreading across her skin and she found herself wishing they were back home in Pittsburgh right now, and the housemaid was out on errands and they had the apartment to themselves...

The concierge returned with a steaming cup of coffee. Allan gave Faith's hand one last squeeze and set the coffee down after taking a sip. Then he sat back in his chair and snapped the newspaper open. Faith drank her tea and looked out the window, watching the trees scroll past with a whisper. The city of Johnstown had disappeared from view, though she could still see the valley and the river running through it. After spending most of her life on farmland and in forests, Faith hadn't thought much about the beauty of nature. But three years in Pittsburgh had changed that, and now she was filled with delight at the sight of rolling hills and blue skies dotted with puffy white clouds.

I want to see this every day, she thought to herself.

Another voice spoke up in her heart.

You used to, before you abandoned your home and went search-

28

ing for a new life.

Faith pursed her lips and told the voice to hush. She looked down at the fine silks she wore, and at the opulent lounge car she was riding in, and the handsome and wealthy man that she was married to.

I found my new life. And I love it.

The voice in her heart didn't raise any objection. A proud smile turned up the corners of her lips.

She was right where she wanted to be.

****

Pittsburgh was about eighty miles from Johnstown and the train ride took two-and-a-half hours. Dusk had fallen by the time the train pulled into the Pittsburgh & Lake Erie Railroad Station, a proud granite monument to the railroad's industrial power.

The train whistle blew and Faith awoke with a start.

I fell asleep again?

A sticky strand of saliva tethered her hand to her cheek, which she had apparently been leaning on while she slept. Mortified, she hastily wiped her face and hand with her kerchief, looking around to see if anyone had noticed. She often found herself falling asleep at awkward moments, like an old man.

Allan put his newspaper down on the table. Faith supposed that he had been reading it during the entire journey. He probably didn't even realize that she had fallen asleep.

She reached out for his hand.

"Are you hungry, darling?" she asked.

Allan helped her to her feet.

"A bit," he said, looking around. "You can go on home ahead of me. I think I'll pop by the office for a moment and take a look at some charts for – "

Faith touched his face and brought his eyes level with hers. "The office can wait till the morning," she whispered. "Come home with me."

Allan stared into her eyes and brought her hand to his lips. "As you wish, my lady."

They stepped out of the car onto the platform, which was already crowded with disembarking passengers. Allan kept a firm grip on Faith's hand as they made their way to the exit, squeezing through the crush of people. Faith used her other hand to hold her hat down on her head and she gasped with surprise when a large man bumped into her without so much as an apology.

I can't wait to leave here, she grumbled to herself.

The air tasted of soot and a dim haze blanketed the street outside the station. Faith swallowed hard and squared her jaw. This was still home for a while longer, and she wasn't going to let the Steel City get the better of her.

"Quite a bit different from Johnstown, eh?" Allan said.

"Yes," Faith said quietly, like she was admitting a secret. "I miss the trees already."

"We'll go for a walk in the park tomorrow morning."

"After church?"

Allen hesitated. "Of course. After church."

Faith gave him a grateful smile. He only went to church because of her, though she hardly knew why she went herself, except perhaps out of duty ingrained in her since she was a child. Her father had died when she was just a baby and her mother had raised her and her sister Mary Beth on a steady diet of daily Bible readings. Even after her sister caught a fever and died when she was thirteen and Faith felt like her whole world was falling apart, her mother held onto God's word, her nose buried in its pages day and night. Just like Allan and his stock re-ports.

Entering the rowdy world of the *nouveau riche* and climbing the social ladder had left Faith's conscience with more than a few stains, which was probably another reason why she sought solace in going to church. She was no saint, but God couldn't hold that against her for-ever, could He?

Allan whistled sharply for a carriage as the two of them exited the depot. Faith looked around at the gas-lit streets teeming with activity. Even in the twilight, every shoe, whether human or horse, stirred up black dust. Stifling a cough, she pressed a kerchief to her mouth. Just a day spent in Johnstown's fresh air had made her lungs fragile.

Allan, on the other hand, seemed to be completely in his element. Faith noticed how he stood up straighter and lifted his chin, like he was a prince surveying his kingdom. And in some respects he was. Men like him were the future leaders of this country.

A carriage pulled up to the curb and the driver jumped down.

"Madam," he said as he opened the door.

"Thank you," Faith murmured, scrambling inside the carriage. She didn't know why she suddenly felt flustered but her anxiety evaporated when Allan climbed in alongside her and the carriage started moving. A weary sigh escaped her lips and she laid her head on his shoulder.

It didn't matter where she was as long as she was with him.

****

The carriage came to a halt in front of a stately apartment building on Grant Street. Faith stared out the window at the polished brass door and smartly-dressed doorman standing at attention. It was a sight she had seen almost daily for the last six months, but it felt different somehow. Like she was looking at a hotel and not her home.

Allan put his hand on her knee.

"Doesn't feel the same, does it?"

Faith grinned. *How does he always know what I'm thinking?*

The carriage door swung open and the driver offered his hand to help her out. Standing on the sidewalk, she craned her neck and looked up at the towering building and she thought about the seven flights of stairs to get to their apartment. Some of the newer buildings in town had electric elevators but this building was constructed before the War Between the States and had no such amenities. Faith had little trouble keeping a trim figure with the exercise.

Images of the big, beautiful house waiting for her in Johnstown drifted through her mind and she made a face as she stared up at the soot-streaked granite facade. Allan came alongside her and looked up as well.

"Ready to climb the mountain?"

Faith groaned and leaned on his arm. The doorman opened the door for them with a smile as they walked into the elegant lobby. It wasn't the fanciest apartment building in the city but it certainly tried to make an impression with its fashionable flourishes and copies of European masterpieces. A marble sculpture of Venus de Milo topped a burbling fountain in the center of the lobby. Faith had always felt it was a bit inappropriate for public display, and as she walked past, she felt relief that she wouldn't have to look at it for too much longer.

A young man behind a desk nodded as they walked toward the stairs, where another young man opened a second door for them. Faith took a deep breath and lifted her dress as she followed her husband up the stairs. Several people were also going up or down, and the stairs were wide enough to accommodate two people at a time, but there were a few traffic jams when women with wide skirts would have to pass by one another. Luckily there was a server waiting on the landing of the fourth floor with a tray filled with cups of water. Faith took a cup and drank greedily. She looked down over the railing and shook her head.

Why did people enjoy living up so high? And why couldn't Allan have rented an apartment on the second or third floor?

None of that matters, she told herself. In a few weeks, she wouldn't be living at the top of a soot-stained box. She would have a spacious house and a luxurious garden all to herself.

With sweaty brows and burning leg muscles, they finally made it to the seventh floor. Faith dreaded the thought of having to go back down for church tomorrow and then come back up again, but at least they were home now. Allan opened the door that led out of the stairwell and she stepped onto the carpeted hallway. It was much more quiet than the stairs where every footfall echoed like a gong. The hallway was almost completely silent except for occasional muffled voices coming from behind hand-carved mahogany doors.

The first thing Faith wanted to do was slip into a warm bath. She hoped and prayed that Meredith, their housemaid, already had a pot of water at a boil. And that the plumbing pipes were working reliably today to pump enough water for a bath into their home. When the residents on the lower floors used their taps, sometimes barely a trickle reached up to their apartment.

A sense of relief washed over her when she saw their door, number 707. Allan pulled a jangly cluster of keys from his pocket and slipped one into the lock, but he paused before opening the door.

"What is it?" Faith asked.

Allan frowned. "It's unlocked."

Faith furrowed her brow as well. Meredith knew to keep the door locked whether she was inside or out running errands, and she had never forgotten even once, despite being almost sixty years old.

"Stay behind me," Allan said, hunching his shoulders and balling his hand into a fist. Faith hadn't considered the possibility that there was an intruder in the house, and suddenly she felt afraid. She stood behind him and put her hand on his back for reassurance.

Allan turned the handle and opened the door as quietly as he could. Cigar smoke gushed through the opening.

Faith looked puzzled.

Who is smoking in our – ?

Allan pushed the door open all the way.

"Hello, Father."

Through the haze, Faith saw a very large man standing in front of the glowing fireplace.

Mr. Allan Charles Shelton, Sr.

He turned around, holding a thick cigar between equally thick fingers. He was dressed in a very expensive suit that looked like it might burst its buttons at any minute. His waxed gray mustache rose

35

like wingflaps as he smiled and held out his hands.

"My boy!" he said in a booming voice. "Welcome home."

His hawk-like eyes fixed on Faith. "And you as well, my dear."

Faith dipped her head. "Thank you, sir."

Allan took his wife's hat and hung it up on the hat rack along with his own. "What are you doing here, Father? And where is Meredith?"

Mr. Shelton waved his hand, scattering cigar embers. Faith watched them carefully to make sure they were extinguished before they reached the carpet.

"I sent her out to procure tonight's dinner," he said, ambling over to the sofa and taking a seat. The furniture groaned as if in pain.

Allan glanced at Faith. "You're dining with us tonight?"

"Of course! This is a night for a celebration!"

"A celebration?"

Mr. Shelton's eyes flashed. He leaned forward and set his cigar on an ashtray on the glass coffee table in front of him.

"Have a seat, son. Faith, my dear, would you be a doll and fetch some coffee for us? Two lumps of sugar for me, please."

A taut smile stretch Faith's cheeks. "Of course. For you, darling?" she asked her husband.

Allan waved her away, keeping his eyes on his father. "None for me."

Faith nodded and walked through the dining room to the

kitchen. Once out of sight, she clenched her jaw and inhaled through her nose. This was not what she expected to come home to.

Faith filled a kettle with water and put it on the stove. Then she groaned.

There wasn't any fire in the firebox. She opened the small door and poked the ashes, unearthing a few glowing embers. There was a pile of kindling and small logs in the corner but it would take several minutes for the fire to get hot enough to bring the kettle to a boil. She glanced over her shoulder toward the living room and chewed on her bottom lip for a moment.

Allan and his father looked up as Faith strode into the room holding a gleaming silver platter with two tall glasses of lemonade. She set the platter on the table between them and handed each man a glass.

"We seem to be out of coffee," she announced, avoiding eye contact with either of them. "But I find that a lemon beverage can be even more stimulating than coffee, especially with a splash of brandy."

Mr. Shelton's eyes lit up and he took a generous sip.

"That's mighty fine, my dear." He turned back to Allan. "Your mother, God rest her soul, never brought me lemonade with brandy."

"Probably because she drank all the brandy," Allan grumbled, setting his glass aside without drinking it.

Faith stood between them, her hands folded dutifully.

"Can I get you gentlemen anything else?"

Mr. Shelton opened his mouth but Allan headed him off.

"Have a seat, darling. You just had a long trip. Besides, Father was just going tell me how he knows so much about the recent developments in our life."

Faith sat down on a French-style wingback chair and looked at her father-in-law, who took another gulp of lemonade. He plucked his cigar from the ashtray and settled back on the sofa, which creaked dangerously.

"Okay, you've got me," he declared before blowing a massive cloud of smoke into the air. Faith began to strategize how she could politely get up and open a window.

Allan's face grew dark. "Father...what did you do?"

Mr. Shelton grinned and pointed his cigar at Allan. "Never let it be said that I didn't do everything I could for my one and only son. A courtesy I expect you will extend to your own progeny, which I hope won't be too far in the future." He shot a disapproving glance toward Faith.

"Father," Allan said slowly as he rose to his feet, "tell me you didn't get me the job at Cambria Iron Company in Johnstown."

"Of course I did."

Allan groaned and walked over to the fireplace. Faith felt nervous.

What is going on?

"You couldn't let me do one thing by myself, could you?" Allan spat. "Just one thing?"

Mr. Shelton stood up. "Son, I know the people in this city. They'll eat you alive. You're still too young to play their games. I had to get you out so you can build up your strength. Then, when you're ready, you're going to come back to Pittsburgh and show them what we Sheltons are made of."

"Then why did you let me think that it was my own doing? I feel like a fool!"

"Because if I told you the plan, you would have dragged your feet and possibly even turned down the job. But look what you did, all on your own I might add. You bought a very nice house within two weeks! Would you have been that excited if you knew that it was me who had gotten you the job there?"

"But why Johnstown? Why Cambria Iron?"

"Because Johnstown is going to be the next Pittsburgh. And because just a few miles up river, there is a little place called the South Fork Fishing and Hunting Club. Have you heard of it?"

"I've heard the name."

"You'll be hearing a lot more of it. That club is where all the big boys go to play. The Carnegies, the Fricks, the Mellons, the Husseys, all coming to your backyard during the spring and summer. Do you have any idea what a great opportunity this is?"

Allan sighed and hung his head. Faith rose from her seat and walked over to him, putting a comforting hand on his arm. She turned around and glared at her father-in-law.

"Your son isn't a puppet on a string."

Mr. Shelton exhaled a billow of smoke.

"I don't recall asking your opinion," he said with a smirk. "Besides, tell me I'm wrong. Both of you. Tell me this isn't what both of you want. Huh? Does it matter who made it happen? No. What matters is that it is happening. Allan, son, I want you to fill my shoes one day but you've still got a long way to go. Don't you see? You could rule a place like Johnstown. And don't tell me you wouldn't rather have a nice big house all to yourself, little missy."

Faith pursed her lips and looked away. Mr. Shelton was right, but it hurt her to see Allan's pride crushed like this. He had been so proud of himself, and she could tell that he thought he was finally getting out of his father's shadow, when in fact he had never been more overshadowed.

The front door swung open and Meredith stood in the doorway, holding two large bags of food. The little woman stared through the hazy smoke at the three people standing in the living room.

"I hope everyone's hungry for mutton stew," she said with an uneasy laugh.

****

Dinner was delicious, though hardly anyone at the table spoke a word, either to each other or to compliment the food. The two men sat at opposite ends of the table with Faith in between them on her husband's right. She kept her eyes on her plate but she would occasionally sneak a glance at Allan and see him glowering at his father. Mr. Shelton hardly seemed to notice as he slurped up two large bowls of stew.

When dinner was finished, Meredith proceeded to clean the table while the three of them went to the sitting room. Mr. Shelton lit up another cigar and Faith's eyes pleaded silently with her husband.

Allan smothered a sigh.

"I'm really sorry, Father, but Faith and I have had a long day and we need to retire. Faith insists that we attend church in the morning."

Mr. Shelton shot a condescending look toward Faith and stubbed out his cigar and put it in back in its case.

"Very well. I wish you both a good night's rest. You've earned it."

He went to the door and grabbed his hat and coat. Then he turned around and fixed his eyes on Allan.

"I know you're upset with me, son, but trust me, you will thank me when you realize the track I have set you on. There is no shame in accepting help."

"Except when that help is neither offered nor needed."

Mr. Shelton smiled. "So says the hatchling right before it plummets out of the nest. I don't demean your accomplishments. I've just given you a nudge in the right direction. And I know that you'll go farther than I ever could."

Allan looked away, though Faith could tell he was encouraged by the compliment. She stepped forward and bowed her head.

"Thank you for joining us, Father. And we appreciate everything you've done."

"I know." Mr. Shelton slapped his hat on his head. "Enjoy your church tomorrow."

Faith suppressed a scowl as he exited the apartment and slammed the door with enough force to shake the walls. She closed her eyes and drew in a long, slow breath.

Soon you'll be living eighty miles away from that man.

Allan was slumped in his chair and she went over and knelt beside him.

"Is it really so bad?" she asked gently.

Allan rubbed his forehead and looked off into space. "I suppose not," he mumbled. "And he's probably right about the whole thing. It's just...it's the principle of it. You said it earlier; I feel like his puppet."

Faith reached up and stroked his strong jaw. "He's just jealous of the man you've become and will continue to become. But he also wants to help you. One day, you will be king of the Shelton name. Every son builds on the foundations laid by his father. And you will do the same for your son one day."

42

"I hope I have a little more compassion than that when I'm his age."

"You will," Faith said. She took his hand in hers and pressed it to her cheek. Then she kissed his palm and looked at him with adoring eyes.

He was staring off into space again.

Chapter Three

MEREDITH POKED HER head in the dark doorway. "I'm going home now, madam. Is there anything you'd like me to do before I leave?"

"No, thank you." Faith looked at her in the vanity mirror as she brushed her long brown hair and frowned. She turned around when she saw Meredith fidgeting with her hands. "What is it?"

Meredith stepped into the boudoir. "I don't mean to be eavesdropping, madam. But I couldn't help overhearing you and Master Shelton talking with his father about moving out to Johnstown."

"Yes. Master Allan purchased a home for us there. It was quite a surprise."

"I'm very happy for you, madam."

When she didn't say anything more, Faith clicked her tongue with impatience.

"Meredith, what is it?"

"Well, madam, I'm just wondering what will I do? I was lucky enough to find a job here at my age, and I'm afraid that after you leave, I'll – "

Faith walked over to the little woman and took her hand.

"You don't need to worry about any of that."

"I don't?"

"Of course not. You're coming with us."

Meredith's mouth fell open. "I'm...I'm coming with you? To Johnstown?"

"Unless you'd rather stay in Pittsburgh."

"Heavens, no! I'll gladly come to Johnstown! Please tell me you're serious, madam!"

"Yes, I'm serious. You're indispensable. I don't know anyone in Johnstown and I'll need someone I can trust to manage the house."

"The whole house?"

"Yes. It's a big job, though. Far bigger than this apartment. And there is a garden to tend to as well. You'll have to live in the house, of course."

"Live in the..."

Meredith looked like she was going to faint. Then she squeezed Faith's hands with surprising strength.

"Oh madam, I don't know what to say! It sounds too wonderful to be true."

Faith smiled. "I'm still trying to wrap my head around it. Wait till you see the house. It's like a castle!"

"Lord have mercy!" Meredith fanned herself with her hand. "I won't be able to sleep tonight! When are you planning to move?"

"I'm not entirely sure, but I suspect it will be a few weeks. I'll need plenty of help packing up."

"Just point me in the right direction, madam. I'll have this place buttoned up in two shakes of a lamb's tail!"

"Good. Now go and try to get some sleep. This is still our home for a little while longer, and we'll need to save our strength for the move."

"Okay." Meredith's giddy smile looked like it was going to pop right off her face. "Thank you, madam! You don't know how happy I am. And you can be sure that you will have the cleanest and most orderly castle in Johnstown."

"It's not really a castle," Faith laughed, "but it feels like one. I know you'll do a great job. Now go on home."

"Yes, madam." Meredith turned to leave but she paused. "I will make an extra-special lunch tomorrow when you and Master Shelton get home from church. Something my mother used to make. I've never prepared it before because I wasn't sure if you would like it, but I feel like tomorrow is a cause for celebration and trying new things."

"Sounds wonderful. Good night."

"Good night, madam."

Meredith left the room and Faith finished brushing her hair. Then she stood up and leaned forward to examine her face in the mirror. She noticed a dozen minor flaws but overall, she was pleased with how she looked. She pinched her cheeks to give them a bit of color and then she sprayed a dash of perfume under her neck. After appraising her appearance one more time, she gave herself a smile of approval and took the kerosene lamp with her as she stepped out of the boudoir. Her bare feet tread softly on the long rug that led down the hall to Allan's bedroom. The door was closed but a gentle light shone underneath the gap on the floor.

Allan was reclining on the bed and reading his newspaper when she entered the room.

"He's always been like this, you know," he blurted out, his eyes still fixed on the page. "Treating me like a little schoolboy. He wouldn't let me cross the street without holding his hand until I was ten years old!"

Faith set the lamp on the dresser and went over to the window to draw the curtains shut.

"You're right – he's just jealous," Allan continued, turning the newspaper page. "He came up from nothing so he has to make it as hard as he can for me. It may look like he's handing everything to me on a silver platter, but the message is clear: *he* worked for it, not me. He always wants me to remember that. No matter what, he's in charge. Oh, I'm going to show him one day. I'm going to show him!"

"Allan."

"Hmm?"

"Stop talking."

He looked up from his paper. His eyebrows rose and a grin spread across his face.

****

The warmth from almost two hundred people packed into the First United Presbyterian Church on the corner of 7th and Mason made the sanctuary feel like an oven. Mindful of maintaining the proper tune on "Rock of Ages, Cleft for Me", Faith wiped her damp brow and glanced over at her husband. Allan was almost asleep on his feet. She poked him with her elbow and he snapped his head up, loudly singing the wrong verse. Faith smirked and pointed to the correct place on the hymnal page. Allan gave her a sheepish smile and fell into harmony with her.

It was hard to stay annoyed at him, especially when he had such a good singing voice. He did nod off during the sermon, though. Faith sat up straight, secretly looking around to see if anyone was staring. She prayed that Allan wouldn't start snoring.

When the service was over, she woke him up as gently as she could, and after taking a moment to come to his senses, he accompanied her out of the sanctuary. A brisk wind blew in from the river, stirring up black dust that had accumulated on the cobblestone street. It hadn't rained in almost two weeks and the coating of soot and grime grew thicker each day.

Faith coughed and waved her fan in front of her face.

"Goodness! Can't they hose down the streets or something?"

Allan offered his arm and she took it.

"They do in the neighborhoods where the politicians live," he said as they meandered down the sidewalk.

Faith coughed again and Allan squeezed her arm.

"Just have to grin and bear it for a little while longer, darling."

"How much longer?"

"That depends."

"On what?" Faith asked with a pout.

"There are several matters I need to attend to before I can transfer to my new position at Cambria. It will take some time."

"How much time?"

"A few months."

"A few months? I thought we were going to move to Johnstown in a matter of weeks?"

"This is why it depends on you."

"On me?"

"Faith, you don't have to stay here while I get everything in order. In fact, I think it would be best."

"For me to go to Johnstown without you?"

"Just for a short time, my dear."

Faith shook her head. "I couldn't be away from you that long. I

50

will go mad with missing you."

"But you will have your hands full arranging our new home. Remember what a task it was furnishing our small apartment? This will be a much bigger job."

"I suppose..."

"The time will pass quickly, I promise. And I can come to see you now and then. It's just a hop, skip, and a jump away. But you will languish here if you wait for me to get everything sorted. While I wrap up my business here, you can prepare our home."

Faith clicked her tongue. "All right then. But you better come visit me often. You know I can't stand to be away from you."

"Nor I from you."

"You are very shrewd, Mr. Shelton."

"How so?"

"By waiting to tell me this now instead of last night. It would have spoiled my celebratory mood."

Allan laughed. "Regardless of what my father thinks, I do have a knack for business, and I've learned that one thing is important above all else."

"What is it?"

"Timing."

Faith nodded. "Well, I think it's time you took me home. Meredith is making an extra-special lunch for us."

Allan raised his hand to hail a passing carriage. "Is that so?"

"She was ecstatic when I told her that she would be coming with us to Johnstown."

"Ah, well. I had quite forgotten about the old bird in all of this."

"We couldn't possibly get on without her, especially if I'm going to Johnstown alone."

"Come now, darling, don't rub it in. My heart aches just thinking about it."

Faith took his arm and held him close. She wanted to savor every moment with him.

****

The next three weeks were a dizzying blur.

After making peace with the fact that she was going to Johnstown without her husband, at least for a little while, Faith got busy preparing for the move. That meant packing up their apartment and purchasing items for the new home.

Meredith was a huge blessing. On top of her normal housekeeping duties, she helped Faith clean and pack all of the delicate items on the shelves and take down the pictures from the walls and sort through the linens and fabrics and curtains. Faith was thankful that she and Allan had lived in the apartment for less than a year, which hadn't given them too much time to accumulate a lot of possessions. Yet after growing up in a shack in the Allegheny mountains, she had been determined to surround herself with opulence, and she had spent much of those first months as a married woman perusing the fashionable home decor shops uptown. Allan never objected to anything she bought, regardless of price. Sometimes she would test him to see if there was a limit to his generosity. When he came home to see a four-hundred-dollar painting hanging in the parlor, she kept her eyes glued to his face to analyze his reaction. He had nodded his approval, but Faith clearly caught the tension in his jaw, and guilt began gnawing at her conscience after having spent his hard-earned money on a painting that she didn't even like.

She kept the painting, though. She would never admit defeat.

Now the painting was on the floor, leaning against the wall with half a dozen other pictures. Faith looked around at the crates overflowing with brown wrapping paper. There was still so much to do, so much to sort, not to mention things that needed to be bought for the new house. Some things would have to be purchased in Johnstown but she didn't know what kind of stores she would find there, so she planned to purchase decorations here in Pittsburgh and have them shipped.

Even though she was glad to leave these crowded, coal-dusted streets behind, she was still proud to have made it in this city, and she was going to make sure everyone knew where she was from.

Just hope no one asks you about your childhood.

Faith silenced the cynical voice in her heart. As far as she was concerned, her life began when she stepped off that train three years ago. Everything before that was smoke in the wind.

Right at that moment, her eyes fell upon the Bible on the end table next to the sofa. She didn't know why she hadn't packed it up yet. Taking the weather-beaten book in her hands, she sat down and gently opened the pages. The leather cover was worn smooth but wasn't cracked, and the pages were yellow and crinkled from being left out in the rain many times, yet the words were still vibrant. An earthly smell emanated from the pages, transporting Faith to a place far away from the busy streets of Pittsburgh, to a wooden shack tucked away in a grassy hollow, where a woman with rough hands and sad eyes rocked on a hand-made rocking chair.

As Faith scanned the words, she heard them in her mother's voice.

"And I say unto you, ask, and it shall be given you; seek, and ye shall find; knock, and it shall be opened unto you. For everyone that asketh, receiveth, and he that seeketh findeth; to him that knocketh, it shall be opened."

A droplet of water fell on the page. She gasped and touched her wet cheek.

"Madam? Are you all right?"

Faith looked up and saw Meredith studying her with concern.

"Yes," she muttered, closing the Bible and wiping her eyes. "Just this old dusty book. I suppose it's God's way of telling me I should

54

read it more often."

"That's surely so," Meredith said with a smile. She reached out her hand. "Would you like me to pack it with the other books?"

"Yes, please. Be very gentle."

"Of course, madam."

Meredith took the book and went over to a crate. Faith dabbed her eyes again, groaning at the dark spots on her kerchief. Her makeup was ruined. In her mind's eye, she saw her mother glaring at her with disapproval. Faith shook her head to clear away the image and went to her boudoir to fix her face. A few minutes later, she emerged, looking pretty as a picture.

"Meredith," she called out as she grabbed her hat and gloves. "I'm going out. I will be back for supper."

"Will Master Shelton be home for supper too?"

"I'm sure he will be. Prepare the goose tonight. And remember he likes the dark meat."

"Yes, madam."

After checking the mirror next to the door, Faith stepped out of the apartment. Downstairs, the doorman pulled open a large brass door. Faith stepped outside, her eyes sweeping the street and buildings in front of her. She started walking with no particular destination. She just wanted to think and remember.

When she had first arrived in Pittsburgh, she was so full of defiant energy and excitement, she barely gave any thought to the more practical concerns of daily life, such as money and a place to live. The first thing she did when she got off the train was find a dress shop and buy the most expensive dress she could afford. It wasn't much, but she had compensated by choosing a dress that was hardly modest. She was determined to stand out one way or another. After that, it wasn't difficult to find an audience. Even though her heart was pounding in her chest, she had walked down the street with her head high, stopping at a tavern that looked at least moderately upscale.

The rest was history. Her attractiveness, charm, and wit was enough to ingratiate herself to men with money and an eye for beauty, and she bounced from one mindless job to the next, which was really just a way to pass the time as she built her reputation as a socialite. The aristocratic women were too steeped in their polite ways to be very expressive, and their husbands found Faith captivating because of her outspokenness. After all, she didn't have anything to lose, and this devil-may-care attitude served her well.

The only problem was that men with money always wanted something in return. There were some with whom she became intimately familiar but nothing ever came of it, and thankfully these men eventually moved away, sparing Faith the awkwardness of running into them at parties again. Sometimes when she would be lying in a strange bed, she would stare out the window and wonder what her mother would have thought of her. She told herself that practicality was more important than morality, and when she finally found the right man, any compromises she had made along the way would be worth it.

She told herself this over and over again.

Yet find the right man she did. She met Allan at a New Year's Eve party and she hooked him right away. At first their relationship was one of mutual selfishness: he wanted her for her beauty and she wanted him for his money. But somewhere along the way, love blossomed. Faith tried to hold her feelings for him at bay, knowing that someone of his social status would never marry someone like her, even though her background was still a secret. She knew she had to tell him sooner or later, and one moonlit night as they held each other close, she confessed. Allan told her that he already knew, or rather had made an educated guess, and it didn't change his feelings for her one bit. That was when Faith decided that she wouldn't hold back any of her love for him. They married two weeks before Christmas 1887.

As her life had grown from a dream into a reality, she sometimes heard a stern voice in her conscience. Sometimes it was her mother's voice, and sometimes it was a voice she had never heard before, and it always said the same thing.

What has happened to your faith?

An unusually chilly gust of wind made her gasp, bringing her back to the present moment. She looked around, startled to discover that she was walking along the Allegheny River, just a short distance away from the ruins of Fort Pitt. She had walked nearly a mile and a half without even realizing it. There were a few people around but it was much quieter here than on the busy city streets.

Faith hugged her elbows, feeling a bit nervous. She had never come down here before. Actually, that wasn't true – she had walked along this very spot once with that dashing gentleman from Atlanta during her first summer in Pittsburgh...

She frowned and tried to push the memory out of her mind. Just thinking about it felt like cheating on Allan. Faith huffed in annoyance and hurried down the riverwalk to get back to the street where she could take a carriage home.

There was too much shame here. Johnstown would be the start of a new life.

This thought made her smile as her hard-heeled shoes clacked on the stone sidewalk.

Chapter Four

Early November, 1888
Johnstown, Pennsylvania

A COLD, GENTLE RAIN fell as Faith stood on the front porch of her new home and watched her husband march down the stone walkway to the gate. A carriage waited beside the curb to take him to the train station and back to Pittsburgh for the next couple of weeks. He had only been able to visit her in Johnstown for two nights, but Faith savored every moment with him.

Before he stepped inside the carriage, Allan turned and looked at her. Faith's heart fluttered and she felt the urge to rush down the walkway, throw her arms around his neck, and press a desperate kiss to his lips. But she remained on the porch, calm and composed, the picture of elegance.

He will come back to you. And he will be true while he is away.
You are his home.

The carriage door closed and the horse's hoofbeats clopped

down the street, eventually fading into the sound of the rain. Allan was gone.

Meredith touched Faith's arm.

"Let's go inside, madam. It's quite chilly out here. I'll fetch some tea."

Faith followed the little woman inside and shut the door. Now that the house was filled with furniture and crates and tapestries and pictures and carpets, the door didn't echo as loudly when it was closed, nor did footsteps reverberate throughout the entire house.

She and Meredith had arrived two weeks ago to begin the process of turning the house into a home, while Allan had remained in Pittsburgh. He had commissioned an entire boxcar to transport their belongings to Johnstown, and unpacking everything had been a frightful ordeal, even though Faith had hardly lifted a finger. She was certain that something expensive was going to get broken with how clumsily the hired hands unloaded everything, but miraculously, only three plates met their demise. For the next several days, the house bustled with activity. Carpenters, movers, painters, gardeners, every sort of labor imaginable was going in and out and up and down. Faith felt like she was conducting a chaotic orchestra. Decorating the apartment in Pittsburgh had seemed overwhelming when she was first married but this was an entirely new level of stress.

Yet despite the confusion and chaos, Faith had never felt happier. Slowly but surely, she could see the house taking shape. The work was put on hold during Allan's visit, though she felt a bit guilty for not having the house looking more presentable. Allan had insisted that she pace herself, which made her relax a bit. She was happy to spend her attention on him for a few days rather than on curtains and carpets.

But now, it was just her and Meredith. Faith could already feel Allan's absence. They had never spent more than a few days apart since getting married, and she honestly didn't know how she was going to handle him being away for weeks at a time during this transition.

She glanced around at the boxes and crates that surrounded her and she put her hands on her hips.

Time to get back to work.

****

Johnstown's weather in autumn was similar to Pittsburgh's: damp and dreary. Faith hardly saw the sun during those first couple of weeks, and it rained in some form almost every day. The continuous moisture did help the garden remain lush, but the house would get a musty smell sometimes, especially in rooms with little or no light.

Then one Sunday morning, the sky was blue and the sun shone with cheerful brightness.

"Meredith!" Faith called out. "Get your hat! We're going to

church."

"Where are we going, madam?"

"I don't know yet," Faith answered as she opened her closet and began shuffling through her dresses. "We'll just follow the bells."

The air was filled with the crisp, clear clangs of church bells as the women walked down the street towards the center of town. It had taken Faith the better part of an hour to get ready, and even as she strolled down the shaded sidewalk, she worried that she had chosen the wrong color for the day. She hadn't seen any women wearing light blue.

You haven't seen any women at all, because they're all at church.

Faith couldn't argue with that. She just wanted to make a good impression. This was her first time to be out and about on Sunday, after all. She felt like this was her debutante ball and she needed to give the people of Johnstown a proper introduction.

That was another thing she needed to do: insert herself into the social scene. Considering how small Johnstown was compared to Pittsburgh, she figured her chances of making a name for herself were pretty good, something that was difficult in the well-established pecking order she had left behind. Here, the possibilities were endless. A fresh start. A chance to really shine.

But first, church. As houses gave way to storefronts and hotels, Faith spotted several steeples rising above the rooftops. Her church back in Pittsburgh had been Presbyterian, and she found herself wondering if she should try something new.

"What do you think, Meredith?"

"Madam?"

"Which church should we go into?"

"I have no idea, madam. Which one do you think?"

"I think that one."

"Why, madam?"

"Because it looks very nice and well-kept. That means it's expensive. And that means the people in the congregation have money."

"If you say so, madam."

Faith held her head high and walked with measured steps as she and Meredith crossed the street towards the grand church on the opposite side. There were a few people milling about, mostly laborers by the looks of their clothes, and several of them stopped what they were doing and stared as she walked past. She pretended to ignore their gaping mouths and wide eyes, though she couldn't hide the slight curl of a smile in the corners of her lips.

A handful of people were heading into the church as the bells rang loud and clear from the steeple, and Faith figured they had arrived just in time. As she glided up the steps to the sanctuary door, she spotted a placard affixed to the stone facade that read "First Methodist Episcopal Church."

A peppy young man in a white robe stood just inside the door.

"Welcome," he said, his smile almost painfully bright.

Faith nodded and stepped into the sanctuary, taking a moment to scan the space. It was tastefully decorated in the Gothic Revival style but was nothing like the churches back in Pittsburgh.

She looked at Meredith and gestured to an empty space in the pews at the back.

"You can sit over there," she said quietly.

"What about you, madam?"

Faith cocked an eyebrow. Meredith bowed her head meekly and went to take her seat. Keeping her eyes straight ahead, Faith started walking down the center aisle. The pews were quite full and a number of people in the congregation turned around to take a look at this young lady striding confidently into their midst. A few people whispered and murmured. Faith smiled to herself. She knew her dress was a little too tight and her neckline just a little too low and her makeup just a little too prominent, but she intended to make an impression, and so far, it was working.

About six or seven rows from the front, she stopped and looked at a man with spectacles and wearing a wrinkled suit sitting next to his long-faced wife.

"Might I scoot in here, good sir?"

The man swallowed nervously. He glanced at his wife who gave him a sour look, and then he nodded hesitantly. His wife rolled her eyes and shifted over as much as she could, and her husband pressed in alongside her, clearing a space for Faith to sit down.

"Thank you," she said with a smile.

Thunderous notes bellowed from an organ. Faith rose to her feet with the rest of congregation as a number of people in robes took their places in the choir. A round man with a shock of white hair made his way to the altar.

"Please open your prayer books to page one hundred and twenty-one."

Faith looked down and noticed two books in a small compartment on the back of the pew in front of her. One was black and the other was gray. She didn't know which was the book of prayer and which was the hymnal, and when she saw the man next to her pick up the black book in front of him, she followed suit. She gave him a quick nod and a smile of thanks, and he hastily smiled back, though not before his scowling wife noticed. He cleared his throat loudly and began to read along with the minister. Faith joined in as well.

"O Lord, bless our assembly. Prepare our hearts to sing Thy praises and to heed Thy commands. Thy love is everlasting and fills the Earth with joy and gladness..."

Faith's eyes drifted from the page and she glanced to her left across the aisle. A man with sandy blond hair and a well-trimmed beard was looking at her with a strange sort of smile. It would have been unnerving if he wasn't stunningly handsome. Faith looked back to her prayer book but she snuck one more glance at him when the reading was over. He wasn't looking at her.

The service was simple and a bit boring, but Faith made sure to keep a good posture while she sat. She also wore one of her larger hats, which obstructed the view of those seated behind her. A few grumbled words reached her ears but she didn't mind. She wanted people to be talking about her, and not all of that talk should be positive. Back in Pittsburgh, she had come to realize that jealousy and complaints could raise one's social currency a lot faster than good manners.

After the long-winded sermon was finished and the concluding prayer was offered, the minister bade everyone to go in peace. Faith smothered a sigh of joy and rose from her seat, giving the man next to her one more grateful smile, much to the annoyance of his wife. When Faith looked across the aisle, the handsome man with the beard was nowhere to be seen. She thought nothing more of it and slowly made her way through the sanctuary to find Meredith. Several women complimented her on her dress along the way and she hastily acknowledged their kind words. She didn't plan to stop and chat with anyone; she wanted to keep them guessing. Mystery and intrigue was irresistible to genteel society.

She found Meredith and they walked out of the sanctuary, once again greeted by the impossibly cheerful young man in the white robe.

"Go with God!" he declared with teeth as white as snow.

"The same to you," Faith answered, hurrying down the steps with Meredith.

The man with the beard and sandy blond hair stepped in front of them.

"I beg your pardon, sir," Faith said.

The man tipped his hat. "I beg yours, Mrs. Shelton."

Faith raised one eyebrow. "You know who I am?"

"It's not a secret," he said. "I would wager a number of people in that church know your name."

"Is that so?" Faith gave him what she hoped was a cold glare. "And you are...?"

The man bowed with a flourish. "Stephen Baldwick, at your service."

Faith and Meredith exchanged glances. "Pleased to meet you, Mr. Baldwick," Faith said flatly. "But you still haven't told me how you know my name."

Stephen put his hat back on his head. "I am a colleague of your husband's at the ironworks. Or, at least I will be once he relocates here."

"I see. But how do you know who I am?"

Faith wasn't sure but she thought she saw Stephen blush.

"I hope you don't think me forward, ma'am, but I recognized you."

"Recognized me from what?"

"From the picture."

"What picture?"

"Your husband showed me and a few other fellows at the ironworks a daguerreotype of you that he keeps in a pocketwatch. Remarkable sharpness and clarity. I recognized you right away."

Now it was Faith's turn to blush. She knew exactly what Stephen was talking about, and she was particularly proud of how she looked in that image. She usually hated what few pictures of herself Allan had taken of her, but that one was very flattering.

"I must have some words with my husband the next time I see him," Faith said with an air of condescension. "It's not proper for a man to show off his wife in such a manner."

"All I can say is that your husband seemed to be very proud of you," Stephen said. "Those of us at the office who saw your picture were quite enchanted, and now I can see why."

"Mr. Baldwick," Meredith interjected, taking a step forward, "my mistress needs to get home out of this cold air."

Stephen looked at the little woman with a bemused smile and then he bowed again. "Of course. My apologies. If I may offer my carriage?"

Faith lifted her chin. "Thank you for your generosity, but we walked here and we will be walking back. Good for the blood circulation."

"If you insist. I do have one more proposition for you: what are your plans this Friday evening?"

A moment passed. Faith blinked.

"I beg your pardon?"

Stephen shifted his feet. "I know it sounds forward, forgive me. A humble bachelor like myself with the audacity to inquire about a married woman's evening plans. Dreadful. But I assure you that my intentions are as honest as the late Mr. Abe."

"And what are your intentions, exactly?"

"To invite you to Thanksgiving dinner."

Faith blinked again. "Thanksgiving dinner?"

"Yes. Well, more of a pre-Thanksgiving dinner, since the holiday isn't until the following Thursday. But it is more or less a tradition among the upper echelons of Johnstown society to attend a banquet at the home of Mr. Winston Archibald Rathbun, or Mr. War as he is affectionately termed when he is not around."

"Who is this Mr...War?"

"He's the man responsible for bringing the iron and steel business to Johnstown. Mr. Carnegie would never admit it, though."

"I see." Faith glanced at Meredith, who pursed her lips, and then she turned back to Stephen. "Thank you very much, Mr. Baldwick. Your invitation is very kind, but I'm afraid I would feel out of place without my husband. I don't think it would be appropriate to be the guest of another man, especially one I've just met, though I do find him quite charming."

"You flatter me, Mrs. Shelton. But you wouldn't be my guest. I will be bringing my fiancée with me."

"Oh." Faith didn't know why she felt a twinge of disappointment, but her polite smile didn't falter. "Well, that may be even worse. A married woman turning up at a party unaccompanied would invite all sorts of gossip."

"I suppose it would." Stephen frowned and rubbed his chin. "Could you persuade Mr. Shelton to come down from Pittsburgh? I'm sure he would find the event fascinating and beneficial."

"I will send him a telegram tomorrow, though he likes to maintain control of his schedule."

"Tell him that Mr. War is having a banquet and that the two of you are invited. That will get his attention."

"I hope it will. But are we?"

"Are you what?"

"Invited?"

"Of course! Mr. War is my uncle. I live at his estate. His guests are mine and vice versa."

"Well, that's good to know." Faith offered her hand. "It was wonderful to meet you, Mr. Baldwick."

"Stephen." He took her hand and pressed it to his lips. "May I call you Faith?"

"I...I suppose." She ignored Meredith's look of consternation. "Yes, you may."

"Good."

His brilliant smile made her skin tingle and she hoped she wasn't blushing again.

"Well, I'm afraid we must be getting home," she sputtered, locking arms with Meredith. "Good day, Stephen."

"Good day, Faith."

She held his gaze for a moment before walking down the street. She could feel his eyes following her and she considered looking over her shoulder but she thought better of it. Besides, Meredith was shooting her a matronly look of disapproval. When they turned a corner down a tree-lined street, she let out an exasperated groan.

"All right Meredith, out with it!"

Meredith turned away. "It's not my place, madam."

"It is if I say it is."

Meredith drew her lips in a line. "They say that absence makes the heart grow fonder."

Faith furrowed her brow. "Yes, I've heard that too."

"Absence can also make the heart wander."

"Oh come now, you know it wasn't like that."

"As I said, not my place."

The two women walked in silence for a couple of minutes. Then Faith clicked her tongue.

"Besides, he has a fiancée. If he were a lout, he would have invited me to accompany him, but he didn't. He is quite a gentleman."

Meredith looked up at her with a haughty grin. "It's already started."

Faith's mouth fell open and she mumbled something unintelligible. She unhooked her arm from Meredith's and quickened her steps.

"Move along," she commanded. "I'm hungry and I want roast beef for lunch."

"But madam, I didn't prepare –"

Faith shot her a stern glare. Meredith hung her head and walked faster.

"Yes, madam."

****

The next morning, Faith scribbled a note on a card with instructions for Meredith to take it to the telegraph office. It read:

"My dear A.S. If possible, can make trip to Jtown? Invited to Friday banquet at home of Mr. War by your colleague, S. Baldwick. All my love. F.S"

After Meredith left to send the telegram and take care of various errands, Faith found herself alone in her large, elegant house. Her silk chiffon robe whispered across the floor as she moved through the rooms. All of the furniture was now in place, all pictures had been hung, all repairs had been made. The house was absolutely gorgeous, a sanctuary of peace and comfort.

And Faith had never felt more lonely.

Her hands brushed the ornate flourishes carved into the woodwork and the soft curtain fabrics, but she hardly felt anything. It took a few minutes for her feelings to coalesce, and she realized that the sense of satisfaction she had been expecting once the house was finished had yet to materialize.

You just miss your husband, she told herself.

Another question drifted through her mind: *If he were here now, would you feel content?*

Faith hesitated. She had to admit that she honestly didn't know. She had gotten a bit used to him not being around, and she liked having complete control of the house. When he came home to stay for good, he would be king of the castle, though she didn't think that he would have much interest in the carpets or tapestries. Still, she would have to ask him for permission to change this or that, or to throw a party. Right now, she had her little oasis all to herself.

All to yourself. Such a wonderful feeling. You are practically glowing with joy.

Faith rolled her eyes at the sarcastic tone. Sometimes the voice in her heart was quite annoying.

Without really planning to, she found herself outside in the garden. There was a chill in the air but it was refreshing compared to the stuffiness of the house. Faith wrapped her robe tighter around herself and walked slowly through the foliage. She smiled when she spotted a cluster of chrysanthemums underneath a small maple tree that had shed its leaves. The pink, white, and red colors brightened the otherwise drab bedding that surrounded the tree, and Faith made a note to plant flowers in every available space come spring.

She turned her head to the right. Had she heard something or was it just her imagination?

She waited, holding her breath for a few moments. All she heard was the slight rustling of tree branches in the breeze. Wait, there it was again...a faint mewling sound coming from a hedge of boxwood bushes. Faith hurried over to the hedge, gasping when she heard the pitiful sound again.

Bunching up her robe to keep it from getting dirty, she knelt down and peered beneath the bushes. A tiny black kitten stared at her with eyes that were fearful and hungry.

"Oh my word," she whispered. "Come here, little thing!"

She stretched her hand under the hedge, hoping that the tiny animal didn't have sharp claws yet. The kitten shrank back for a moment and then crept forward. Faith forgot about holding her robe up out of the dirt and reached out both hands.

"Come here," she repeated softly, hardly daring to breathe.

The kitten drew close enough for Faith to touch its tiny nose. It flinched but didn't retreat. Faith kept her hands open, afraid that the slightest movement would send the tiny animal scurrying away. For a few tense moments, neither Faith nor the kitten moved. Faith tried to keep her hands from trembling.

"I won't hurt you," she said, her voice barely a whisper. "Come on out."

The kitten meowed once more and crept closer. Faith reached out and grabbed it gently. The kitten's body stiffened but it didn't try to escape.

"Oh my word..." Faith stood up and looked at the adorable little creature, a female. "Aren't you precious?"

She cradled the kitten in her arms and it snuggled against her warmth. Faith thought her heart was going to melt right then and there.

"Are you hungry?" she asked, stroking the soft fur. "Where is your mama?"

She glanced around but didn't see or hear any other animals.

"Well," she declared, "you're just going to have to come inside with me."

She wrapped her robe around the kitten and hurried up the stone pathway back to the house.

Maybe this was what she had been missing...

Chapter Five

"I'M HOME, MADAM!" Meredith called out as she entered through the back door, her arms laden with paper bundles and bags. "There was quite a fuss at the market. Someone decided to let their donkey off its lead and–"

She walked into the kitchen and stopped.

"What is that, madam?"

Faith looked up at her from the floor where she sat watching the kitten lap milk from a saucer.

"This is Precious," she announced. "She'll be staying here with us."

Meredith's face was stern. "Well, I hope you won't mind replacing the curtains every couple of months."

Faith chuckled. "I'll teach her to be good."

Meredith turned on her heel and walked over to the counter to open the bundles. "Then you'll be the first person to ever teach a cat to do anything."

The kitten raised its head from the milk, white droplets around its mouth. Faith picked it up and held it close.

"Don't listen to her," she said to Precious. "I know you're going to grow up to be a perfectly delightful cat."

Meredith clicked her tongue but didn't turn around.

Faith set Precious on the floor and watched it finish its milk. What would Allan say? He had never been a big fan of animals and pets weren't allowed at the apartment in Pittsburgh. But how could he say no with a big house like this?

You know what? I don't care what he might say. Precious stays and that's that.

She smiled down at the tiny kitten and touched its tail, which flicked side to side. Then the door chime rang out. Precious jumped with fright and scurried into her arms.

"Hush now," she said gently, cradling the kitten and nuzzling it against her cheek as Meredith went to answer the door. She craned her neck to peer around the corner but she couldn't see who Meredith was talking too. After a moment, the door closed and Meredith came back into the kitchen with a telegram.

"What is it?" Faith asked.

Meredith handed her the note. "Only one person would send you a telegram, madam."

Faith opened the telegram and read out loud.

"My dearest F.S. – I will be arriving on the Thursday eve train. Yours, A.S."

78

Faith looked up at Meredith with wide eyes.

"Allan's coming on Thursday!"

"I suppose that fellow at church yesterday was right about the banquet," Meredith remarked.

Faith looked down at the telegram. "I suppose he was…"

If Allan was ready to drop his plans and make the trip here at the mere mention of a banquet at the home of Mr. War, it must have been more important than she realized.

She rose to her feet with Precious in her arms.

"Come upstairs, Meredith. We need to start planning my outfit for the banquet."

"But what about the food?"

"Fashion is more important than food. Now come along."

****

The darkened window reflected her image like a mirror. Faith perched on the edge of the couch in the parlor, twisting her fingers as she stared out into the twilight. She always fidgeted when she was nervous, which was strange because she really didn't need to be. After all, it was just her husband coming home on Thursday like he had promised.

She smoothed her dress and looked up at the clock on the wall. 6:37. The train was scheduled to arrive in Johnstown at 6:15, which meant that Allan would come walking in the door any moment. When he was eighty miles away, Faith thought of him and missed him, but now that he was so close to home, she yearned for him. So much so, she could hardly keep still.

Everything had to be perfect for Allan's arrival. She and Meredith had cleaned the entire house, which was something Faith decided she would never do again. But there was still a sense of satisfaction knowing that she had put her own sweat into the job, and the house was now a gleaming gem. Meredith had also prepared a sumptuous meal of lamb chops, greens, sourdough bread, and pumpkin soup. The mouthwatering aromas drifted through the house, making Faith's stomach growl impatiently. She told her stomach to wait for her husband but it was getting harder with every passing minute.

Besides making the house as welcoming as possible, Faith had also dolled herself up quite nicely. She caught her reflection in the window again, pleased with how her hair fell about her shoulders in coquettish ringlets, her eyes smoldered with dusky mascara, and her lips glistened like cherries. Sapphire earrings sparkled on her earlobes, twin moons orbiting the gem-studded necklace draped over her neck. Every movement made her glitter in the candlelight. Yet she knew Allan's attention would be drawn to her dark red dress, a relic from her early Pittsburgh days when modesty was not an advantage. In anticipation of his amorous mood, she had laid out perfumed linens on the bed upstairs and sprinkled a few rose petals as an afterthought. Pre-

80

cious had curled up on the bed and fallen asleep, but Faith didn't have the heart to shoo the poor creature away.

She hoped Allan wasn't allergic to cats.

A solitary candle lamp flickered outside, illuminating the empty stone pathway leading up to the front porch. Faith sighed and looked at the clock again.

6:46.

Where is he?

The sound of horse hooves on the street made her heart leap. She looked out the window and nearly squealed with delight when she saw a carriage stop in front of the iron gate.

"He's here!" she cried out, bolting up from her seat and rushing into the foyer.

"Goodness gracious!" Meredith exclaimed as she wiped her hands on a rag and hurried into the dining room to stand at attention.

Faith positioned herself in the center of the foyer, right below the shimmering chandelier. She couldn't wait to see the look on her beloved husband's face when he opened the door.

A few agonizing moments passed, and then she heard footsteps on the stone path. She also heard muffled voices, and she was puzzled about whom Allan could be talking with. Probably a footman helping to bring his luggage up to the house. The footsteps reached the porch, sounding loudly on the wooden planks. The door handle turned.

Faith drew in an anxious breath.

The door swung open and the round face of her father-in-law appeared. His eyebrows rose.

"Allan, my boy," Mr. Shelton called over his shoulder, keeping his eyes locked with hers. "Your wife would like to say hello."

Faith instinctively pressed her hands to her chest. She felt paralyzed by Mr. Shelton's glare, but the spell was broken when Allan appeared in the doorway.

"Darling!" he said with a grin, setting down his suitcases and taking her in his arms.

Faith clung to him like her life depended on it. She felt the overwhelming urge to kiss him but the presence of Mr. Shelton made her pause. Allan caught her looking at him over her shoulder and he cleared his throat.

"My dear," he began in a tone that tried to be authoritative but sounded more apologetic, "my father will be spending the holiday with us. Thanksgiving is a time for family and that is what we are, so I trust that we can make him feel at home here."

Faith looked at Mr. Shelton standing in the open door, letting all of the warm air out. She forced a smile to the surface and dipped her head.

"Of course. We are happy to have you stay with us. For the holiday."

Mr. Shelton offered a smile that looked more like a smirk and he closed the door. "This is a bit of a step up from that hovel," he re-

82

marked, scanning the foyer. "I bet it's—"

His words broke off when Precious appeared from behind Faith's dress.

"What in the blazes is that hideous thing?" he cried.

Faith bent down and scooped the kitten into her arms.

"This is Precious," she said, giving her husband a sweet, demure look. "She's been a faithful companion for the last several days, and she hasn't damaged anything in the house."

"Just give it time," Mr. Shelton retorted.

Faith ignored him and held the kitten out towards Allan. He scratched behind its ears and Precious purred softly.

"She likes you!" Faith beamed.

Allan heaved a quiet sigh. "All right, it can stay. But I don't want to see a single claw-mark anywhere in this house!"

Faith bounced with joy and gave her husband a quick peck on the cheek. Mr. Shelton grumbled.

Meredith poked her head into the foyer. "Welcome home, Master Shelton! ...And Mr. Shelton. Supper is on the table. I've set an extra place."

"Good," Mr. Shelton bellowed as he shed his coat and hat and dropped them into Meredith's arms. "I'm starving. Hope it tastes as good as it smells."

After he went into the dining room, Faith locked eyes with Allan. He didn't say anything but the look in his eyes said, *"I can ex-*

plain."

Faith's eyes replied, *"I sure hope so."*

She set the cat on the floor and took Allan's hat and coat. It felt so good to have him home, even with the unexpected company. She also took Mr. Shelton's hat and coat from Meredith and hung them up in the closet in the hall. The suitcases and trunks were still piled up next to the door but they would have to wait. She smoothed the fabric of the dress over her waist and hips, yanked the neckline a couple inches higher, took a deep breath, and marched toward the dining room. It was important for everyone to see that she was the queen of this castle.

****

Both men were apparently quite famished. Faith would have been annoyed at the barbaric manner in which Mr. Shelton stuffed his pudgy face with food, but she was glad that he didn't have much time in between bites to talk. She was sure that she wouldn't like whatever he had to say.

When the meal was over and nothing remained except bones and crumbs, Mr. Shelton announced that he was going out onto the porch for a smoke. Before anyone could acknowledge his words, he sat up from his seat and left the room, grabbing his coat from the closet in the foyer and stepping outside. Faith and Allan exchanged amused glances, and Faith waited for him to finish his food before walking with him to the parlor while Meredith cleared the table.

Giving Allan a sly look, Faith peeked through the curtain and saw her father-in-law bundled in his coat with a massive cigar pinched between his fingers, its end glowing red and sending up a lazy stream of fragrant smoke. He looked like he would be occupied for a while.

"Allan, dear," she said, taking her husband's arm and leading him to the far side of the room by the fire. "I'm so happy you're home."

"Me too." Allan sank into an easy chair and swirled the bourbon in his glass. "As the weather started getting colder in Pittsburgh, I found myself thinking more and more about coming here."

Faith sat down across from him. "So why wasn't that your plan already? Why did it take my telegram to bring you here?"

Allan rubbed his head. "If it were up to me, I would already be here permanently. But before I go to Cambria, old Mr. Jenson is squeezing every bit of work out of me. And my father is encouraging him."

"What changed, then?"

"Well," Allan began, shifting in his chair, "you mentioning Mr. Rathbun – Mr. War, as you called him – certainly got my attention. Did you meet him?"

"No. I still don't really know who he is. Your colleague, Mr. Baldwick, mentioned him to me. He was very charming in his invitation."

Allan took a sip of bourbon and cleared his throat. "Yes, and that's another reason why I came so quickly."

"Mr. Baldwick?"

"Mm-hmm."

"My dear husband," Faith said with a grin, "are you jealous?"

"Of course not," Allan blustered. He looked at the floor for a moment and then added, "Well, maybe not 'jealous', just concerned."

"About what?"

"About Mr. Baldwick. The fellow is a cad, pardon my language."

"Allan! I met him at church."

"Precisely. I've only met him a couple of times myself but I know for a fact he is always on the prowl and he preys on the most unsuspecting women."

"That's not a nice thing to say."

"Oh, really? Did he flatter you?"

Faith blushed. "Yes."

"Was he dressed a bit too garish for church?"

"Yes..."

Allan leaned forward. "Did he offer you a ride home?"

Faith's cheeks felt like they were on fire. "Yes."

"And did you accept?"

"No."

"Good." Allan settled back in his chair with a victorious smile.

Faith tried to grab the reins of her flustered thoughts. "But...but he said he has a fiancée."

Allan moved closer and took her hand in his. "Faith, my darling, you lived in Pittsburgh for three years. You know that a man having a fiancée means very little when it comes to his social life."

"Oh stop it now." Faith turned away to hide the redness returning to her cheeks. "He spoke so fondly of you. I refuse to believe he was trying to poach me from your side."

"I'm sure he wasn't poaching, at least not yet. But give an inch, and he'll take a mile. Trust me."

Faith watched the fire for a few minutes. Then she looked over her shoulder at the cigar embers glowing outside the window.

"Well?"

"Well, what?" Allan said, swirling his bourbon again and watching the legs cling to the glass.

Faith turned to him and folded her hands on her lap. "Aren't you going to tell me why your father is here?"

"He's my father. I can't leave him alone on Thanksgiving."

"He didn't join us last Thanksgiving. He was on a hunting trip in Canada."

"That's not a precedent for all future holidays."

Faith pursed her lips. *If only...*

She inhaled slowly and forced herself to speak in a pleasant tone.

"I'm not unhappy that he's here. I just wish you had told me beforehand so I could have prepared his room and sent Meredith to the market for some of his favorite foods."

Allan raised an eyebrow. "Really? Is that why you wish I had told you that he was coming?"

Faith looked down at her hands. "Well..."

Allan put his hand on her knee. "I'm sorry."

She could see the honesty in his eyes.

"I wasn't planning on bringing him along," Allan added. "But he came over on Wednesday and saw me packing and asked where I was going. I couldn't lie to him. Plus I figured he already knew because I had requested the time off from Mr. Jenson. And I know you'll hate me for this, but I could only get the time off by promising to make it up next month. I can only stay until next Friday, and that means I'll have to add a week to my December schedule."

"But that means you'll miss Christmas! And our anniversary."

"I know. I'm sorry."

Allan reached for her hands but she pulled them away and got up from her seat. She walked over to the hearth to stare into the flames.

"Faith?" Allan asked quietly, rising to his feet and moving closer to her. "Are you all right?"

A tear escaped from her eye and she quickly wiped it away before turning around.

"This is our first Christmas in our new home," she said, trying to hold her voice firm. "I don't want to spend it alone."

"Then come back to the city with me."

Faith made a face. "Ugh. No!"

"Why not?"

The thought of spending a cold, gray Christmas in Pittsburgh made her feel sick, even though she had done so many times before.

But it might be worth it to be with Allan...

No! This is your home now.

A home that she had worked tirelessly to prepare and that she had eagerly planned to share with her husband for the holidays.

"I'm staying here," she declared. "It may not be apparent but I have worked very hard to make this house into a home and I expect my husband to be here to enjoy the Christmas holiday with me."

Allan's face fell. "Are you being serious?"

"Very much so. You have to make a choice, dear husband: spend Christmas here with me, or in Pittsburgh without me. I will not subject myself to Christmas in a cramped, empty apartment. I can only imagine what it looks like as a bachelor pad now."

"But my dear," Allan pleaded, "I can't get off work!"

Faith reached up and touched his face. "You were charming enough to get this time off. I'm sure you can work your magic again."

Allan stood dumbfounded as Faith glided past him and picked up Precious, who was perched on the edge of a small table. "I'm going to bed," she said, glancing at him over her shoulder. "Tomorrow is going to be a busy day, and I need my rest. Please tell your father good night for me."

A twinge of guilt pricked her heart when she saw Allan looking like a crestfallen little boy.

You did the right thing, she told herself as she walked up the stairs. *But will you make good on your threat?*

After a moment of consideration, she decided that yes, she would. Allan needed to know that she came first, not the job. She looked down at Precious and smiled. Standing up to her husband was the last thing she had expected to do tonight, but it felt good in a way, even if meant a lonely Christmas. But she also knew that Allan was a very resourceful man and if he wanted something badly enough, he would find a way to make it happen.

The question was, did he want to spend Christmas with her badly enough?

Only time would tell. Right now, all Faith could think about was shedding this uncomfortable dress and slipping into her nightgown. Nothing about this night had gone according to plan, and her heart sank when she saw the perfumed bedsheets strewn with rose petals.

At least my dreams will smell nice...

Chapter Six

FAITH FELT A SLIVER of morning sunlight brush against her cheek like a gentle finger and she opened her eyes. A gap in the curtains let in the light but she didn't mind. She stretched her arms over her head and arched her back, feeling a satisfying *crrrack!* travel up her spine. Then she looked over at the empty space in the bed next to her.

I wonder how Allan slept?

She went over to the vanity by the window and glared at her reflection.

I hope he tossed and turned all night. And that he's come to his senses.

After completing her morning toilette, Faith made her way downstairs for breakfast. Mr. Shelton sat alone at the table reading a newspaper and smoking a cigar. The room was half-filled with smoke and Faith couldn't stop a sneeze in time.

"Oh, so sorry my dear," he said without looking up from his paper. "I'd open a window but it's quite chilly out this morning."

"Good morning," Faith replied with a taut smile. "Meredith? I will take my breakfast in the parlor."

Meredith waved tendrils of smoke away from her face. "Yes, madam."

Faith turned to leave and nearly smacked into Allan.

"Oh!" she exclaimed, feeling her cheeks flush. "Good morning."

Allan took her hand and raised it to his lips. "Good morning, my dear. And to you, father."

Mr. Shelton lifted a finger in acknowledgment.

"Meredith is bringing my breakfast to the parlor," Faith said, avoiding eye contact with her husband. "Would you like to join me?"

Allan hesitated before answering. "I'd love to, but I need to discuss some things with my father."

"Now?"

"I'm afraid so."

Faith tried to hide her disappointment but she failed. Allan touched her shoulders. "After breakfast, I'm all yours."

"Okay," Faith said with a bowed head. She shuffled into the parlor and sat down, annoyed at her feelings. Precious appeared at her feet and she brightened immediately. She picked up the kitten and stroked its soft fur as she stared out the window at the leafless tree limbs trembling in the wind.

I hope Mr. War's house is warm.

Faith gasped. Tonight was the banquet!

All thoughts of her grudge against Allan and her disappointment about his Christmas plans evaporated. She had to get ready for tonight! Meredith had helped her pick out her dress and jewelry and accessories several days ago, but what about Allan? Did he have a suit to wear? Did he knew where Mr. War's house was? What time did the banquet start, anyway?

She grit her teeth. Why did he have to be in there chatting with his father in that smokey room when she was in here with so many questions to ask him?

Precious screeched and leaped out of her hands. She hadn't realized that she was squeezing the poor thing too tightly.

"I'm sorry, sweetheart," she called out as the cat fled into another room. She groaned and slumped in her seat. Then she pounded the armrest. "Meredith! Where is my breakfast?"

"C-coming, madam," Meredith stammered as she rushed into the room, carefully balancing a tray of food. She set it on the table next to Faith's chair and proceeded to butter the toast.

Faith waved her away. "I can do it," she snapped. "Go open some windows and let that dreadful smoke out."

"Yes, madam." Meredith scurried off.

Guilt rose to the surface in Faith's heart but she told herself that Meredith was the hired help, not a friend or relative that she had to be nice to. And she had burnt the toast. Faith breathed slowly to calm her frayed nerves and drank her glass of juice.

When she was nearly finished with her breakfast, Mr. Shelton

93

marched past the parlor, grabbed his hat and coat from the foyer closet, and headed out the front door. A moment later, Allan came into the room with his hands in his pockets.

"Is everything all right?" Faith asked offhandedly, dabbing her lips with her napkin.

Allan nodded.

"Where is your father going?"

"He, uh, he's going fishing."

"Fishing?"

"Of sorts."

Faith frowned but she got the feeling that Allan didn't want to be transparent so she let the issue drop.

"Allan," she said quietly, "I apologize if I was too blunt last night. I didn't plan to ruin your first night home." She paused, then added, "It wasn't what I was expecting either."

Allan paced the room for a moment. "The fault is mine. Bringing my father along without letting you know in advance, changing our Christmas plans..."

"Which you will change again, correct?"

Allan gave her a warm smile. "Yes. Against all odds, and possible unemployment, I will be here for Christmas."

Faith's heart leaped, but she just gave a curt nod. "Good. Now, a more immediate matter: tonight is the banquet at Mr. War's home. I bought a wonderful dress that I hope you will love."

Allan stared out the window, watching his father march down the stone walkway. "Mm-hmm."

"And," Faith persisted, "I'm hoping you'll look as handsome as ever. Shall we go into town to find a suit for you to wear?"

"I already brought one," Allan said, stepping to the side and grabbing a bite of food from her plate. "Have Meredith steam it smooth for me."

Faith cleared her throat. She was losing his attention. "Darling," she cooed, "perhaps you'd like to see my dress a little early. Perhaps I might need your help when I try it on..."

"Soon, sweetheart." He gave her a quick peck on the cheek and went to the closet to get his hat and coat.

"Where are you going?" Faith demanded.

"I have a meeting to get to."

"But...your father's carriage has already gone."

"I know," Allan said, shrugging into his coat. "I'm not going where he's going."

Faith folded her arms. "At least tell me when you'll be back."

"As soon as possible. In plenty of time to go to the banquet."

He leaned in for another kiss but Faith turned away. He smiled and touched her chin.

"I'm sorry, sweetheart. I don't mean to be distant. I just have some important things to attend to today."

"I'm important," Faith whined, immediately wishing she hadn't

95

sounded so petulant.

"More than anything." Allan lunged forward and pressed a kiss to her lips before she could react. Her eyes went wide and she pushed him away, but she couldn't hide her smile.

"Go on then," she said with exaggerated annoyance. "Go do your important business. Don't worry about your wife whom you haven't seen in weeks."

"And she misses me so much because she loves me to the moon."

Faith smirked. "Maybe..."

Allan slapped the top of his hat. "See you soon."

He whisked out the door, shutting it quickly before the warm air inside could escape. Faith watched him hurry down the path and disappear out of the gate.

Will it always be like this?

When she turned around, she saw Meredith standing in the parlor doorway, hands folded dutifully in front of her. Faith pretended she wasn't startled and wandered to the other side of the room for no particular reason.

"Meredith," she said in what she hoped was a casual tone, "Master Shelton asked you to—"

"Steam his suit. Yes madam, I heard."

"Oh. Well...steam his suit, and polish his shoes, if he brought another pair."

"Yes, madam. What about Mr. Shelton?"

Faith looked up at the ceiling. She hadn't asked Allan if his father was coming to the banquet or not.

"Did you see a suit in his closet?" she asked.

Meredith shook her head. "I haven't been in his room yet. I was going to head up there after I cleaned the dishes."

"All right. If you do see one, steam it just in case."

"Yes, madam."

Meredith started to leave, then stopped.

"He's a good man, madam."

"Who?"

"Your husband."

Faith looked away, feeling like she was going to laugh and cry at the same time.

"Do you think he meant it? That I'm important to him?"

"Of course, madam. Don't you see? He does all of this for you. He so desperately wants to impress you."

"Why? I'm already his wife."

Meredith smiled. "Madam, men want to be idolized by their women."

"Well if that's what he wants from me, he needs to do a better job."

Meredith had a knowing look on her face as she left the room.

"Oh, I think he knows exactly what he's doing."

Faith sulked for a moment, mulling over her words. As much as she didn't want to admit it, Meredith was right. She absolutely worshiped Allan Shelton III, which was why she yearned for his undivided attention, even though she knew she would never have it completely. And perhaps that made her admire him even more.

Precious purred and rubbed against her leg.

"Come here, sweetie," Faith said as she picked up the kitten and snuggled it against her cheek. "Are you hungry? Let's get you something to eat."

****

The day crawled by. Faith spent as much time staring out the window as she did getting ready for the banquet. Where was Allan? He needed to try on his suit. And Faith couldn't wait to see his face light up when he saw her dress and jewelry.

It was just after four o'clock when the front door blew open and heavy footsteps stomped around downstairs. Faith looked up from her mirror in surprise. She was wearing just a slip and wasn't decent enough to be seen out of the room, so she went to the door and cracked it open. Allan and his father were in the foyer, and by the sound of his voice, Mr. Shelton wasn't in a good mood.

Faith only caught bits and pieces of their conversation, but she did hear one phrase very clearly: *"Allan, you need to secure an invitation to that club. If you ever want to be somebody in this town, your*

98

name must appear alongside theirs."

"A club?" she whispered to herself. "What club?"

She heard footsteps coming up the stairs and she hurried back to her mirror. A few moments later, there was a knock at the door.

"Faith?" Allan called out.

"In here, darling!"

The door opened and Allan stepped into the room. Faith turned around, hoping to see his face brighten at the sight of her half-dressed and her neck adorned with diamonds. But his brow remained furrowed and his eyes were fixed on the floor.

Faith huffed in annoyance. "Well, how do I look?"

Allan looked up and gave her a fleeting smile. "Beautiful, darling." He went over to the window and toyed with the curtain. He was clearly distracted, but Faith wasn't about to indulge his absentmindedness.

"All right," she said, rising to her feet and putting on her silk robe. "Out with it!"

"Out with what?"

Faith put her hands on her hips and her eyes shot daggers at him. Allan cleared his throat.

"You heard?"

"A few words. But I could tell that your father was pretty upset."

Allan sighed and sat down. "Yes, that's an understatement."

Faith sat next to him. "Tell me."

"He'd probably be mad if you knew."

"Darling, he's just your father. I'm your wife."

Allan smiled, giving Faith a measure of relief. He shifted in his seat and took her hand.

"My father didn't receive an invitation to the banquet. So he decided that he was going to go fishing."

"Fishing?"

"Fishing for an invitation. He has a few acquaintances in town and he took a tour of the hotels and restaurants where they might be in the hopes of being recognized, invited to lunch, and then invited to the banquet. But he didn't see anyone of note. I was at the Cambria office and he sent a message for me to come and meet him at The Red Horse downtown. He was in quite a foul mood by that point and had had a few glasses of Scotch. So, all this to say, my father won't be joining us tonight."

"Oh." Faith tried to keep the smile from materializing on her face. "I'm sorry to hear that. So...just the two of us?"

"Looks that way. I suspect my father won't be in the mood for dining at home so you can tell Meredith not to worry about dinner."

Faith laid her head on Allan's shoulder. "I missed you today. It will be nice to have you to myself."

"Not all to yourself, I'm afraid. There will be many important people there whose feet I must kiss."

"What did your father mean when he talked about a club?"

Allan frowned. "What did you hear?"

Faith shrank from his gaze, wondering if she should have kept her mouth shut. "I didn't hear much. And I wasn't spying or anything; your father has a loud voice and it came through the door."

"I see." Allan didn't sound convinced. "So what did you hear?"

"Only something about you getting an invitation to a club. "

Allan rubbed his chin and then fixed her with a stern glare. "Can I give you a mission for tonight?"

Faith's heartbeat quickened. "Yes! Anything to make this banquet more interesting."

"All right. There is a club, very exclusive, called the South Fork Fishing and Hunting Club. Do you remember me telling you about it?"

Faith shook her head.

"It's several miles upriver," Allan went on. "At the top of the South Fork Dam. A paradise for the rich and powerful, so I've been told. If you're a member, you are the cream of the crop. Men like Carnegie and Allen and Frick are members."

"Do you think you could get a membership too?"

Allen chuckled. "Right now, no. It is a very elite and secretive club, the kind that people gossip about. Sometimes the men bring their wives and children, and sometimes they have parties without the wives and children."

Faith pursed her lips. "So why would *you* want to become a

member?"

"I don't want to be a member, not yet anyway. But getting invited as someone's guest is a big stepping stone towards becoming a major player, especially for me since I'm relocating here permanently. Most of these men live in Pittsburgh and this is just their weekend retreat. I need to establish myself in Johnstown and this is a good way to do it."

Something stirred in Faith's heart and she touched Allan's cheek.

"So how do we get ourselves invited to this mysterious club?"

Allan grinned. "Something tells me that you're going to be better at it than I am."

****

Faith's silk-gloved hand slid down the banister with a whisper and the sequins in her teal-blue dress sparkled and shimmered in the light from the chandelier. She knew she looked marvelous, but she still felt a bit nervous about what Allan would think. Yesterday's attempt at making his jaw drop had failed, which put more pressure on tonight's outfit.

Just don't trip and fall down the stairs...

She glanced down into the foyer and saw Allan wearing a trim black suit, looking every bit the dapper gentleman that he was. But his back was turned to her. Faith lifted her chin and set her foot down on the next step with a sharp *clack!*

Allan turned. His mouth fell open and his eyebrows flew up.

"My word..."

Faith tried to hide her smile. A blushing warmth crept through her cheeks and she unfurled her fan to hide her face. Her smoldering eyes peeked over the top and fixed on his. A giddy smile spread across his face.

She reached the bottom of the stairs and snapped her fan shut. Allan offered his hand with an exaggerated flourish.

"Faith, my dear, you look like a dream."

"Thank you," Faith said, giving a small bow in reply. She took his hand and followed him to the door where Meredith stood at attention. Her smile was also ear-to-ear.

"Well don't you two look a fine pair," she remarked as she turned the door handle.

Faith drew in a sharp breath when the November air nipped at her skin. Her shoulders were wrapped in a warm fur shrug but the air bit through the thin fabric of her dress. She couldn't wait to get into a carriage and snuggle with Allan.

For warmth, of course.

"Thank you, Meredith," Allan said as he placed his hat on his head. "I hope my father won't give you too much trouble when he returns home tonight. Heaven knows when that will be."

"Not to worry. I purchased his favorite brandy last week."

Faith's eyes grew wide. "You knew his father was coming too?"

"Not exactly, but I had a good feeling."

"Why didn't you tell me?"

"I didn't want to cause you any more worry, madam. I knew how anxious you were about getting the right dress for this evening."

Faith blushed again and Allan laughed.

"I'm not at all surprised," he said. "Come along, darling. Don't wait up for us, Meredith."

"Yes, sir. Enjoy yourselves."

After Meredith closed the door behind them, Allan's hand slipped down to her waist and pulled her hips close to him.

"Patience, dear husband," Faith said with a smile. "The night's still young."

"So are you."

"Let's enjoy the banquet," Faith whispered, touching his nose. "Then we'll see about dessert."

Chapter Seven

A CARRIAGE TOOK THEM to the outskirts of town and then to the foothills by the river. Dark trees rose up on either side of the road as it fed into the forest and the driver had to navigate by lamplight. The road was surprisingly smooth, even more so than the cobblestone streets in town. After several minutes, Faith spotted torches lining the road. She peeked through the carriage curtains and saw two rows of flickering flames leading the way up to a grand mansion bathed in electric light.

"Allan!" she cried, grabbing his arm. "Look!"

Allan ducked low to look out the window and whistled. "Sweet mercy! That's a palace."

Faith felt her fingers tingle. It had been so long since she had attended an elegant gathering and she couldn't wait to get a taste of Johnstown high life. Along with her excitement, though, came flurries of doubts.

What if they don't like me? I don't have a fancy pedigree and I'm only a year married. What if they think I'm just a trollop digging for gold?

The voice in her heart replied in a stern tone.

Well, are you just a trollop digging for gold?

Faith looked at Allan.

No. I'd marry this man even if he didn't have a cent to his name.

The voice answered, *Good. Carry yourself that way and people will see you for who you really are, a devoted wife and a woman with sophisticated tastes.*

It was a comforting thought. Faith smiled to herself and settled back in her seat.

They will see me for who I really am.

A line of carriages crawled toward the house like a giant chain, and this gave Faith ample time to study the courtyard and grounds. The driveway was bordered by leafless trees and encircled an ornate fountain ringed with meticulously trimmed shrubbery. Several marble statues patterned after classical masterpieces dotted the yard. Or perhaps they were the actual masterpieces...

Faith glanced over at Allan, studying his face. He was looking intently out the window but he didn't seem to be admiring the landscaping or the house. He appeared deep in thought, his mouth drawn tight.

The carriage lurched to a stop and the driver hopped down to open the door.

"Watch your step, madam."

Faith tugged her fur tight around her shoulders and took the driver's offered hand, stepping out of the carriage onto the gravel driveway. Allan got out after her, paid the driver, and took her arm. They both stood still for a moment, staring in awe at the white marble Georgian-style mansion that loomed large in the darkness with every window brightly lit. Several guests were scattered about, chattering happily and hurrying towards the house to get out of the cold, and Faith and Allan joined in the current.

As they approached the house, Faith heard chamber music coming from inside. She glanced at the people around her, noting that most of them were much older than her and her husband. Well, at least the men were. There were some middle-aged and older women but several men had fresh-faced girls wrapped in clingy dresses on their arms. One of them looked at Faith and smiled, as if to say, *You hooked one, too.*

Faith gave her a cold glare.

Several smartly-dressed footmen stood at attention by the front door. In one fluid motion, they gestured for Faith and Allan to enter, but then a man appeared in front of them.

"Allan!" Stephen Baldwick cried, stepping down to shake hands. "So glad you could come."

Allan's expression was somewhere between a smile and a smirk. "Good to see you, Stephen."

Stephen looked at Faith and his mouth dropped open. "Mrs.

Shelton. You are a vision from heaven. If you had come to church looking like this, they would have thought an angel was in their midst."

Faith giggled, and Allan's smirk became more pronounced.

"That is the most exaggerated flattery I have ever had the joy of hearing," she said.

"Please, step inside," Stephen said with a sweep of his arm. "Make yourselves at home. I will introduce you to my uncle soon."

"Thank you," Allan said, taking Faith's arm and hurrying her up the large stone steps. Faith started to protest but she thought better of it.

He's just jealous. Let him simmer a little bit. It will make him appreciate you more.

The tension evaporated when they stepped into the expansive foyer. Marble columns rose up to the ceiling and the floor gleamed with fresh polish. Massive paintings adorned the walls and everything sparkled and shone. Faith felt like she was standing inside a cathedral.

"This house is gigantic!" she whispered to Allan, who laughed.

"Indeed. And the funny thing is, Mr. War probably only spends a couple months a year here. His first home is the top floor of the Westgate building in Pittsburgh. I heard he has an entire garden up there."

Faith clicked her tongue. "These people must take baths in their money."

Allan turned to her with a sparkle in his eyes. "And we'll be one of them someday."

"You promise?"

"I promise."

A servant approached and offered to take their coats. Allan surrendered his hat and coat and Faith removed her furs. Despite her bare shoulders, she didn't feel cold. The house was warmed by so many people inside, along with fires roaring in numerous fireplaces. She followed Allan into the house and spotted the string quartet in the corner of a large room where a number of guests were mingling and chatting with drinks in hand.

"Champagne?"

A man in a tuxedo held out a tray. The glasses were filled to the brim and yet his hand was so steady, he didn't spill a single drop. Faith thanked him and took two, one for herself and one for her husband.

"Cheers," she said, carefully clinking her glass against his.

"To the future queen of Johnstown," he added, downing his glass.

Faith sipped hers and frowned. "Take care, Allan."

He gave her a wolfish grin and pulled her close. Faith gasped as some champagne spilled from her glass and landed on someone's shoes. She turned and saw Stephen and another woman standing right beside her.

Her hand flew to her mouth. "Oh, Mr. Baldwick! I mean,

Stephen. I'm so sorry!"

"Don't worry about it," Stephen said with a chuckle. He snapped his fingers and pointed at his feet. A dark-skinned young man in a spotless white uniform appeared out of nowhere and hastily wiped Stephen's shoes with a rag, and then he vanished again.

"See?" Stephen lifted his shoes one by one. "Good as new. Better. Champagne is a great shoe polish."

"Well, I apologize again," Faith said.

"Accepted, and immediately dismissed."

He turned to the woman next to him. "This is my fiancée, Charlotte Greenburg."

Charlotte held out her hand. "How do you do?"

"Pleased to meet you," Faith said, giving her hand a delicate shake. She appraised Charlotte in half a second.

By her estimation, Charlotte looked about twenty-two or twenty-three years old, and she was beautiful. Her blonde hair was curled in perfect ringlets and her face was accented by unusually bright make-up. Her figure was quite voluptuous and her shimmering red dress bordered on immodesty, but there was a sweetness in her expression that made her seem like an innocent girl who just happened to be blessed with an overabundance of beauty. And Faith also saw something in her eyes that she recognized: her instincts told her that Charlotte had come from poverty and was capitalizing on her good genetic fortune. Faith immediately felt a sort of kinship with her.

"This is quite a party," Allan declared, taking another glass of champagne from a passing tray.

Stephen nodded and looked around, as if he had just realized where he was. "My uncle is around here somewhere. Probably in his study with his inner circle, plotting and conniving."

"Is that not what you do?" Faith asked.

Stephen blinked. "I beg your pardon?"

Faith offered a disarming smile. "I mean 'you' in general. Men like you and my husband, and I would assume most of the men here. Businessmen, plotting and scheming and cooking up deals. I dare say the world turns on the hushed conversations of powerful men in their studies under a haze of cigar smoke."

Allan's eyebrows rose and a knowing smile spread slowly across Stephen's face as he wagged a finger.

"I'm beginning to think there might be some thorns hidden behind your roses, Mrs. Shelton."

Faith let out an airy laugh and reached back to touch Allan's face. "Mr. Baldwick, as my husband already knows: all you need is Faith."

Allan's mouth fell open. Stephen blinked again. Charlotte looked away to hide her smile.

The string quartet stopped playing and a stout fellow with an immaculate mustache and a crisp uniform clapped his hands twice before speaking in a booming voice. "Ladies and gentlemen! Welcome to the humble home of Mr. Winston Archibald Rathbun. We are honored that you have accepted his invitation to share this Friday evening before Thanksgiving with us. Dinner will be served shortly and we request that you find your seats. Please ask a footman to assist you, as there are a number of tables throughout the house. Thank you."

Stephen turned to Faith and Allan with a penitent expression. "I must apologize profusely. I had hoped to find seats for both of you in the main dining room but my uncle had given away all of the good seats by then. And adding to the misfortune, Charlotte and I are seated in that room, so I'm afraid we won't be seeing each other during the meal."

Allan started to reply but Faith interjected, "No need to apologize. We make friends wherever we go. I hope that your table is filled with lively conversation."

"Doubtful," Stephen snorted. "Remember that inner circle I was telling you about? I guarantee there will be at least two or three of them sawing logs at the table with bellyfuls of turkey."

"Then come and find us as soon as you can and we'll make up for lost fun."

Stephen cocked an eyebrow. "Indeed we will."

Both he and Charlotte bowed and headed deeper into the house. Allan gave Faith a quizzical look, but she just countered with a coy smile and took his arm. They went back to the foyer where Allan gave his name to a footman, who led them down a corridor to a spacious room adjacent to the kitchen. The aromas were intoxicating and

Faith's stomach growled loudly, but the noise in the room saved her from embarrassment. The footman took them to a table with folded cards that read *"Mr. Allan Shelton Jr."* and *"Mrs. Allan Shelton Jr."* on top of china plates with gold trim. Several other people were seated around the table, though Allan didn't seem to recognize any of them. Faith didn't mind, and after a few smiles and well-placed compliments, she had the attention of nearly everyone at the table.

Wine was poured a couple of minutes before the food came out. Faith was practically ravenous when the servants laid platters laden with turkey, quail, mutton, gravy, vegetables, fresh baked rolls, soups, sauces, and salads.

"Bon appetit!" the servants declared before hurrying off.

Decorum was cast aside as everyone dug into the food. Forks and knives and spoons and tongs dipped and scooped and stabbed and sliced. It wasn't complete chaos but it was a bit messier than expected, which added quite a bit of merriment to the whole process. People smiled and laughed as they passed the food around, and within minutes, they all felt like good friends sharing a meal together.

Faith looked at Allan with a mouthful of food.

"Thith ith duhlithith!"

Allan nearly choked. Faith swallowed and laughed loudly.

As appetites were sated, the bites became less frequent and the conversation picked up. Once again, Faith was the center of attention, though as she talked, she carefully examined the expressions of the other ladies at the table to see if there were any hints of resentment. She was pleased to note that they all seemed as enchanted as the men were. Allan simply ate his food and watched with amusement and mild surprise as Faith told stories of their life in Pittsburgh and her adventures in setting up house in Johnstown, some of which were news to him.

About an hour later, the head butler announced that dessert would be served and that the guests were free to mingle as they wished. Spirits and cigars were available in the great room, and that's where many people headed if they were too full for pumpkin and apple pie.

Faith wasn't in the mood for dessert so she tugged on Allan's arm. They excused themselves from the table and melted into the swirl of guests. It took several minutes to make their way to the bar, where Allan asked for a gin and tonic and Faith took another glass of champagne. Shortly after, a group of men with red faces and big smiles came up and shook Allan's hand and slapped him on the back. He looked a little embarrassed and introduced Faith to his colleagues. She politely shook hands and then excused herself, not interested in hanging around a raucous group like that.

Allan chatted with his pals and tried to keep an eye on his wife, but he lost sight of her after a couple of minutes. He started to go out into the crowd to look for her but one of his colleagues ordered the bartender to fill his glass again, despite Allan's protests. His friends would hear nothing of it, and soon they were clinking glasses and laughing loudly enough to cause the guests around them to move away.

After finishing his third gin and tonic, Allan announced that he needed to go find his wife. His friends chastised him but he ignored their jibes and made his way through the crowd, which had started to thin out a bit since the hour was getting late. He sometimes had to press a hand to the wall to steady himself but he made a valiant effort to walk with confident steps. He searched the faces but didn't see Faith anywhere. A cloud passed over his face and darkened his eyes as he went from room to room, scanning the faces and coming up empty.

Then he heard a woman's laugh rise above the din, not because it was particularly loud, but because it sounded like music to his ears. He hurried around a corner and saw Faith standing beside a bookshelf with Stephen Baldwick, his fiancée Charlotte, and an older gentleman that he recognized immediately.

William Archibald Rathbun. Mr. War.

Faith caught a glimpse of her husband out of the corner of her eye and her blood turned cold.

He's had too much to drink. Goodness sakes, Allan, stand up straight!

Allan must have heard her telepathic message because he drew in a deep breath and walked over to the group looking as sober as a judge, though Faith could still see the glassy look in his eyes.

"Darling," she said with a smile as she took his arm, feeling his weight shift onto her. "We were wondering where you had wandered off to."

"Just admiring the view," Allan said, mirroring her smile.

Stephen cleared his throat. "Uncle, this is Allan Shelton. I believe you've met his father, Allan Shelton, Jr. Allan here is number three."

Mr. Rathbun took the cigar from his mouth and looked at Allan with a hawk-like expression. "You do resemble your father quite a bit, though the canvas isn't quite so stretched."

Allan laughed and Faith joined in, though she could hear the nervousness in his voice.

"I'm afraid you're quite right, Mr. Wa-Mr. Rathbun. My father certainly knows how to occupy a room, if you know what I mean."

Mr. Rathbun chuckled and stuck his cigar back in his mouth. "I do, indeed. I've only met your father once or twice. He struck me as a very ambitious man. Perhaps a bit too ambitious."

He kept his eyes fixed on Allan, seeing if he'd take the bait. Faith gave his arm a subtle squeeze.

"You may be right," Allan said as he held Mr. Rathbun's gaze. "But I have his ambition to thank for getting me on my start, and I have no doubt by the time I reach his age that my ambition and achievements will have surpassed his."

Mr. Rathbun narrowed his eyes and then nodded.

116

"I don't know if I'll be around long enough to see that come to pass, but I certainly hope it does. My nephew here will be the one to watch your saga unfold. I hope that maybe some of your impetus might rub off on him."

Stephen frowned. "You have your father's shadow to struggle out from under," he said to Allan with a roll of his eyes, "and I have my uncle's."

Mr. Rathbun laughed dryly. "As did I and your father and the fathers and uncles before them. But I must commend you, Master Allan. You have done very well for yourself already, so I am told. A new job at Cambria, a house on Main Street, and this delightful young lady on your arm. Before you came in, she was entertaining us with some humorous anecdotes about her adventures in Pittsburgh. She's a marvelous storyteller."

Faith blushed. "My life has changed in so many ways since I met this man."

Charlotte sighed and gave Stephen a longing look, and he rolled his eyes again.

Mr. Rathbun puffed on his cigar. "Well, I wish you both the utmost happiness. My blessed wife Sheila died seven years ago. That woman was my rock. She helped my dreams to soar and brought them down to earth if their wings weren't big enough. We had three daughters, all married now, but with no male heirs, my nephew Stephen has stepped into the role. And despite my ribbing earlier, he is doing a fine job."

"Thank you, Uncle," Stephen said, visibly relieved.

There was a lull in the conversation and Faith knew it was her moment to make her move. She laid her head on Allan's shoulder and pouted.

"I'm sad to have to send this man back to Pittsburgh next week, so soon after he arrived."

Mr. Rathbun frowned. "Oh? Why is that?"

Allan looked flustered. "Well, it's just...I still have some unfinished business with my old company before I can formally start at Cambria. I only got the time to come here by agreeing to stay on during the Christmas holiday."

"You mean you traded one holiday for another?"

"I'm afraid so."

"Preposterous!" Mr. Rathbun drained the whiskey from his glass. "You will do no such thing."

"Sir?"

"Your business in Pittsburgh is finished."

"But sir, my boss, Mr. Jenson—"

"Edward Jenson will not refuse a favor from an old friend who saved his head from nearly being taken off by a rebel cannonball."

Everyone in the group looked stunned. Stephen started to ask a question but Mr. Rathbun waved his words away and pointed his cigar at Allan.

"Your place is here in your new home with your wife. Whatever business was left over in Pittsburgh is not your concern anymore, and whatever things you still have there will be delivered to you next week. You will not spend your first Christmas as a citizen of Johnstown away from home."

Allan and Faith stared at each other and then turned together to stare at Mr. Rathbun.

"You are too kind," Faith stammered, helping her husband stay upright. "Whatever can we do to repay your generosity?"

"You can be my guests for the New Year's party at the South Fork Fishing and Hunting Club," Mr. Rathbun declared as a servant refilled his glass.

Now it was Faith's turn to be struck speechless. She struggled valiantly to find her voice.

"Oh Mr. Rathbun, we couldn't."

"Why not?"

Faith's mind raced. Now was the time to dance very carefully.

"Mr. Rathbun," she said with a demure tone in her voice, "we are flattered beyond words. It would be a dream come true to visit the club. I've heard so many wonderful things about it. But you've only just met us, and being your guests would be an honor that we wouldn't know what to do with."

"Don't fret about that, my dear," Mr. Rathbun said, taking a sip of whiskey. "Membership is very exclusive, that's true, but people bring guests up there all the time. And you won't be my only guests, so you needn't worry about elbowing out a jealous social climber."

"Oh, but that's not why we would—"

Mr. Rathbun waved his hand. "Motives and aspirations are one's personal business, unless it affects my business. I care about the bottom line. Will you accept my invitation, Mrs. Shelton?"

Allan leaned in. "We would be very happy to."

Mr. Rathbun silenced him with a look. "I was asking your wife, Master Allan."

"Yes, sir." Allan bowed his head and looked sheepishly at Faith.

She smiled and clasped her hands. "Absolutely, Mr. Rathbun. We would be delighted to be your guests."

****

The massive grandfather clock in the hall chimed eleven o'clock.

Faith stifled a yawn, nodding politely to an elderly couple walking past. Then she reached out and discreetly but firmly shook Allan's shoulder.

"Wake up, dear husband," she said while maintaining an immovable smile.

Allan snorted and jolted awake, stretching his limbs that had been tucked under the easy chair where he slumbered. He gathered his senses with moderate success and pushed himself to his feet.

120

"Time to go?" he asked, regarding her with unfocused eyes.

"Most certainly."

After a number of goodbyes, she stood shivering outside with Allan, waiting for an empty carriage to pull up. She clutched his arm and stood close to him for warmth, resisting the unladylike urge to stamp her feet.

She heard footsteps behind them and turned around to see Stephen and Charlotte both wearing their coats.

"All done for the evening?" Allan asked with comically raised eyebrows.

Stephen smiled. "My uncle treats me like his son in many respects but fortunately, I don't live in his house as a son would. I like to have my own space."

He grinned at Charlotte. Faith pursed her lips but said nothing.

A carriage pulled to a stop in front of the sprawling stone steps and the driver stepped down to open the door. Allan took Faith's hand to lead her down the steps, and she turned to Stephen.

"Thank you for inviting us to this lovely banquet," she said. "We had a wonderful time."

"Yes, we did," Allan added. "Come along, dear."

Stephen raised her other hand to his lips with a smile. "You made quite an impression tonight."

"You mean on your uncle?"

"On everyone."

She caught the twinkle in his eye and faltered for a moment. Then she reassembled her smile and bowed her head.

"You are too kind, Mr. Baldwick. And it was lovely meeting you, Charlotte. I hope we can have lunch together soon."

"I would like that," Charlotte said.

"Come along, dear," Allan repeated. "We don't want to catch cold."

Faith let him help her into the carriage and she settled on the seat next to the window. The driver closed the door, climbed back up into his seat, and gave the reins a tug. As the horses pulled the carriage around the driveway toward the road, Faith saw Stephen standing on the steps watching them ride away.

Allan took off his hat and set it down on the carriage seat.

"You certainly did make an impression," he said, his eyes half-open.

"Don't I always?"

Allan let out a short laugh. "I can't believe we got invited to the South Fork club. Did you have a strategy that you were executing throughout the evening?"

Faith smoothed the fabric of her dress. "Men have the luxury of making it up as they go along. A woman always has to have a plan."

"Oh yes?"

Allan moved from his seat to hers and wrapped his strong arms around her. She looked into his eyes. They were more clear than before and there was a twinkle in them.

"So," he went on, "what do you have planned next?"

"You'll have to wait and see," she whispered and kissed him.

Chapter Eight

MR. SHELTON LOOKED UP from his newspaper as Faith and Allan entered the breakfast room.

"It's almost nine o'clock," he remarked. "Did you two enjoy yourselves last night?"

Faith took a seat at the table across from her husband, catching his eye for a moment.

"Yes, Father," Allan said as he sat down. "Very much. It was an entertaining and enlightening evening."

Mr. Shelton folded the paper and set it on the table. He gave both of them a leering gaze. "So how would you rate the impression you made on Johnstown high society?"

Meredith brought in plates with their breakfasts. Allan scooped a large bite of scrambled eggs into his mouth and chewed for a moment before answering.

"I don't know how much of an impression *I* made," he said, "but I believe Faith's name is on quite a few lips this morning."

"Oh?" Mr. Shelton looked at her again, this time with barely concealed disdain. "Did you fall into old habits?"

Faith took a small sip of coffee and dabbed her mouth with a napkin. "I would hardly dare to imagine what habits you mean, sir, but I did find it quite easy to converse with a number of people there. They must be starved for good conversation, especially from a woman. Mr. Rathbun seemed especially eager to chat."

Mr. Shelton sputtered in his juice glass, sending droplets all over the table. Meredith hurried forward to clean it up.

"Mr. Rathbun?" he said, though his question sounded more like an accusation.

"Yes," she answered as she scooped sugar into her cup. "His nephew introduced us, but after just a few minutes, I felt like we were old friends. He even complimented me on my necklace, saying that his late wife used to wear very similar pearls. I didn't expect the owner of such a grand house to be so warm and affable, though I was taken aback by his invitation to visit the South Fork Fishing and Hunting Club."

Mr. Shelton's mouth fell open. Faith stirred her coffee and took another sip, looking at the wall. After a moment, her father-in-law composed himself, snapping his newspaper open in front of his face.

"Well done, my dear."

"Thank you."

Mr. Shelton looked over at his son. "When do we get to see this fabled ground? Before or after Thanksgiving? I can extend my stay a day or two if need be."

Allan paused with a slice of bacon in his mouth. "Um, well the invitation was for their New Year's gala. Oh, and apparently I'm not going back to Pittsburgh. Mr Rathbun assured me that he would settle things with Mr. Jensen so I can stay here for the Christmas holiday."

"I see."

Faith saw the faintest sparkle of victory in Allan's eyes. He had enjoyed telling his father the news. She smiled to herself as she took a bite of toast. It felt good to know that he was fully on her side.

After a few minutes, Mr. Shelton announced that he was going out. Allan made a brief acknowledgment and continued eating his breakfast. Mr. Shelton left the room in a huff and stormed out of the house.

When the plates and cutlery had stopped rattling, Faith reached across the table and touched Allan's hand.

"Do you also have to go out today, darling?"

Allan wiped his mouth and dropped his napkin on his empty plate. "As a matter of fact, I don't."

Faith beamed. "And as luck would have it, neither do I."

"So what shall we do today?"

Faith picked up Precious, who was rubbing against her feet, and stroked the kitten's soft fur.

"I would like to explore Johnstown with you."

"All right. You can get ready and I'll go out and call for a carriage."

"No carriage. I want to walk."

Allan frowned. "It's rather cold outside."

"Will you keep me warm?"

"Of course." Allan rose to his feet. "I suppose that since I'm here for good, I should get to know my new city by foot."

Faith hurried around the table to kiss him before bounding up the stairs to get dressed for the brisk November weather. She was so excited, she wanted to squeal. This would be the first time she and her husband would be seen about town as proper Johnstown residents, and for people to see that she did indeed have a husband. She got the feeling that some of the neighbors and shopkeepers were beginning to wonder if she lived alone in this house, but now her man was home and she wanted everyone to know.

Despite the temperature, it was a beautiful day outside. Faith and Allan strolled arm-in-arm down the lane, smiling at neighbors and passersby. It was a short walk to downtown, which was fairly busy at this hour. Carriages and pedestrians hurried back and forth across the streets. As she observed the tension on the faces of the busy people, Faith was glad that Allan didn't have to go to work today.

"Where is your office?" she asked him as they walked.

Allan pointed towards the smokestacks on the other side of town. "About a mile that way. My office isn't right next to the works but it's near enough to have the constant smell of iron in the air."

"Do you have a big office?"

"Big enough. I have a nice view of the river."

Faith squeezed his arm. "I'd like to see your office one day."

"Of course, darling."

They walked through the town center and Faith pointed out the church she had attended on Sunday.

"I'd like to go again," she said.

Allan nodded absently but didn't say anything. His attention was focused on a building across the street.

"Is that an opera house?"

Faith shrugged. "That's what the sign says. Think the shows are any good? Can't be worse than the shows in Pittsburgh."

"Want to get out of this cold?" he asked.

She nodded, giving him a blue-lipped smile.

Allan flagged down a carriage and helped her inside.

"Where to, sir?" the driver said.

"Where should we go?" Allan asked Faith.

"How about the library? Your company paid for it."

"Sounds good. Cambria Library."

"Yes, sir." The driver tugged on the reins and the carriage started down the street.

The library stood tall and proud, looking like a large mother house flanked by smaller house children. Its brick structure had a castle-like quality but it still felt inviting. And it looked warm, which was the most important thing to Faith as she and Allan hurried inside.

The main hall was very quiet but bright, due to the large windows that let in abundant sunlight. The furnishings and decor were also impressive, consisting mainly of wood and brass. The number of books wasn't particularly large considering the size of the building, but it did seem like a good place to spend an afternoon reading. As Faith wandered among the shelves, she wondered if she might put some of her leisure time to good use in acquiring some new knowledge or perhaps learning a new language.

Allan found several newspapers and settled in a chair to peruse the articles. Faith opened a book on tales of the grotesque and took a seat opposite her husband. Reading together was something they would often do back in their apartment in Pittsburgh and it was nice to bring back old habits, even if it was in a new setting.

When lunchtime came, the two of them took a carriage to the Fifth Avenue Hotel, which was also owned by Cambria Iron Works. Allan declared with great gusto that the meal was to be charged to his company expense account and Faith acted impressed. He was so cute when he tried to show off. A few of his colleagues were also dining there and he exchanged pleasantries but politely refused the offer to join them, which actually did impress her.

The meal was delicious – filet mignon with greens that should have been out of season but were surprisingly still fresh. Faith could only eat about half of her serving.

"Where is your father?" she asked as she added sugar to her coffee.

"Who knows," Allan said in a grumbling tone as he took another bite of meat. "That man vexes me."

"He was happy about our invitation to the hunting and fishing club."

"But not happy that it was going to be after he'll have gone back to Pittsburgh."

Faith swallowed her nervousness. "Do you think he'll come back for Christmas and New Year's?"

Allan shrugged. "It's possible. He has a new mistress in Philadelphia and she might want him to spend time with her."

"A new mistress? When did this happen?"

"I don't know. Could have been recent, could have been a while back. I just found out about her a few days before coming here, but he acted like it had been going on for a long time. I thought he was still visiting that dame over in Newark."

Faith reached across the table and touched his hand. "So...did you ever get lonely while you were away from me?"

"Sure. But lonely just for you."

"Did anyone try to steal you away from me?"

Allan leaned across the table and flashed a sideways grin. "You know gals are always trying to steal me away from you. And you know

131

it'll never work because they can't hold a candle to you."

"I love you, Allan Shelton."

"I love you too, Faith Shelton."

"Will you take me shopping?"

Allan threw up his hands. "Love is a business, apparently."

"But you get quite a return on your investment, don't you?" Faith said with a sultry look in her eyes.

A smile reappeared on Allan's face. "Worth every penny. Come, let's get out of here."

****

Rays of setting sunlight tracked over the roof of the house as Faith and Allan walked up the stony path to the front door. After lunch, they had spent the next couple hours browsing shops and storefronts. Faith asked her darling husband to purchase an elegant collar for Precious, and Allan had quickly agreed. It was only after they left the shop that Faith realized he had been so eager because he was glad she wasn't buying something more expensive for herself.

They made their way through the town, not lost but not knowing exactly where they were either. Faith got an uneasy feeling when they found themselves in a rather rundown district made up of clapboard houses and unpaved streets. Children and dogs ran around as women prepared food and hung clothes. Few men were in sight. Faith studied the passing faces and was surprised that most of the women seemed happy. Tired, but happy. They didn't have the desperate look in their eyes that she had seen among the working poor in Pittsburgh. Perhaps that was because these women weren't actually poor. Allan later explained that the neighborhood was entirely owned by Cambria Iron Works and that all of the men were employed there. Most of the families came from Dutch, German, and Italian backgrounds, and compared to what their home countries had to offer them, life in Johnstown was a dream. Faith thought back to her own barefoot childhood, amazed at how her perspective had changed in just a few short years.

After taking a stroll along the river and having tea by the water, Faith was ready to go home. She held onto Allan's strong arm as they walked towards the house, feeling bright and happy in her heart. Allan led her up the steps and opened the front door for her, but she stopped short of walking inside.

"Allan...why is there luggage by the door?"

Allan looked over her shoulder and saw the trunks piled up in the foyer. "They're my father's," he noted with a frown.

A fountain of delight bubbled up in Faith's heart.

Is his father really leaving?

Mr. Shelton came down the stairs with heavy footfalls.

"Ah, children," he said as he finished buttoning his cuff links. "I was hoping you'd come back before I headed off."

Allan shut the door behind him and spread his hands wide. "Headed off? Father, what are you talking about?"

"I'm going back to Pittsburgh," Mr. Shelton said. His voice was chipper but he avoided eye contact. He went to the closet and extracted his hat and coat. "I thought I would be able to stay longer but something has come up and I must hurry back."

"Well..." Allan's words evaporated. He looked back at Faith, who put on her best surprised face. "Father," he pleaded, "you just got here!"

"I know. And I'm sorry to rush off like this – "

No, you're not, Faith said to herself.

" – And I'm heartbroken that I'll miss Thanksgiving, but I'm sure you'll have a splendid time with your new friends."

"But where will *you* go?" Allan asked. "Thanksgiving is meant to be spent with family."

Mr. Shelton wrapped his scarf around his neck. "I have some friends in Philadelphia. But I think I will probably be too busy to take time off anyway."

At the mention of Philadelphia, Allan gave Faith a knowing look. He turned back to his father.

"Well, what about Christmas?"

Faith's heart fell. *I'd rather him be here for Thanksgiving instead of Christmas.*

"I don't know," Mr. Shelton said, a touch of melancholy in his

134

voice. "There's still so much work to do."

"Hang your work!"

The house shuddered with Allan's shouted words. Faith and Mr. Shelton stared at him in surprise. Precious raised its head from the couch cushion. Meredith also peeked around a corner from where she had obviously been spying.

Allan looked away for a moment to compose himself. "Forgive my outburst," he said in a voice that still trembled with irritation. "I know you're busy, Father. And I also know that we sometimes butt heads, especially around the holidays. But we're all the family we have, and you are not going to spend Thanksgiving *and* Christmas alone."

Mr. Shelton's mustache quivered like he was going to say something, but the words didn't materialize. Then he smiled darkly and waved his finger at Allan.

"You are a shrewd negotiator, son. Very well. I shall return for Christmas."

Faith's veins ran cold. *No, please, no...!*

Allan's eyes met hers for a moment, but he looked away before she could glare at him.

"Good," he said to his father. "And I don't want you running off after just a day or two."

"You have my word. I shall push aside all thoughts of work for a week."

Faith smothered a gasp. *A whole week!*

135

Mr. Shelton turned to her and she caught a strange look in his eyes, like a flash of victory. "I hope that is all right, my dear," he said. "I don't want to be an imposition on your first Christmas in your new home."

She managed to force a smile to the surface. "Of course not. Like Allan said, we're all family."

"Yes," Mr. Shelton echoed, *"we* are."

Faith was puzzled his emphasis on the word *"we"* but her thoughts were interrupted by footsteps on the porch. A moment later, the doorbell clanged.

"That will be my coach," Mr. Shelton said as he shrugged into his coat. Meredith hurried to open the door and let the footman in to start gathering the trunks.

Mr. Shelton patted the top of his hat. "Well," he announced, "I shall be seeing you both again soon."

Before Allan or Faith could reply, he spun on his heel and marched out the door behind the man carrying his luggage. Allan stood in the doorway, staring into the twilight. In a huff, Faith turned and marched up the stairs. She stormed down the pictured-lined hallway to her boudoir and slammed the door.

I could just strangle him!

Her jaw clenched tight as she started ripping off her jewelry and throwing them onto the vanity. She squeezed herself out of her dress and put on her nightgown, then sat down in front of the mirror and began yanking the brush through her hair. It hurt when she raked through tangled knots but the pain helped her focus.

Why did Allan have to be so dense? Why couldn't he let his father just leave like he wanted, or at the very least, make him stay for Thanksgiving? That way they could have a delightful Christmas all to themselves. But no, he had to act like a whipped little puppy and now Christmas was ruined.

A timid knock sounded at the door.

"Faith?"

She didn't answer.

"Faith?" Allan called out again.

"I'm tired," she snapped. "Good night."

There was a sad pause.

"Good night."

Faith waited for him to speak or knock again, but she heard nothing. She let out an exasperated sigh and set the brush down. She didn't know why but she felt her eyes drawn to the picture on the far wall, a gentle image of Jesus praying.

She stared at the picture for several moments before tightening her jaw again.

I'm not going to pray. I'm going to bed.

****

Faith didn't know where Allan slept; she just knew that it wasn't in her bed. In the morning after she awoke, she dressed and came down for breakfast, ready to give him the coldest shoulder she could muster. Meredith dutifully informed her that Master Allan had already had breakfast and left the house, mentioning that he would be gone all day. Faith pretended not to care, but as the day crawled by, she found her thoughts drifting back to him. It was silly, she knew, and she told herself to get dressed and do something productive. Perhaps go to church, since it was Sunday morning. Yet the time crawled by and she found herself still lounging about the house in her robe, browsing through books or absentmindedly stroking Precious in her lap.

You're an embarrassment to modern women everywhere, she scolded herself. The condescending voice in her heart was right: she was the epitome of the bored, spoiled housewife, pining for her husband after a spat. After all, he was the one in the wrong! Inviting his overbearing father to the first Christmas in their new house? Was he *trying* to turn their marriage bed cold?

Faith looked down at Precious. "Don't fall in love," she said with a wry smile. "Especially since it would mean a whole litter of kittens in your case."

Precious mewled quietly and burrowed deeper in the folds of her dress. Faith looked out the window at the leafless trees and sighed.

She knew what was missing; she had felt it almost since the day she had moved into this house.

A baby.

A rosy-cheeked little angel to cuddle and feed and play with in the garden. And now that Allan was home to stay, she figured the odds had improved quite a bit.

So are you going to hold onto grudges or focus on more important things?

Faith blushed. The voice in her heart certainly knew how to get right to the point.

Allan is a good man, she had to admit. *And a good man is supposed to love his father, even when his father is hard to love. Like it or not, his father is part of your family.*

Faith pursed her lips and looked across the room.

Well, he still should have talked to me about it first.

At that moment, she spotted Allan walking up the pathway to the house. He looked so handsome and dashing with his hat and suit and broad shoulders and that self-assured look on his face that had caught her eye almost two years ago.

Her pulse quickened and she could heart the voice in her heart laughing at her. She didn't care.

She loved him.

And she wasn't going to sleep in a cold bed again tonight.

Chapter Nine

WHEN THANKSGIVING DAY arrived, Faith awoke with butterflies in her stomach.

She saw this holiday dinner as her home's debutante ball, and she had spent nearly every waking hour that week planning, preparing, and decorating. Meredith accompanied her as she flitted to and fro like a busy bee, and she wisely avoided telling Allan the full amount of how much she was planning to spend on the dinner. Since Thanksgiving had been instituted only a quarter of a century earlier by the late President Lincoln, many people didn't celebrate it, or if they did, it was more of a social event, like the soiree at Mr. War's home last week. Faith herself hadn't even heard about the holiday until she had come to Pittsburgh.

But Johnstown was a fresh start, a new beginning, and she was determined to make her home as festive as possible. As long as she was mistress of this house, every holiday would be celebrated to the fullest.

A nagging sense of worry had been plaguing her all day, beyond the usual trepidations about food and decor and the guest list. About midday, she realized what was making her nervous. The epiphany happened as she was passing a mirror in the hall. She caught her reflection and stopped, nearly dropping the platters she held in her hands. The face that stared back at her was that of a dirty-cheeked girl wearing hand-sewn clothes. And the look in the girl's eyes was stern, even accusatory.

You are just a pretender.

Faith had heard those words whispered in the back of her mind many times before, especially when she had first inserted herself into Pittsburgh high society. She had willingly sacrificed her principles upon the altar of social advancement, telling herself that she had made the right decision when Allan Shelton had asked for her hand in marriage. And now she had a big, fancy house and was fast becoming a respectable member of Johnstown.

But those eyes staring back at her didn't believe it. They told her that she was an impostor, a low-born mountain girl who just happened to have a pretty face.

You don't belong here. You're just playing house. You got lucky with Allan, and perhaps he simply has lower standards than the other men who were interested in you as a distraction but hardly as a wife. Maybe your father-in-law is right.

The platters shattered on the ground. Faith clenched her jaw tight and looked herself right in the eyes.

I will decide what, and who, I am.

Meredith came running up to her.

"Are you all right, madam?"

"Yes," Faith stammered, looking at the shards around her feet. "I suppose I overestimated how much I can carry. I'll clean all this up."

"You'll do no such thing. I'll clean it up and fetch the large plates to serve in their place. You need to go lie down for a bit, then come down all bright and fresh and tell me everything that's wrong about how I set the table."

Faith laughed. "I'm sure it will be fine. But I would enjoy a few minutes of rest."

"I insist, madam. I can see you're under a lot of pressure."

Faith glanced back at the mirror. She saw an elegant young woman who was preparing to host her first social event in her new home.

"Perhaps. But nothing I can't handle."

****

After lying down on the bed for a few restless minutes, Faith decided it was time to get herself ready. It was so hard to choose which dress to wear...and which jewelry to go with it...and how to wear her hair...and which shoes looked best...and when she was all finished, she still wasn't completely pleased with the results. She studied her reflection in the mirror and groaned in frustration.

A knock sounded at the door. "Come in!" she barked.

Allan poked his head into the room, his smile bearing a hint of nervousness. Faith sighed and closed her eyes for a moment.

"Sorry," she said, holding her hands out to him. "I'm glad you're home."

"You look marvelous."

"Really?" Faith looked in the mirror again, this time noticing the bright glow in her cheeks. "Thank you," she said, giving him a gentle peck on the cheek. She didn't want to ruin her lipstick, after all.

"The house smells delicious," Allan added. "I had to put the cat out because it keeps trying to get into the kitchen."

Faith clicked her tongue. "Oh Allan, it's freezing outside!"

She rushed past him as he held up his hands in surrender and hurried down the steps. She could hear Precious mewling outside on the front porch and when she let it in, the cat jumped into her arms. Faith didn't care about keeping her outfit pristine; she nuzzled the cat's soft fur and held it close to warm it up. She gave Allan a look as he came down the stairs. He just shook his head and headed to the kitchen.

The guests started to arrive shortly after nightfall, ten altogether. Mr. War had been invited but as expected, he already had holiday plans. Stephen and Charlotte were the only guests that Faith knew personally before tonight but she quickly charmed the other guests, most of whom were Allan's work colleagues and their wives. The evening went off without a hitch – everyone talked and laughed and

144

ate and shared what they were thankful for, although Faith noticed Charlotte would sometimes stare off into the distance, uttering short chuckles on cue when everyone else would laugh. Stephen didn't seem to notice her despondence, joining in the mirth along with the other guests.

Even though she was seated at the other end of the table, Faith managed to catch Charlotte's eye and give her a sympathetic smile. Charlotte seemed to brighten for a moment and began pecking at her food without much interest.

After the meal was finished, the guests moved out of the dining room and into the parlor where Allan served brandy and bourbon for the gentlemen and sherry for the ladies. Meredith brought coffee for those who weren't having spirits, and Faith took a cup from the tray and lifted it towards her husband.

"Cheers, darling," she announced. "Happy Thanksgiving, everyone."

Glasses were raised and cheers were echoed. Faith entertained the group with an Irish folk song about a lost lover wandering in a forest. The men were enchanted and the women looked on with jealous admiration. After the song, Faith bowed to their applause, then noticed that Charlotte was absent. She excused herself and began searching the rooms downstairs. She finally found Charlotte standing out on the porch, smoking a cigarette.

Charlotte flushed with embarrassment. "Oh, Faith. I..."

Faith rubbed her arms to keep warm and walked out onto the porch. "It's all right. Everyone needs a moment to themselves now and then."

Charlotte took a quick puff and exhaled almost immediately. Faith noticed her hand trembling slightly.

"Are you all right?" she asked.

Charlotte nodded and took another pull from the cigarette, longer this time. "I'm fine."

Faith sat against the porch railing. "It's not the cigarette that makes you feel like the odd one out, is it?"

"No. It's not the cigarette."

"Then what is it?"

A chilly breeze made the branches chatter, though Charlotte seemed unaffected by the cold. She just stared out into the darkness, her beautiful face completely motionless.

Then she turned and looked at Faith with a tear sparkling in her eye.

"I'll never be one of you."

"What do you mean?"

Charlotte raised the cigarette to her lips but let it fall again.

"I've had a wonderful evening. Really, I have. Your home is beautiful, and you and Allan seem so happy together. And I heard your song, even though I was out here. But all of this just reminds me of what I'll never have."

146

"What won't you have?"

"This. A warm, cozy house with a husband and food and happy guests."

"Why not? You and Stephen are engaged to be married. And Stephen has quite a bit of money. I'm sure you will outdo all of us."

Charlotte smiled joylessly. "In a way, yes. I may have a big fancy house and host big fancy parties. But I fear I will never have the warmth that I feel here."

Faith moved closer and took her hand. "Charlotte, what's wrong? Why are you saying this?"

Charlotte looked away. "I'm nobody, Faith. Stephen Baldwick's arm candy, nothing more."

"That's not true! You're his fiancée. He loves you."

"Loves me? What makes you say that?"

Faith blinked. Her mouth started to form words but they evaporated on her tongue. She squinted her eyes, as if trying to focus on Charlotte's question.

"Are you being serious?" she sputtered after finding her voice. "Why wouldn't a man marry a woman unless he loves her, at least to some degree?"

Charlotte heaved a sigh and puffed on her cigarette. "Oh, he loves in part. I'm sure you can guess which part."

"Come now. Men are men. They may not be the fairy tale princes we dream of but the good ones hold deep affection in their hearts, even if it only manifests in limited ways."

"If that's the case, my fiance has love for quite a large number of women."

"Charlotte..."

"Everyone knows it," Charlotte added offhandedly, cocking her hips and striking an exaggerated pose of nonchalance. "So did I before we were a couple."

"So why did he ask you to marry him? And why did you say yes?"

Charlotte looked at her with startling intensity. Faith wondered for a moment if she was going to lash out and strike her.

But as quickly as it had flared, the fire in Charlotte's eyes died down. She took one last pull from the cigarette and stubbed it out on a brick ledge.

"I suppose the easy answer would be to say that we were what we both needed," Charlotte said. "He's looking to rise in the company ranks, and he can only get so far as a bed-hopping playboy. Not that he's changed much, but in order to attend social functions like this, he has me to show off as a testament to his propriety."

Something stirred in Faith's heart. "And what about you?" she asked, somewhat fearful of the answer.

Charlotte shrugged. "Why does any girl marry an unscrupulous man? Because he has money. Because she thinks she can change him. Because she's just as attracted to his power as those around him, and she's proud of herself for being the closest to it."

Faith's eyes fell. *Sound familiar?*

She pushed the voice deep down. "But if you knew what kind of man he was, why did you agree to marry him?"

"Because if I didn't, someone else would, and I'd just be another fish in the sea, trying to get reeled in on a golden hook."

"Don't sell yourself short like that. You are smart, insightful, and very pretty. Any man would be happy to marry you, and if he knew what's good for him, he'd be devoted to you alone."

"Thanks," Charlotte said with a blushing smile. "That's what every girl hopes, and I suspect it's not true more than it is, especially the higher you go up the ladder."

"Charlotte," Faith said gently, putting her hands on her arms, "there is no reason you can't have the life, and the love, that you dream of. You don't have to go down a road that you don't want to. I'm hardly a marriage expert but I know enough that a nice home or fancy clothes are no substitute for a union without true love."

"Is that what you have? True love?"

"Yes. Allan and I truly love each other."

Charlotte wore a look of amazement on her face. "I swear, you must have found the only honest man among the whole bunch."

Faith wrestled with whether or not she should share her own story. It was a bit unsettling hearing Charlotte put into words the thoughts that would often run through her own head, especially in the early days when she first came to Pittsburgh. And she certainly had a

149

rough road paved with regrets before she and Allan fell for one another.

But it is true love, isn't it? It must be. Allan isn't a dallying playboy like Stephen. And his expressions of affection go beyond physical intimacy. Maybe she's right...maybe Allan is one of the few good ones out there.

She looked at Charlotte with sympathetic eyes. "Are you free on Saturday afternoon? The weather should be nice, and it would be a wonderful excuse to spend some time together."

Charlotte's face lit up. "Oh, I would love that!"

Faith grinned and led her toward the door. "Wonderful. Let's go inside before we turn into icicles."

They stepped into the warm house and Meredith seemed to materialize out of thin air, handing them saucers with cups of hot tea. She gave them a polite smile and headed off to tend to her duties.

"She's amazing," Charlotte remarked.

"Yes, she is," Faith said, taking a careful sip. "Let's get back to the party."

****

"Where did you run off to?" Allan asked from the bed as he flipped a page in the *Johnstown Gazette*.

Faith finished buttoning her nightdress and closed the bureau.

The party had been wonderful but exhausting, and she was grateful to be out of that constricting dress and uncomfortable shoes.

"Run off to?" she echoed.

"Yes. After your song."

"Ah." The gears in Faith's mind whirred frantically, processing what she should and shouldn't say. "I had to go to the toilet and I saw Charlotte outside on the porch. She was...smoking."

"Smoking?"

"Yes."

"Was she upset?"

Faith hesitated again. "I couldn't tell at first, but I didn't want to leave her out there alone, so I went out to chat with her."

"And?"

"It took a little while but she opened up to me, confiding in me how she felt a little out of place."

"Out of place? What does that mean?"

Faith drew back the goose down duvet and sat down on the bed. "She's like me, Allan. Just a girl trying to find her way in a man's world."

Allan put down the paper. He reached out and touched her face. "I doubt she's anything like you."

"I'm sure we're different in a lot of ways but we're also similar. I got the impression that she comes from humble beginnings, like me. And we both managed to find good men with lots of money."

Allan laughed. "Well, I'd say I'm more 'good' than Stephen and he has more money than me."

"What do you mean?"

"About the money or being good?"

"Being good."

"Come now, dear, I told you about Stephen Baldwick's reputation. I'm a little surprised that Charlotte puts up with it. They are not yet married and they carry on like a married couple, so I don't think her scruples are particularly keen either."

"Allan, don't say such things!"

"It's not me saying them. It's everyone around town. Of course, it's better for Stephen than for Charlotte. Stephen's a bit of a legend at the company. Many men are secretly envious of him. Charlotte is quite fetching but he doesn't let that stop him from chasing Johnstown's co-quettes. And perhaps Stephen isn't the only one stepping out at night. I wouldn't be surprised."

"I won't hear anymore of this," Faith grumbled, extinguishing the bedside lamp and burrowing under the blanket.

"I'm sorry, darling," Allan said with a chuckle. He wrapped his arms around her shoulders. "I don't mean to speak ill of her. You two seemed to hit it off. And I would bet she needs a friend."

Faith turned around and looked at her husband. "Are you like him?"

"Who? Stephen? No, sweetheart, of course not. Ever since I met you, you've been the queen of my heart."

"But do you think it's wise to spend time with him? Bad company corrupts good morals."

Allan sighed. "Honey, don't worry about me. I work with him, so naturally I'm going to spend time around him. But that doesn't mean he's going to rub off on me."

Faith searched his eyes, seeing the reassuring sparkle of honesty in them. "Really?"

"Really. Besides, I would never do anything as stupid as stepping out on you."

"You better not."

She gave him a poke in the ribs. He yelped and grabbed her, making her giggle. Then their lips found each other's.

"Happy Thanksgiving, darling," Allan whispering, drawing her close.

Faith could feel herself melting into him. "Happy Thanksgiving, my love."

****

Faith was glad that the first holiday in her new home had gone off without a hitch, but the true test would be Christmas, especially with her father-in-law coming back into town. That's why she was so happy to spend her Saturday afternoon around town with Charlotte.

Their conversation while they dined at a French cafe on Main Street was a bit more lighthearted than their chat on the porch had been. Charlotte opened up right away, and Faith saw her own struggles in her, the doubts and uncertainty. But since Charlotte looked up to her, Faith tried to soothe her own misgivings about the path she was on, though it was hard to be encouraging after what Allan had said about Stephen. Faith didn't want to be the one to break up a potential marriage but she definitely felt uneasy about telling Charlotte to stay the course and hope for the best.

What would I do if I were her? she asked herself.

The answer was clear.

Run.

But who was she to give marriage advice, especially since she was in Charlotte's shoes not too long ago?

Just be a listening ear and a kind heart.

She and Charlotte spent most of the day together, and they went out again the following week. There was something freeing about being with Charlotte. On one hand, she felt like she could be herself—open and honest about her feelings, her worries, her delights. But on the other hand, she had to maintain the ideal image that Charlotte had imposed on her: a young married woman of sophistication and taste with impeccable virtue. She had to be careful not to let too much information about her past slip out. Charlotte would sometimes try to pry, and Faith would be clear enough to give the impression of answering her questions but vague enough so as to avoid letting any scandalous anecdotes slip. Yet the more she strove to hide her days before marrying Allan, the more those days were on her mind. Sometimes they would prick her heart with regret, and sometimes she would have to hide her smile. She did have fun and exciting memories, and on blustery days when she would stay in the house and put up Christmas decorations, her thoughts would sometimes drift back to those wild times, swirling and twirling through Pittsburgh nightlife.

It really was a miracle that Allan agreed to marry her. And it was no surprise that his father disapproved.

Are you going to keep measuring your worth by how men think of you?

She wanted to answer with an emphatic "No!" but if she was being honest with herself, she did care very much what other people thought of her, especially her husband. And there wasn't anything wrong with that. She was just tired of feeling like an impostor here in Johnstown, and the only way to put an end to those thoughts was to stop comparing herself to those she perceived as genuine. Who was to say that the high-society women she met at these parties didn't have sordid pasts even more scandalous than hers or Charlotte's? How many of them were having affairs right under their husband's noses? At least Faith could boast that she was a chaste wife.

It was going to take time, she knew, but she was determined to make a name for herself in Johnstown. Allan was building his legacy in

155

the steel industry, and she was going to build her legacy in society.

One of the best ways to do that was to have a stunning home.

She stepped back to look at the garlands that twisted around the banisters of the sweeping central staircase. Her eyes narrowed as she studied the bursts of holly among the spruce needles and pine cones.

This house was going to become a Christmas wonderland.

Chapter Ten

One week before Christmas, 1888
Johnstown, Pennsylvania

THE TRAIN WHISTLE BLEATED as the locomotive rumbled into the station, its massive wheels screeching to a stop. Steam gushed from vents and filled the platform. People waiting to board the train moved forward a few steps, anxious to get out of the cold.

The conductor stepped out of the first car and blew his whistle. Allan didn't react but Faith winced. Shrill sounds normally didn't bother her but today the noise pierced her eardrums like needles. She shivered and rubbed her arms, hoping Allan would notice, but his attention was on the passengers disembarking from the train.

A shadow passed over Faith's eyes as a rotund shape materialized out of the mist.

Think on the bright side, she told herself. *At least he wasn't here to ruin your wedding anniversary last week.*

"Hello, Father," Allan said, reaching out to shake Mr. Shelton's hand.

"Feels ten degrees colder here than in Pittsburgh," Mr. Shelton grumbled. He glanced at Faith and squeezed out a polite smile. "How do?"

"Fine, thank you," Faith answered with equally taut politeness. "I think the fresh mountain air lends itself to a cooler, more crisp feeling. I find it refreshing myself."

Mr. Shelton pursed his lips. "Make sure those monkeys don't drop my trunks," he said to Allan with a glance over his shoulder. "Last time the whole pile fell over and dented one of the corners."

"Don't say 'monkeys,' Father." Allan gave him a stern look and headed towards the baggage car.

Mr. Shelton straightened his jacket and checked his pocketwatch. "So, how is small town life?" he asked, looking at no one in particular.

"It suits both of us just fine," Faith answered, keeping her gaze parallel with his.

"Good to hear. I was a little nervous about Allan, to be honest. He's been a city boy all his life and after getting the job for him here, I began to have second thoughts about how he might handle being away from everything he's used to."

"He has adjusted quite well. And to be honest myself, I don't think he misses Pittsburgh much. All his needs are taken care of here."

Mr. Shelton raised an eyebrow. "I'm sure."

Allan returned, looking slightly flustered. His father's face fell.

"Don't tell me those mon...those men dropped my baggage again."

Allan shook his head. "No. They're just trying to *find* all of your bags."

"What do you mean, all my bags? There were three trunks and two small suitcases."

"Yes. And they have three trunks and one small suitcase."

Mr. Shelton's face reddened like a beet. "Why, of all the..."

He stormed off towards the baggage car, trailing a string of curses. Allan put his arm around Faith and heaved a sigh.

Faith gave him a dark smile. "It's going to be a lovely Christmas, isn't it?"

Allan laughed, though it sounded more like a whimper.

****

Charlotte took a sip of her tea and fixed her eyes on Faith over the rim of the cup.

Faith shrank back from her gaze. "What?"

"You have that look again."

"What look?"

"Faith, you can tell me."

"Tell you what?"

Charlotte didn't answer; she just kept her eyes steady.

159

Faith looked around the restaurant, trying desperately to find a distraction. Then she sighed.

"He's ruining Christmas."

"Your father-in-law?"

Faith nodded. "He's been here for just two days and he's driving everyone crazy."

"How so?"

"He hardly says anything nice to anyone, especially to me. It's no secret that he doesn't think I'm a good match for Allan."

"But you know that's not true."

"Of course I know. Allan and I are perfect for each other, but no one likes being judged."

"Welcome to my world."

Faith reached out and touched her hand. "I'm sorry, I didn't mean—"

"Don't worry about it. We're all in the same boat, to one degree or another. How does Allan like having his father around?"

"Allan is conveniently finding himself rather busy. He can't wait to leave the house in the morning and he comes home later than usual, just so he won't have to be around his father too much."

"You both saw your father-in-law a good deal in Pittsburgh, right?"

"Yes, but he didn't live with us. He was barely tolerable then, and everything is compounded tenfold now. And poor Meredith..."

"That woman is made of steel."

"Don't I know it. I would positively lose my mind if she weren't around. She does the work of four women. How many domestics does Stephen keep?"

Charlotte laughed dryly. "At least five. That man is a slob like no other."

"Will that change once you two are married?"

"I doubt it."

"Why not?"

"Because we're not getting married."

"Charlotte! What happened?"

A few patrons looked over at their table, startled by Faith's outburst. She gave an apologetic smile and leaned forward.

"What's wrong?" she asked in an urgent whisper. "Did he hurt you?"

Charlotte fidgeted with her hands for a moment. "I suppose you could say that. He didn't put his hands on me or anything. He just..."

"Just what?"

A tear escaped from the corner of Charlotte's left eye. "He told me that I was a liability for him."

"A liability? What did he mean by that?"

Charlotte shrugged and dabbed at her eye with a napkin, careful to avoid smudging her makeup. "He said that if he was going to make something of himself, he needed a partner of 'higher status'."

"So he's saying that he's too good for you?"

"That's the gist of it, I suppose."

"What a pig. Everyone knows the company he keeps. He's no better than the ironworkers who go to the whorehouses after their shifts."

Her eyes grew wide and she covered her mouth with her hands. "Oh Charlotte, I'm so sorry, I didn't mean it like that..."

Charlotte waved her words away. "No, no, you're right. He was a pig. He *is* a pig."

"Maybe you're better off not marrying him after all. We can't live our lives being dishonest to ourselves, no matter how nice things may look on the outside."

"You're right. I always knew what kind of man he was, and it bothered me, of course, but I told myself that the life I was getting in return was worth it."

"When has that ever been true?"

Charlotte's smile was tinged with sadness. "Everyone thinks that their life is special and unique. It's kind of tragic how we keep reliving the same mistakes throughout history."

"You're not the first woman to be seduced with diamonds and gold and gotten a rotten deal out of it. Besides, you don't need someone like him in your life. You're smart, you're beautiful, you're sociable."

"Thank you," Charlotte said with a blush. "But you said we need to be honest with ourselves, and I want to be honest. Don't you think he has a point? He's going to be king someday, and I'm just a peasant. Those kinds of stories only happen in fairy tales."

Faith reached out for her hand again, and she squeezed it with enough force to make Charlotte gasp.

"Now you listen to me," Faith said, her voice almost a growl. "Don't you *ever* let anyone tell you what your life ought to be. Where you were born, where you grew up, your father's last name – none of it matters. You are who you make yourself into. Stephen Baldwick may be steel company royalty, but that doesn't make him less of a pig. Probably even more so. And he's got it all backwards. He's not too good for you; you are too good for him."

Charlotte said nothing. She picked up her tea, cold by now, and took a small sip. Faith watched her carefully, trying to peek into her thoughts.

"What will you do?" she asked.

"Well, Stephen was kind enough to give me a 'severance package', as he put it. Enough to last me through the winter. Though I'll have to budget my money, since I suppose I was getting a bit spoiled spending so much time with him. I got used to him taking care of me."

"Are you going to stay in Johnstown?"

"I don't know." Charlotte dabbed at her eye again. "It's not like a big city where you can disappear. I already have a bit of a name here, good or bad depending on who you talk to. Now I'll just be known as

163

Stephen Baldwick's cast-off, doubly scandalous because we were engaged to be married. Everyone will assume it's my fault the engagement broke."

Her lip trembled and then the tears came. They streamed down her face in almost perfectly straight lines, carving paths through her makeup.

Faith glanced around at the other restaurant customers who were starting to look their way again.

"Charlotte," she said in a hushed tone, "we should get out of here."

Charlotte nodded, struggling to get her tears under control. Faith got the attention of a waiter and asked for the check and she paid the bill while Charlotte kept her head low. After the check had been paid, Faith helped Charlotte to her feet and took her outside. They stood shivering out on the snowblown street, facing one another.

"Thank you for the coffee," Charlotte said, mist spurting from her lips. She seemed frail, almost child-like.

Faith reached out and took Charlotte's hand. "Come home with me. You really shouldn't be alone."

"Thank you. You're very kind, but I think it might do me some good to be alone. My life was so wrapped up in Stephen, I forget who I was before I met him."

"But Christmas is only a few days away."

"I'll be fine. I do have a few acquaintances around. I know what you're going to say, and I don't want you to say it."

"What?"

"Don't invite me over for Christmas dinner."

Faith couldn't stop the guilty smile from spreading across her face. "Never crossed my mind."

Charlotte laughed. "You're a good friend. I'm glad we met."

"Me too."

The two women stood with their hands clasped for a moment, and then Charlotte pulled hers back.

"Merry Christmas, Faith."

She turned and walked down the street, leaning against the wind. Faith's heart broke for the poor girl and she almost called out for her to wait so that she could at least pay for a carriage to take her home, but something held her back.

Maybe she's right. Maybe she does need to be on her own for a while.

Faith shook her head and hurried to a carriage waiting in the road.

"Is the carriage available?" she asked, her teeth chattering.

The driver nodded and hopped down to open the door for her. Faith breathed a sigh of relief as she shut the door, feeling better almost instantly. The carriage slowly made its way through the streets, the horse's hoofbeats muffled by the snow. As she relaxed on the plush cushions, Faith found her thoughts drifting back to what Charlotte said over coffee, about Stephen wanting a partner of higher status.

Does Allan ever feel the same about me?

Faith pictured her husband's face in her mind. She had spent many nights watching him sleep next to her, that handsome face gently illuminated by the moonlight. Her heart overflowed with love for him, and she knew he felt the same about her, but she couldn't help but wonder if he felt it *all* the time. Her brief immersion in Pittsburgh high society made her realize how easily these men would cast aside a woman when they grew tired of her, and it was usually for carnal reasons. She had met a number of girls like herself, big dreams and pretty faces, all willing to sacrifice their principles if it meant they could remain in the clouds a little longer, hopefully long enough to rope a man into marriage. Some of them didn't mind the inevitable divorce because they would take a sizable chunk of their husband's money with them, but Faith wanted more than that. She wanted to put down roots, to weave her family name into the fabric of high society, to ensure her children's place in it.

A warm feeling spread over her skin and her lips turned up in a gentle smile. She couldn't wait to –

The carriage lurched to a stop, nearly throwing Faith from her seat. She heard the horses' hooves clomp loudly on the cobblestone and the driver calling out to calm them.

"Apologies, madam," he said after he had gotten the animals settled. "A stray dog ran across the street and frightened the horses."

Faith exhaled through her nose and smoothed her dress.

"It's all right," she said as he opened the door and offered his hand. She stepped down onto the snow-covered sidewalk and gasped in the brisk air.

"Best get inside, madam," the driver said.

Faith paid him and hurried up the stone pathway. When she drew near the house, she noticed someone sitting in a chair on the porch.

"Allan?" she said as she walked up the steps.

Allan reached out his hand to her. She took it, noticing it was quite cold.

"You're freezing!" she exclaimed.

Allan sighed. "Father is in the parlor smoking a cigar. The whole house reeks of smoke."

"Did you tell him to smoke outside?"

"He was already halfway through his cigar when I came home."

"Well, did you at least tell Meredith to open the windows?"

"Yes. Can't you smell it?"

Faith sniffed the air and made a face. "Goodness, you're right."

Allan patted the chair next to him. Faith wasn't enthusiastic about sitting outside but she figured it was better than going inside. She snuggled up against him for warmth.

"Allan?" she said after a moment.

167

"Hm?"

"Do you ever wish..."

"Wish what?"

"Wish that I came from a better family?"

Allan frowned. "What are you talking about?"

Faith smoothed her dress, feeling very self-conscious all of a sudden.

It was a stupid thing to say.

But she had already said it, and besides, it would be nice to have his assurance. She lifted her head and met his eyes.

"Marriage is a bond between a man and a woman," she said, "but we all know that when you marry someone, you marry their family. I'm quite proud of the Shelton family name, probably more than I let on. Me, on the other hand, I'm just a little bird in the wind. You don't get to tell people about my family money or titles or history, because there isn't any, and sometimes I feel bad for you."

Allan covered her hand with his. "I speak the truth when I say that the thought has never entered my mind."

Faith's heart melted. "Truly?"

"Truly. I don't mean this in a harsh way, but there is a measure of relief for a man to find a woman who is unfettered and free. I have so many friends whose parents-in-law make them miserable. Sometimes I wonder if you don't have the same thought about me."

"Oh, Allan. I don't deserve you. And I never had such a

thought."

That's not entirely true, but it's what he needs to hear.

Allan smiled. Then he slapped his knees and got to his feet.

"Family or no family," he declared, "I'm making him put that wretched thing out or smoke outside."

Faith tried to hide her smile as he marched back inside.

"Good luck!" she called after him.

****

Some grumbling and sour looks ensued, but Mr. Shelton agreed to smoke outdoors. In fact, for the next few days leading up to Christmas, his demeanor seemed to soften quite a bit. By contrast, Faith noticed Allan walking around the house with his head held higher and he spoke to his father like a colleague, as opposed to a son living in his shadow. This new-found bravado made him even more appealing and Faith would steal secret kisses when no one was watching.

One night, she lay with her head on his chest listening to his heartbeat.

"Allan, what is happening with your father?"

"What do you mean?"

"Your father. He's different. He's changed. He's *nice!*"

"Nice?"

Faith raised her head to look at him. "Well, he hasn't given me a

169

disapproving frown for days. He doesn't talk to me much, but as far as I'm concerned, that's nice behavior coming from him. So what did you do? It can't be just insisting that he smoke outdoors."

A devious smile spread across Allan's face. He looked so handsome that Faith's heart fluttered.

"Well?" she prodded.

Allan let the smile linger for a moment longer. "I had lunch with Mr. War last week."

"And?"

"I mentioned that my father was in town for the holiday, and Mr. War remembered our invitation to the South Fork Fishing and Hunting Club."

"Well, I should hope so. I've been looking forward to seeing it ever since that magnificent dinner."

"And see it we shall."

"So what does this have to do with your father?"

"Mr. War said he recalled meeting him once. 'He reeked of cigar smoke,' he said with a laugh that wasn't entirely funny. I politely agreed. Then he told me to bring him along with us when we head up there for the New Year's gala."

Faith looked puzzled for a moment, then her face brightened with understanding. "My dear husband," she said, mirroring his smile, "are you holding this invitation hostage in exchange for your father's good behavior?"

Allan couldn't hide the playful guilt in his eyes. "Perhaps," he said dismissively. "It will probably backfire and he may be twice as ornery after the event. But I figure it will guarantee us a cordial Christmas at least."

"How very enterprising of you." Faith leaned up and kissed him. "And I will pretend to be none the wiser. Perhaps his cordiality might actually become genuine."

"One can only hope," Allan replied.

Chapter Eleven

Christmas Day, 1888

FAITH WAS SO EXCITED when she woke up, she thought she might pop. The first Shelton family Christmas in Johnstown!

Snow fell gently outside but inside was warm and cozy. Scents of spruce and peppermint wafted through the air, mixing with the delicious aromas coming from the kitchen. Faith glided through the house in a velvet and silk gown, wearing a diamond necklace that Allan had surprised her with when they woke up. She wondered if she should give him his gift early but she figured it was best to wait.

The Shelton men made their way downstairs, enticed by the aromas coming from the kitchen. Breakfast was still a few minutes from being ready, so Faith insisted that they sing Christmas carols in the study. Allan and his father protested at first but Faith wasn't going to let the merry moment slip away, and she grabbed both men by the hand and pulled them down the hall.

She took the lead and sang alone for the first couple of songs but

Allan joined in for "Jingle Bells." Then to her surprise, Mr. Shelton sang along for the final chorus. Faith had to admit he had a marvelous bass voice. Even Allan seemed taken aback.

"I haven't heard you sing in ages, Father," he exclaimed.

Mr. Shelton shrugged, a surly smile tugging at the corners of his mustache. "All this merriment is like a plague. You can't help but get infected by it."

"That's one way to put it," Allan said with a laugh.

A warm feeling washed over Faith's heart and her eyes shone with tears.

Well, aren't you getting all mushy over the holidays!

Faith told the voice in her heart to shush. After all, it was natural that she was going to be emotional since –

"Breakfast is on the table!" Meredith called out.

Mr. Shelton practically leaped out of his chair and hurried into the dining room. Allan offered his arm to Faith, and the two of them walked together. She placed her head on his strong shoulder and exhaled a quiet sigh.

"Are you all right?" he asked.

"Yes. I just love being with you at Christmas."

He gave her hand a squeeze. "Me too."

They were stunned when they entered the dining room and saw the feast laid out on the table. Meredith had really outdone herself this time. Ham, sausage, and duck anchored the center table, surrounded by platters of corn meal, biscuits, potatoes, greens, jam, gravy, and sauce laid out in a picturesque array fit for a painting. Allan helped Faith into her seat and then motioned to Meredith.

"Sit down, Meredith."

"Oh, no sir," Meredith said, standing in the doorway with her hands folded together. "I have too much cleaning to do."

"And it shall wait. I insist that you sit down and enjoy this marvelous meal that you have worked all morning to prepare."

Meredith bowed her head. "Yes, sir."

She sat down on the other side of Mr. Shelton, who gave her a hint of a smile. Everyone joined hands and Allan said, "Faith, my dear, would you please bless our food?"

Faith nodded. "Our Father in Heaven," she prayed, "thank You for Your many blessings. Thank You for home, food, family, friends, and most of all, the gift of Your Son Jesus Christ. Bless this meal and the hands that prepared it. Amen."

"Amen," everyone echoed.

The dishes were passed around and plates were heaped full of mouthwatering food. Meredith was hesitant at first but Allan insisted that she try every dish she had prepared, and soon she was eating happily. There wasn't much conversation at first; the only sounds were clattering silverware and food being chewed. Meredith ate the fastest, asking to be excused and hurrying off to the kitchen to prepare tea and coffee. Allan and Faith exchanged grins, and then Allan looked at his father and clicked his tongue.

"Uh uh, father. You know the rules."

Mr. Shelton put away his cigar. "My apologies. Old habits. Too cold out to smoke anyway."

Faith looked at her husband. *He is a genius.*

Meredith informed them that tea and coffee and cakes were served in the great room, and Mr. Shelton declared that it was time for presents. Faith's heart began pounding. What if Allan didn't like his gift?

Stop being silly. He's going to love it.

She followed the men into the large room where a fire roared in the hearth and the yuletide tree sparkled and glittered in front of the window. Several boxes were piled underneath and Allan once again called Meredith into the room.

"Everyone in this family gets gifts," he told her. Meredith smiled and couldn't stop a tear from trickling down her cheek. To cover her embarrassment, she hurried to the tree and started distributing the presents.

"Merry Christmas!" Allan declared.

"Merry Christmas," Faith echoed, giving him a kiss on the cheek. Mr. Shelton snorted but she ignored him, turning her attention to the gifts on her lap. She opened the largest one first, gasping at the beautiful dress she unwrapped.

"I'm going to wear it to the New Year's Eve gala," she said.

Allan's eyes lit up. "Splendid idea!"

Her next gift was from her father-in-law, a small box that jingled. She opened it carefully and her eyes widened.

"What is it?" Allan asked.

She held up two silver bracelets carved with ornate patterns. Allan looked surprised as well, and Mr. Shelton wore a smug smile across the room.

"Do you recognize those, son?" he asked.

Allan nodded.

"Those were your mother's," his father said. "I gave them to her for our fifth wedding anniversary. It felt like a good time to pass them along to you, my dear. I trust you will keep them in your care."

"Absolutely," Faith gasped, clutching the bracelets to her chest. "Thank you!"

It took all of her willpower to keep the tears back. She clenched her jaw in annoyance. Was this how it was going to be for the next several months?

Allan opened his gifts, delighted with the pocketwatch with a recent photograph of Faith inside the front cover. The back of the casing was engraved: "To My Beloved Allan, From Your Beloved Faith. 1888." He stared at the watch for a long time, and it made Faith happy to see him so entranced. Then he opened his father's gift, a heavy tome on the history of American railroads. He politely thanked his father, though Faith could tell that he was much happier with her present.

Precious was presented with a small cat-sized stocking stuffed with a knitted mouse toy, a new collar, and a small pouch with some treats from a gourmet pet food store on Main Street. Faith had never heard of such a place but when she went inside and saw the wealthy customers fawning over their pets, she understood the appeal.

Mr. Shelton's gifts were a bottle of Scotch whiskey and a very elegant ink pen set. He mumbled his gratitude and proceeded to pour himself a generous glass of Scotch. Meredith gushed over a butterfly brooch from Faith and a pair of warm leather gloves from Allan. She was about to head off to do some cleaning when Faith asked her to stay.

"I have one more gift," she said, handing a small box to her husband. He opened it and stared in confusion at its contents.

"Well, what is it?" Mr. Shelton demanded.

Allan held up a pair of tiny white socks. Meredith shrieked and ran over to embrace Faith's neck. A moment later, Allan gasped.

"Is it true?" he cried.

Faith couldn't stop the tears this time. "Yes," she said, taking his hands in hers. "You're going to be a father."

Meredith cried out again and danced a little jig in front of the Christmas tree. Mr. Shelton downed his Scotch and slapped his knees.

"Good on you, son. I hope it's a boy. Carry on the strong Shelton family name."

Allan was grinning from ear to ear. "How far along?" he asked

Faith, touching her stomach.

"About two months. We'll have a baby in this house by autumn."

"Sakes alive!" Allan jumped up from his chair and threw his arms wide. "I'm going to be a father!"

Faith giggled and stood up as well, and the two of them danced to unheard music while Precious watched with drowsy amusement. Mr. Shelton chuckled at the spectacle while Meredith sobbed tears of joy and clutched the tiny white socks.

****

New Year's Eve, 1888

The carriage jostled over a pothole and Allan grabbed Faith's shoulders.

"Oh stop it now!" she protested. "I'm not made of glass."

"Sorry." Allan removed his hands and looked across at his father, who was snoring soundly. He gave Faith an apologetic smile. "I'm just a bit worried, that's all. Are you sure it's all right for you to be out and about like this?"

Faith held up her hand. "Do you see this fingernail?"

Allan nodded.

"That's how small the baby is right now. I could somersault off of Niagara Falls and he wouldn't feel a thing."

179

"He?"

Faith grinned. "Or she. But I get the feeling it's a 'he'."

The carriage jolted again. This time, she clung to her husband. He looked down at her with keen eyes. She sat back in her seat, feigning indignation as she smoothed her dress and adjusted her hat.

"Even if I were in labor," she added, "I wouldn't miss this for the world."

She leaned forward to look out at the wintry wonderland. The road to the South Fork Fishing and Hunting Club had been cleared but the snow-covered woods on either side were untouched. The freshly fallen snow looked as soft as cream and glittered in the afternoon sun like countless white diamonds. Faith gasped when she saw a magnificent whitetail buck with an enormous antler rack on its head. As the carriage passed by, it stopped and stared, seeming to lock eyes with her for a moment. Faith prayed that it would escape the hunters' bullets and live to see another summer.

Since discovering that she was pregnant, she had been doing a lot more praying than usual. Sometimes she felt guilty about her lack of heavenly communication, like a child not quite sure if her father was in a good mood or not. But she figured the best way to get on God's good side was to behave like a proper Christian and pray and read the Bible and go to church and give to the poor. Yet as she did those things, her soul felt uneasy, like she was trying to bribe God. She really wanted a happy and healthy baby boy and she hoped that if she did what God wanted, He would do what she wanted. That was how it was supposed to work, right?

She pushed these thoughts out of her head and looked down at her outfit. Her thick petticoats, heavy satin dress, and fox fur coat should keep her warm enough, or so she hoped. The inside of the carriage was quite comfortable but she worried that the hunting club would be just as its name suggested: a rustic mountain getaway with few creature comforts. After all, hunting clubs were the domain of menfolk that were proud to brave the elements. But since the men often brought their families, Faith hoped it was at least somewhat civilized.

A quiet sigh escaped her lips. Whatever the place looked like, she was grateful for this truly special opportunity. Mingling among polite society back in Pittsburgh, she had heard the name "South Fork" mentioned a few times but she thought nothing of it. Only when she came to Johnstown did she realize this place was revered like Mount Olympus.

Their journey to the hunting club had begun at the Johnstown train depot. Since South Fork was miles from Johnstown, several Pullman cars on the noon train had been booked for the party guests. Faith recognized some of them from the Thanksgiving dinner and she had no trouble renewing acquaintances. She didn't see Stephen Baldwick in the group, though that didn't mean he wouldn't be in attendance. Her thoughts turned to Charlotte, and she wondered where she was these days. She hadn't seen or heard from her since the episode at the restaurant. Faith had made a mental note to invite her to lunch when she got back, to make sure she wouldn't spend the beginning of the new year alone.

The Pullman cars had become quite rowdy by the time they arrived at the South Fork station, thanks to the abundance of alcohol and cocaine being passed around. Faith didn't touch the drug and she hoped that Allan didn't either, but there were a few times when she lost sight of him. She told herself that she was just being paranoid, that the pregnancy was making her more suspicious that normal, but she always got an uneasy feeling when he was with his coworkers, some of whom looked outright wolfish in the way they eyed the pretty ladies around them, who would smile and bat their eyelashes in return.

Faith didn't drink any champagne on the trip, opting for tea with lemon and milk. Ordinarily she would have been soaking up the revelry but she found herself grateful to be observing the festivities with a clear head. She found it easier to charm those with whom she conversed, especially since many of them were already a bit tipsy. She also started thinking strategically about whom she should spend time with, since most of the people around her were Johnstown royalty. When she had been a new arrival in Pittsburgh, she had applied the same analysis, but that was for the purposes of finding a husband. Now that that mission had been accomplished, she turned her atten-tion to how best to climb the social ladder. She knew she was at a disadvantage without any significant family history but there was also an aspect of freedom with that. No one had any expectations when first meeting her, and most people she talked to seemed pleasantly surprised that she was a good conversationalist. She impressed them entirely on her own merits.

Ten miles on a train would usually only take fifteen or twenty minutes, but apparently the conductor had been told to proceed slowly to allow the merry makers to make as much merry as possible before disembarking. By the time the train pulled into the station, Faith couldn't wait to get off. Allan led her and his father, who was already a bit wobbly, to one of the waiting carriages. Mr. Shelton fell asleep almost immediately.

The South Fork dam created a lake for the members of the hunting club to enjoy, and when it came into view, it took Faith's breath away. The crystal clear water lay as still as a sheet of glass, perfectly reflecting the brilliant blue sky and snow-topped trees. More than a dozen buildings lined the bank. Faith had heard them referred to as "cabins" but they were almost as large as her own home, though they were made of wood rather than brick and stone. Yet despite their size, they were quaint and charming. Faith wondered what kind of secrets these unassuming little abodes held within their sawplank walls.

A little further up the shoreline was a large dock with a number of vessels in the water: canoes, paddleboats, and even small sailboats. Towering above the dock was a large building encircled by a railed porch, and Faith figured that this was the clubhouse, much to her relief.

"I'm impressed," Allan remarked, peeking over her shoulder out the window.

"It almost feels like a dream," Faith added. "Like a mirage or something."

"What do you think of the dam? We are riding on top of it right now."

"Is it safe?"

"They wouldn't have built a road across it if it weren't."

Faith angled her view to study the ground. It certainly seemed solid, and the road looked completely normal. One thing did strike her as slightly disconcerting: the waterline was only about eight or ten feet below the top of the dam. If the heavens poured forth a huge rain for days and days, then the water might–

"Hang the devil!" Mr. Shelton exclaimed, flinging his hands and feet up in the air.

"Father!" Allan cried. "Are you all right?"

Mr. Shelton gripped the edges of the padded bench and looked around like a frightened animal. "Where are we?"

Allan spoke in a gentle tone. "We are in a carriage and we've just arrived at the South Fork Fishing and Hunting Club."

Mr. Shelton rubbed his eyes. "So I see."

Faith took Allan's hand in hers as the carriage made its way along the shoreline to the clubhouse. She wished she could calm the butterflies in her stomach. Thankfully her bouts of morning sickness were rather mild, though not limited to just the morning. Faith's worst fear was the sudden, uncontrollable urge to vomit right as she was meeting Andrew Carnegie or Henry Frick or some other illustrious figure.

Oh, stop imagining things! This is going to be one of the best experiences of your life.

Faith exhaled slowly when the carriage halted.

I hope so...

A footman opened the door and offered his hand. Faith stepped out, feeling the bite of the mountain air upon her cheeks. Allan stepped down behind her and rubbed his hands on her shoulders to warm her up.

The carriage creaked as Mr. Shelton eased his way out, huffing and puffing as if he had walked the whole way. He looked at the clubhouse and raised an eyebrow.

"I'd wager they have some wonderful whiskey in there."

The footman swept his hand toward the building. "Indeed they do. Please follow me."

Faith gave her husband an excited grin. She put her arm in his and walked up the steps to the large porch that wrapped the whole way around the clubhouse. The sounds of fiddle music and laughter came from inside, and Faith had a sense of deja vu. The feeling was similar to when she and Allan arrived at Mr. War's estate for his

Thanksgiving banquet.

"Mrs. Walscott!" she called out.

An elderly woman standing on the porch stopped and squinted.

Faith left Allan's side and hurried over to the woman and the gentleman with her.

"I'm happy to see you again, Mrs. Walscott," she said with a smile. "Faith Shelton. We sat at the same table at Thanksgiving."

The woman's face brightened. "Oh yes! Marvelous to see you again."

"My husband and I were over the moon to get the invitation to come up here for the festivities. How is your Boston terrier doing? Phineas, right?"

Mrs. Walscott gasped. "My, what a memory you have! Yes, he's doing much better. Never caught the beast that nearly tore his leg off but he's walking around now. Still in a splint, though. Makes him walk like a peg-legged pirate."

Faith laughed. "Well, I'm glad to hear that. I've got to get back to my husband, but I'll see you inside where it's warm."

"Go on, dear," Mrs. Walscott said with a nod.

Faith walked back to Allan and Mr. Shelton with slow, measured steps, her head held high. She could feel Mrs. Walscott watching her, knowing that her poise would drill a deep impression into the woman's mind.

"Who was that?" Allan whispered.

"Just watering seeds," she answered offhandedly as she took his arm and followed him inside.

She scanned her surroundings as she and Allan stepped into the foyer. Even though the architecture and decor weren't extravagant, Faith could tell that there was a lot of money within these walls. The rustic charm was undeniable, and surprisingly authentic. Studying the wood grain and hand-hewn flourishes on the molding, something inside her flared to life, memories of her childhood in the hills. She had been in cities and towns for so long, she'd almost forgotten what it was like.

"Champagne?"

Faith turned to look at the tray brandished before her.

"No thanks," she said.

"She's expecting," Allan explained with a proud smile.

The footman bowed his head. "Congratulations, madam." He offered the tray to Allan. "Even more cause to celebrate."

Faith looked up adoringly at her husband. "I agree."

Mr. Shelton wiped his forehead with his kerchief. "It feels like an oven in here."

"Why don't you go cool off in the snow?" Allan remarked, prompting a sour look from his father.

"Welcome, Shelton family!"

They turned to see Stephen Baldwick with a smile that took up half of his face. On his arm was a buxom young blonde who looked like she was going to pop right out of her dress. Allan seemed stupefied for a moment.

"How are you, Stephen?" he stammered as he stuck out his hand.

Stephen shook it vigorously. "Splendid, splendid. So wonderful to see you here. This is my guest, Valentina. She's from Madrid. That's in Spain!"

"How do you do?" Valentina said with a silky accent, extending her hand to Allan. Faith felt her blood boil as Allan took her hand and pressed it to his lips.

Being from Spain doesn't make her less of a trollop.

Faith held her breath, fearful that she might have said that out loud, but everyone's persistent smiles put her at ease. If only Allan would stop grinning like an idiot...

"You may have heard that I had to break off my engagement to Charlotte," Stephen said. Valentina pawed at his shoulder like she was comforting a crestfallen little boy. "But," he added, "that gives me the freedom to sample the delicacies of the world."

He touched Valentina's chin and she gave him a simmering stare. "Who knows?" she said, her voice dripping with honey. "Maybe a sample is not enough."

Faith glared at Stephen, hoping she could hear his thoughts.

Being engaged to Charlotte never stopped you in the first place.

He didn't seem to notice Faith's disapproving expression and his smile persisted. "Come, let's get some warm food in those bellies!"

188

They followed Stephen and Valentina into the great room where fires blazed and guests crowded around buffet tables, piling their plates high. Giggling children scampered through the forest of legs and a fiddler moved gracefully through the crowd, playing lively music. Nearly everyone was half-drunk or already drunk. The air was filled with laughter and songs and the guests looked dazzling. The men wore dapper black suits and tuxedos, with an occasional gray or tweed jacket here and there. Some of the women wore heavier outfits, like she did, but a number of them, especially the younger ones, were minimally dressed like Valentina. Faith quickly realized the difference: the more modestly-dressed women were wives, and those who flaunted their figures were either new girlfriends or expensive consorts for the weekend. Faith felt annoyed at the presence of girls like Valentina, drawing men's eyes wherever they went. Allan made a valiant effort but every now and then she would catch him sneak a peek at a form-fitting dress or plunging neckline. Rich men always attracted beautiful women with shallow principles; she used to be one of them, after all. But now that she was married and soon to be a mother, something inside her craved more wholesome company.

Of course, if Allan was going to climb the corporate ladder and enjoy the accompanying privileges, she would have to get used to mixed company like this.

She steadied her nerves and surveyed the room, planning her conversational strategy. It was time to do some climbing of her own.

Chapter Twelve

THE EVENING WAS WONDERFUL. Faith capitalized on the seeds of charm that she had sown during the Thanksgiving banquet and found herself always surrounded by at least three or four people. She would tell them stories of her adventures in home decorating and would drop hints that she and Allan were expecting, though she would play coy when pressed. It was also for her own protection though, since it was still early in the pregnancy and she didn't want to bring on bad luck by spreading the news too soon.

She was sure it was a "he," by the way. Allan Shelton III. No doubt in her mind.

There were moments when a shroud of nausea would descend on her senses, but she would suppress her discomfort and continue talking. One bout was particularly intense and she had to excuse herself from the group. She hurried towards the drinks table to fetch a glass of water to keep from throwing up, narrowly missing a man with a short white beard coming around the corner with two glasses of wine.

"A thousand pardons, miss," he said.

Faith gave him a nod of apology and poured herself a glass of water with shaking hands. After gulping it down, she felt better almost right away, and she leaned against the wall to catch her breath.

Then she gasped.

That was Andrew Carnegie!

She had spotted a few other notable guests throughout the day, some of whom she had crossed paths with in Pittsburgh. Henry Clay Frick owned the club, and Faith saw him out by the lake with a few other men. She had also caught glimpses of Andrew Mellon, Benjamin Ruff (the first president of the club and, from what Faith had heard, the man who had the vision for the club itself), Philander Knox, Henry Phipps, Jr., and many others. Allan had introduced her to his superior, Daniel Morell, the general manager of the Cambria Iron Works. Faith was gracious and polite to the men but she made a special effort to strike up conversations with their wives, especially the older ones. High society matrons liked to feel that the young and pretty members of the next generation looked up to them and valued their insights, and Faith was happy to play the part of an eager hatchling looking to be taken under a hen's gilded wing.

The clubhouse began to feel a bit stuffy after a while and many of the guests made their way out onto the porch or took a stroll around the club grounds. Even though it was quite cold outside, Faith decided that she wanted to take a walk around the lake with Allan.

But she had to find him first.

As she made her way through room after room, she marveled at the size of the clubhouse. It hadn't seemed nearly that big from the outside. After searching downstairs, she made her way to the second floor, which seemed to be a labyrinth of hallways, similar to a hotel. And like a hotel, she spotted a few giddy couples going into rooms and locking the doors. She heard a woman laugh behind a closed door and a frightful thought flashed through her mind: what if Allan had been seduced by one of these vixens and was breaking his marriage vows right now?

You know he wouldn't do that.

She tried to push her fears aside but the thought lingered in her brain. She walked down the hallways, peeking into any rooms that were open and leaving the closed ones be. With her head held high, she went back down to the main floor and made her way to the great room again. Mr. Shelton was asleep in a chair in the corner and she went over to him.

"Father," she said, shaking his shoulder.

"Hmm?" he mumbled, his eyes still closed.

"Have you seen Allan?"

"Hmm?"

"Allan. Have you seen him?"

Mr. Shelton motioned with a limp hand towards a window. "Onna porsh," he slurred.

193

Faith pushed through the crowd to a door that led outside. The chill bit her skin as she stepped out into the open air. She searched the faces and didn't see her husband, and that made her a bit worried.

"Allan!" she called out, hoping she sounded pleasant instead of anxious. "Allan!"

A hand gripped her arm and she spun around, then she drew in a sharp breath.

"Stephen!"

Stephen Baldwick smiled down at her, his eyes shifty and glazed.

"Hello, Faith."

She pulled her arm away as politely as she could.

"Have you seen my husband?" she asked.

Stephen thought for a moment and then shook his head. "I haven't. Is he lost?"

"I should think not. It's a large clubhouse."

"Indeed it is. Larger still if you know where the secret rooms are."

Faith swallowed hard. "How interesting. If you'll excuse me, I need to keep looking."

Stephen stood in her way and *tsk tsked* at her like she was a child. "Oh my dear, you look terribly cold. Let's warm you up inside first and then we can look for little lost Allan."

"He's not little," Faith snapped, "and he's not lost. Besides, I should think Valentina would appreciate being warmed up, if she's not already."

Stephen's face darkened at her comment, and then the wolfish smile reappeared. "Perhaps. But there is something about a married woman; they are much warmer than women like Valentina."

Faith suppressed a shiver and drew herself to her full height. "Mr. Baldwick," she said, looking him straight in the eye, "I sincerely hope you find that warmth one day."

She brushed past him, hoping he wouldn't grab her again, but he just stood by and watched her hurry off. It wasn't until she rounded the corner of the porch that she felt the anger surge in her veins.

Why, that low-down mongrel of a man! How dare he–

A strong hand grabbed her arm. She whirled around, her hand poise to slap Stephen's smile right off his face. Instead, she saw Allan's wide eyes and she pulled her hand back just before impact.

"Goodness' sakes, woman!" he cried out.

"I'm so sorry," Faith exclaimed, putting her hands over her mouth.

Allan took a moment to compose himself. "A bit on edge, aren't we?"

"Perhaps. I'm just a little bit overwhelmed by everything, that's all."

"You're cold as ice," Allan said with concern, rubbing his hands over her arms. "Let's get you inside."

"I came out here looking for you," Faith said as her teeth began to chatter. "Where did you go?"

Allan put his coat around her and led her to the door. "Enjoying a cigar with Mr. War and Mr. Frick and a few other fine fellows. I'm sorry, I should have told you."

"It's all right. I just need to warm up."

Allan opened the door and Faith sighed with relief as she stepped into the warm room. She glanced to her right and caught Stephen Baldwick staring at her through a window. She lifted her chin and then wrapped her arm around Allan's.

"Take me to the fire, darling," she said sweetly, casting one more defiant glance toward the window, but Stephen was gone.

****

After the sun had set over the hills, the wait staff informed everyone that a fireworks display was about to commence outside on the lake. A number of people had retreated to their rooms in the various cabins on the shore but everyone who was still enjoying the party grabbed their coats and filed out the door. Faith held tightly to Allan's arm as she followed him down the snowy path to the water's edge. She felt relieved that Stephen was still nowhere to be seen. Probably in a room with Valentina. Probably making fireworks of their own.

Stop thinking about him! He's a dog and that's the end of it. Valentina will probably be cast off just like Charlotte. And she might even be just hired help for the weekend.

Faith grit her teeth and inhaled a deep breath through her nose.

I know, I know. But he was just so...so...

Her sputtering thoughts dissipated when Mr. War stepped in front of the gathering, accompanied by a servant holding a lantern.

"My family and friends," he said in a loud, clear voice, "on behalf of the South Fork Fishing and Hunting Club, we would like to wish all of you a very happy new year."

Many people wished him the same and he tipped his hat in thanks before continuing.

"Every year, we are happy to share God's blessings in our lives with those closest to us, especially the children. If we are lucky, we still keep the spark of childhood alive in our hearts. It's a great temptation to lose joy as one's life and career looms larger and larger. Life becomes an accumulation and we may think that more things, more wealth equals more joy. While wealth can certainly bring joy, it is merely the conduit, and I have personally found that the greatest joy is in using my wealth to give to others. This is one reason why we want to share this wonderful place with the people that matter to us."

Faith looked up at Allan. "That might be you up there one of these days giving that speech," she whispered.

"You think so?"

"Mm-hmm. You're going to make quite a name for yourself, Allan Shelton."

"No pressure there, right?"

197

"Just some encouragement. I'm in no hurry."

"Yes, you are."

Faith grinned. "Maybe a little bit. But I'll savor the wait."

Allan scanned the lake and the frosted trees. "It's so peaceful up here. So–"

A bright streak erupted from a boat on the water and exploded into bright colors in the sky. The crowd gasped and Mr. War opened his arms wide, a gleeful grin spread across his face. Faith cried out and laughed with delight.

"Just like in Pittsburgh on the river!" she exclaimed.

"But we watched those fireworks from our living room window," Allan remarked, watching the sparks evaporate. "They weren't quite this loud."

A volley of rockets launched from the boat, bursting into brilliant colors and sending *boom* after *boom* echoing across the water. Some people covered their ears but most of them were mesmerized, especially the children. Mr. War didn't look up, not once. He just stood by the water, watching everyone's reactions with a satisfied smile.

Faith was enchanted by the bursts of color reflecting in her husband's eyes. She moved close to him and put her hands on his strong arm and studied his face.

"What?" he asked.

She shook her head. "Just thinking of how lucky I am."

He took her hands in his. "How lucky *we* are."

"Yes." Faith looked down at her stomach. "I hope all this noise doesn't bother him."

"Or her."

"Him," Faith insisted.

"All right then," Allan laughed. He stared up into the sky again, watching the dazzling colors and lights. Despite the concussions, he didn't flinch once.

What a man, Faith thought.

Just then, she spotted someone over Allan's shoulder, standing close to the clubhouse. A rocket exploded in the sky, illuminating the grounds with a yellowish light, and she could see that it was Stephen Baldwick. He looked a bit drunk and disheveled, and his face glowed red from the cigar he held to his lips. His eyes caught hers for a moment, and he looked away. A few moments later, he walked back inside.

Faith watched him go in and then she turned towards Allan. He was a better man than Stephen Baldwick, and most of the other men here who had left their wives at home to dally around with pretty young playthings. She could see his love for her in his eyes every time he looked at her.

Staring up into the fire-filled night sky, she prayed.

Dear Lord, please bless our family. Make Allan a success in his company, keep our love for one another strong, and help me to become a valuable member of this society. I know that we can do a lot of good if

199

we become prominent citizens of Johnstown. We could give much mon-
ey to the church and to charities. Thank You for Your blessings and I
hope this year will bring many more. Amen.

The fireworks ended and the sky was silent. Faith searched the stars, wondering if her prayer had made it to heaven.

****

The winter months crawled by. Faith came to realize that cold weather and pregnancy were not a good combination, though she figured she would be just as uncomfortable if she were with child during the summer. She would feel too cold and would put on more clothing, and then she would feel too hot and shed the extra layers, and on and on. Plus the morning sickness seemed like it would never end. By outward appearances, she looked mostly the same, perhaps even more voluptuous. But she suffered as only she could know, with her hormones fluctuating and her breasts becoming sensitive and her appetite changing and her sleep being erratic, though Meredith assured her that much of this was due to worry and stress.

Faith couldn't help it; this was her first child. What new mother doesn't have a world of things on her mind? Sometimes her thoughts would drift to the memories of her own mother. She must have had it even harder, trying to raise a family on a failing farm in the Alleghenies. Faith looked around at the opulent room she sat in and the ex-

200

pensive clothes she wore. At least she had all the comforts money could buy.

She just wished she didn't feel so alone.

Allan tried his best to keep her in good spirits, but he had made some important new friends during the visit to the South Fork Fishing and Hunting Club, and now he was more busy than ever, taking frequent trips back to Pittsburgh. Mr. Shelton had gone back a couple of days after the new year, but before he left, Faith noticed a distinct difference in the way he spoke to his son, and to her as well. He was more encouraging and generally more positive than he had been in the past. Perhaps he was happy to see his aspirations for Allan starting to come to fruition. Whatever it was, Faith was relieved to see the change. She was also proud to see Allan become more confident in his father's presence. The prince was ready to take the throne.

Yet this meant that she saw him even less frequently than when they first moved to Johnstown. When he was at home, Allan would often come home late, frozen stiff from the cold, and fall exhausted into bed. He insisted that Faith not do anything strenuous for the baby's sake so she would spend much of her time trying to keep herself busy around the house.

There were a few opportunities for the two of them to get out and attend parties and banquets being thrown by Johnstown's elite. Faith hosted afternoon tea a couple of times but she was disappointed with her social schedule. After the celebration at the hunting club, she figured the invitations would come pouring in, now that she and Allan were members of the upper echelon, or so she thought. Perhaps a visit to the hunting club wasn't as special as she had been led to believe. She had hoped she would be the new belle of the ball, especially once word got around that she was expecting, but the visitations were short and far between, and the gifts even less frequent. As the snow fell and the wind blew outside, she had plenty of time inside the house to wonder what she could do to make her company more desirable. The voice of reason in the back of her mind told her that it was the dead of winter, it was cold and icy outside, and people weren't entertaining with the same frequency as during the warmer months. Johnstown's high society wasn't ignoring her; there just weren't as many events happening.

Perhaps that was true...but how would she know either way? The pregnancy had essentially confined her to the house, which was primarily due to Allan's insistence. He wasn't taking any chances with his firstborn child and he never let Faith go out without his escort. He paid for the doctor to make regular house calls, even when the snow was deep. He also instructed Meredith to make sure that Faith didn't do anything more strenuous than lift a book. She appreciated his concern but she was starting to feel more like an invalid than an expectant mother.

Most importantly, she was bored out of her mind. She read nearly every book in the house and went through two sets of pencils, sketching any item of interest she could find. Precious proved to be a willing subject; the cat would sit still for more than an hour, seeming to know that Faith was capturing its likeness on paper.

Faith also turned her artistic inclinations towards decorating the nursery. She wanted to furnish the room with colors and patterns fitting a boy but the small voice of doubt in the back of her mind made her hold off on anything too masculine. That didn't stop her from thumbing through designs and layouts for boys' rooms provided by the visiting interior specialist. Faith told him to hold certain items for delivery after the child was born. She didn't want to appear rash on the chance that she was wrong about the baby's sex.

But of course, she knew it was a boy.

Chapter Thirteen

May 29, 1889

FAITH WRUNG HER HANDS as she watched Allan put on his coat and hat.

"Do you really have to go?" she pleaded, knowing the answer but hoping for a miracle.

Allan placed his hat on his head and stood in front of her. He was so handsome, it made her knees weak. Her skin tingled as he held her hands.

"I wish I could stay," he said, his eyes warm and gentle. "Especially with you needing to stay off your feet."

He touched her stomach, rubbing the bulge at her navel. They smiled at each other, and Faith's heart melted. She couldn't wait to have a family with this wonderful man, but here he was with his bags all packed, getting ready to leave for Pittsburgh for four days.

"What if something happens?" Faith said.

"You're in good hands," Allan said, nodding at Meredith who stood in the kitchen door. "And the doctor will be by tomorrow. Besides, you look like you're feeling better. The time will pass like that."

Allan snapped his fingers, gave Faith a peck on the cheek, and opened the front door. "Oh, rotten luck! It's raining even harder now."

The two women stepped forward to peek outside. Rain poured down in sheets, and a knot of worry twisted in Faith's stomach. It had been raining for three days already and the mountains were sure to be saturated, making falling rocks a risk on the train tracks.

Faith squeezed his arm. "Be careful," she said, trying to sound firm but her voice was as forceful as a feather.

Allan touched her nose, an annoying gesture that he sometimes did when she was acting immature, but this time, she thought it was sweet. She caught his hand and pressed it to her cheek.

"Come home soon."

"I will."

Allan nodded once more to Meredith, hunched his shoulders, and dashed out into the rain. A carriage was waiting for him by the curb and Faith soon heard the horse's hooves *clop-clopping* on the cobblestone street. She stayed out on the porch for a little while, watching water spew from drain pipes, listening to the patter on the roof, smelling the cool, moist air. The temperature was quite pleasant, which was just fine with her. Winter had seemed like it would never end, but now the leaves were budding and the flowers were in bloom.

Yet she couldn't enjoy any of it after watching her husband disappear into the rain.

Stop being so melodramatic! she told herself. *He's only leaving for four days. What about that blizzard back in February? He was stuck in Pittsburgh for a week and a half, and that was when you were as sick as a dog. Besides, if he were here, what could you do anyway? It's pouring outside!*

Faith sighed and leaned against a white painted column. Precious jumped up on the railing next to her and brushed against her hand. She rubbed the cat's head as it purred.

"Why do the men always leave and we get left behind?" she wondered out loud.

Precious wasn't listening; it was savoring Faith's fingernails behind its ears. Faith chuckled and scooped the cat into her arms.

"Let's see what we have to eat," she said as she took the cat back inside. "Mama's hungry."

****

The rain did not stop.

It fell in buckets, straight down without any wind. The incessant drone of raindrops pounding the roof made Faith want to burrow under the blankets even though it was morning. A gray, sunless morning. Allan had left two days ago and it hadn't stopped raining since. Faith

207

sighed and stared out the water-streaked bedroom window. She wished he were back home with her again. Meredith was sweet but she never sat still long enough to make meaningful conversation. There was always something to cook or clean or polish or put away.

Precious hopped up on the bed, meowing for attention. Faith took the cat in her arms. Precious immediately started purring, and that made the baby in Faith's belly squirm.

"Feel that?" she asked. Precious shifted its weight across her belly and continued to purr. The baby moved a few more times before taking a rest.

Faith laid her head on the pillow and watched the raindrops splatter on the windowsill. She rubbed the cat's head with one hand and her bulging belly with the other. The doctor had come by yesterday for her checkup. The poor man was thoroughly drenched when he arrived at the door, and Faith was afraid that he would catch cold, so she instructed Meredith to bring him some warm soup right away. After he had dried off a bit by the fire, he set about examining Faith's vitals and listened to the baby with a stethoscope. Everything was fine, he said, telling her to get plenty of rest but not too much. A little exercise helps the blood circulation, and what's good for the mother is good for the baby. She thanked the doctor and gave him a flask of tea before he headed out into the deluge again.

With another groan, Faith sat up slowly. Precious grumbled and jumped off the bed.

"Sorry, girl." Faith gave the cat an apologetic smile and went over to the mirror, smoothing her satin nightdress over her stomach. There was no noticeable change from yesterday but she felt that her belly had grown during the night.

She drew her mouth into a thin line as she stared at her reflection in the mirror. Despite Allan's repeated insistence that she was beautiful and radiant, she felt the exact opposite. And she still had three months to go...

A knock sounded at the door.

"What?" Faith snapped.

Meredith's voice was quiet. "Breakfast is ready, madam."

Faith closed her eyes to calm her mind. "Thank you, Meredith. I'll be down in a minute."

She looked down at Precious, who stared up at her with curious eyes.

"Don't look at me like that," she sighed. "I'm with child, all right? I'm a little emotional at the moment."

Precious meowed and trotted over to the door and waited patiently. Faith put on her robe, brushed her hair, and opened the door. The cat darted out into the hallway and disappeared around the corner. Faith closed the door behind her and felt a shiver travel through her skin. It was the end of May but there was still a lingering nip in the morning air. Faith told herself to remind Meredith to stoke the fire.

All thoughts of Allan's absence and the dreary weather evaporated when the smell of sausages, eggs, toast, and cheese drifted into her nostrils. Faith hurried down the stairs as quickly as she could, practically salivating by the time she reached the dining room where a sumptuous breakfast was laid out on the table.

"Your favorite, madam," Meredith said with a confident smile.

Faith returned the smile and sat down. She whispered a quick blessing and began devouring the food, which was her favorite as Meredith observed. At least, her recent favorite. She had never been too fond of sausage until about a month ago. Now she craved it almost every day. One more reason to believe it was a boy – why else would she hunger for seasoned meat?

She was halfway through her second helping when the door bell rang out.

"Company!" she gasped, elated and mortified. She was hardly decent to entertain visitors, but she was so starved for company, it was worth the potential embarrassment. Cramming one more bite of toast into her mouth, she reluctantly abandoned her meal and hurried to the foot of the stairs.

"Get the door, Meredith!" she said, her words muffled by the food in her mouth. "I'll go upstairs and change. You can serve them tea and bread in the parlor."

She was halfway up the stairs when Meredith cried out, "Madam!"

Faith turned around. "What is it?" she called out.

"Come quick!"

Faith's heart froze in her chest and she rushed back down the stairs.

It's Allan...Something's happened to Allan!

She rounded the corner and skidded to a halt.

"Charlotte!"

A pool of water had already formed around Charlotte's feet where she stood in the foyer, dripping and shivering like a lost puppy. Faith ran to her and grabbed her hands.

"Dear Lord, you're soaked to the bone! Meredith, fetch some towels and heat up some bath water."

Meredith brought fresh towels and then dashed upstairs. Faith draped a towel around Charlotte's trembling shoulders and ushered her into the kitchen. Precious followed them, mewling with curiosity.

"Sit," Faith said, easing her onto a wooden chair.

Charlotte sniffled and clung to the towel. "Thank you," she whimpered. She sounded like she was on the verge of tears.

"What are you doing out in this awful weather?" Faith asked as she poured a cup of hot tea and held it out to her.

"I...I..." Charlotte's lips trembled as she grabbed the cup and drank greedily, despite the tea being very hot. She looked at Faith's stomach and managed a feeble smile. "I heard. Congratulations."

"I know you didn't run through Noah's flood just to tell me that."

"No." Charlotte's eyes fell to the floor as she set her cup on the table. Faith pulled up a chair and sat down across from her.

"What is going on, Charlotte? Are you all right?"

Charlotte's eyes sparkled with tears.

"I'm such a fool," she whispered.

"Why?"

"I'm sorry I haven't been around for a while. I've been meaning to come by, after hearing about the baby and all. You're going to be a wonderful mother."

Faith pursed her lips. "Charlotte, please. Tell me what is going on."

Charlotte fidgeted with her fingers for a moment. "I've never been good at being alone. Do you ever feel that way?"

"I suppose," Faith said, trying to keep the impatient edge out of her voice. "Every woman does now and then. But what does that have to do with you coming to my house in the rain?"

"I went back to him. I went back to Stephen Baldwick."

"What do you mean?"

"After he cut me loose, the money I had saved up was hardly enough to live for a month. I hadn't been thinking of saving because I was sure that we were going to get married and he was going to take care of me, so why did I need to save? But I found myself with hardly two cents to rub together, and the thought of becoming destitute was terrifying. So I...I did whatever I could to make money."

Tears trickled down her cheeks, and Faith knew exactly what she meant. She took the girl's cold hands in hers and spoke in a gentle voice.

"I don't judge you. We never know what we'll do until we're put in a desperate situation."

Charlotte wiped her eyes and drew in a shaky breath. "I could hardly stand it. After a couple of months, I made up my mind to get him back, whatever it took. I had heard that he was no longer keeping company with that Spanish trollop, though I didn't know if she had been replaced or not. But I wasn't going to wait around to miss my opportunity, so I put on my most fetching clothes, got in a carriage, and walked right up to his front door. He was home alone, and he was surprised to see me, to say the least. I'll spare you the details but I convinced him to take me back. Not as a fiancée or anything, but at least I had a roof over my head and I didn't have to...didn't have to work anymore."

"When was this?"

"About three weeks ago."

"So what happened?"

Charlotte swallowed and folded her hands. "This rain has been making everyone stir-crazy. Stephen has always liked to drink, but for the past few days, he's been drinking himself into a stupor every night. And every night, he gets...he makes me..."

Her voice faltered as fresh tears fell from her eyes. Faith leaned

213

forward to let Charlotte weep onto her shoulder, stroking her hair and shushing her like a mother comforting a child.

It took a couple of minutes for Charlotte to find her composure again. When she spoke, there was a brave, defiant tone in her voice.

"So this morning, while he lay passed out on the bed, I ran. I didn't know where, I didn't pack anything. There are servants in the house and they would surely have alerted him if I had taken the time to gather my things. I didn't even know where I was going; I just ran. And then I found myself on your street, and I came here. I'm so sorry, Faith. I shouldn't have come and gotten you mixed up in this."

"No, no, you did the right thing." Faith embraced her again, but her mind was gripped with worry. What if Stephen deduced where she had gone and stormed over here in a rage? And what was she going to do about Charlotte? She couldn't turn the poor girl out on the street again, but the longer she stayed here, the more danger she was putting all of them in.

Why isn't Allan here?

The voice in her heart spoke firmly.

You are going to be a mother soon; take care of those who need it.

Meredith appeared in the kitchen doorway with a robe draped over her arms.

"The missus' bath is ready," she said.

"Thank you, Meredith." Faith helped Charlotte to her feet and looked into her frightened eyes. "You're safe here, all right?"

Charlotte nodded. "Thank you," she whispered before following Meredith upstairs.

Faith stood alone in the kitchen, slowly rubbing her belly. She turned to stare out the small window above the sink, watching raindrops pitter-patter against the glass.

What do I do?

The answer came immediately.

Pray.

She sat down at the table again and bowed her head.

"Lord Jesus," she said quietly, "I haven't talked to You much these days. I have a lot on my mind, I guess. But I know I should, especially with the new baby coming. Honestly, I'm scared. I feel overwhelmed. I know I'm just being a silly child but I can't help the way I feel. Please show me what to do and how to keep my head on right. And help poor Charlotte. She's been through so much, and she's no saint, but she doesn't deserve to be running scared out in the pouring rain like this. Let her know that You care about her and help her to feel safe. And please be with Allan. I'm sure he's fine but I worry sometimes. Thank You for Your blessings and love. Amen. Oh, one more thing – please make the rain stop."

****

Pittsburgh, Pennsylvania

Cigar smoke drifted through the stateroom in the Pittsburgh Centennial Club, along with hearty male laughter and female giggles. Allan stood beside the towering window overlooking the river as he puffed slowly on Partagas and swirled Old Fitzgerald in his glass. The glowing cigar embers reflected in his eyes as he scanned the low-lit room. He ignored the opulent decor, the expensive artwork, and lavish furniture. His attention focused on the round-bellied men in fine suits with sultry young women draped over their shoulders or perched on their knees, sipping on drinks or feeding them fruit like they were actors in a Greek diorama.

Allan drew in another mouthful of cigar smoke, holding it for a few moments before pushing it through his teeth in thin jets. He looked over his shoulder at the rain pattering against the glass and took a sip of bourbon.

Obnoxious laughter rang out from the other side of the room. Allan watched his father throw his head back as a woman in a skin-tight turquoise dress tossed a grape into the air. Mr. Shelton caught it in his mouth and those around him cheered and clapped. His red face beamed and he threw his arms wide as if he had just won a championship game. Sherry splashed out of his glass onto the floor, and a girl in a green dress jumped to the side to avoid getting her shoes wet.

"Did you see that, my boy?" Mr. Shelton called out.

Allan nodded and gave a half-hearted toast.

Mr. Shelton frowned. "Come over here, son. Tell these girls about the South Fork Hushing and Fishing Club. Ha! Hushing and Fishing! Sounds like the sherry talking!"

Allan looked at the girls coiled around his father, like snakes twisting around the trunk of an old tree. Their eyes sparkled, their flesh glowed, and their teeth shone. One of them reached out her hand to him.

"Yes, tell us," she beckoned with a voice that dripped honey.

"My son is going to run that club one day!" Mr. Shelton declared to no one in particular.

Allan grimaced. He was glad that no members of the Johnstown club were here. Those men usually spent their time at The King's Crest or the Wyndmere, though the Centennial Club did host a number of prominent Pittsburgh businessmen. It was viewed as a sort of waiting lobby for entrance into the top tier. Some made it out of the Centennial and advanced to more prestigious parties; others spent their whole lives enjoying their leisure time behind its mahogany doors.

Mr. Shelton gestured with both arms, splashing his drink again. "Come on over here!"

Allan gulped down the last of his bourbon and walked across the room, past a bearded man snoring loudly in a leather chair and another man old enough to be his grandfather curled up on a sofa with a girl

217

young enough to be his sister.

"I'd love to stay and tell tales, Father, but I need to be off home. I'm going to head back to Johnstown tomorrow afternoon."

"You're leaving a day early?" Mr. Shelton grumbled. "Why?"

Allan glanced at the girls staring back at him. "I feel a bit worried leaving Faith at home for so long while she is with child. She's carrying extra weight and our house has many stairs and – "

Mr. Shelton waved his hand in the air like he was swatting flies. "Oh, hogwash! Faith is a strong girl who is perfectly capable of handling herself for a few days, pregnant or not. And she has that housemaid to take care of her. What's her name? Miranda?"

"Meredith. I know Faith is able to take care of herself but –"

"But nothing! Besides, you said it yourself: she's starting to put on extra weight." Mr. Shelton slipped his hand around the waist of a blonde-haired woman and pulled her close. "As you can see, there are plenty of nymphets here without the inconveniences that a baby brings."

Allan shook his head. "I wouldn't expect you to understand."

A shadow passed over his father's face. "What is that supposed to mean?"

"Nothing. Enjoy your evening, Father."

Mr. Shelton murmured something and looked away. Allan headed to the door, stubbing out his cigar in an ashtray beneath a portrait of George Washington. When he grabbed the door handle, a delicate

218

hand slid over his.

He froze, staring at the graceful fingers and manicured nails. Another hand reached out and a finger touched his cheek, turning his gaze. The woman's emerald eyes sparkled and her ruby lips parted in a fetching smile.

"Going so soon?" she cooed.

Allan tried to keep his eyes above her neck but he failed. The rest of her was just as appealing as her smile.

"Yes," he said, clearing his throat. "I must return home tomorrow. My wife is with child and I've been away for a few days."

"Oh." The woman traced her finger down his chest, keeping her eyes fixed on his. "How about some company on your last night in town?"

Allan drew in a long, slow breath. He took her hand in his and gently set it aside.

"Not tonight, Isabella. Not anymore, I should think."

Isabella pouted for a moment, then the sly smile returned. "You know, when a woman is expecting, her husband's needs can go unattended. Am I right?"

Allan grabbed the door handle again. "I'm fine."

Isabella leaned against the door. "I don't believe you. Come, I'll make you forget about everything that's on your mind."

She reached out to him but he batted her hand away.

"I'm going home," he growled through clenched teeth.

Isabella folded her arms. "Have it your way," she snapped, an eyebrow raised in contempt.

Allan yanked the door open and marched down the hall.

"It only gets worse, you know," Isabella called after him. "Children change everything. Trust me, I know. But I don't hold a grudge. I'll be happy to tell you 'I told you so' anytime, darling."

Allan's footfalls echoed loudly as he hurried down the corridor and stormed through the lobby. The concierge held out an umbrella but he marched right past, out into the pouring rain.

Chapter Fourteen

May 31st

10:15 a.m.

Johnstown, Pennsylvania

FAITH'S FINGERS AIMLESSLY stroked her cat's soft head as she stared out the window. The garden was flooded and water gushed from drainpipes.

Didn't you hear me last night? she prayed. *Haven't we had enough rain?*

She looked over at Charlotte sitting by the fireplace where a small blaze burned. Charlotte caught her eye and gave her a quick smile.

"Breakfast was delicious," she said quietly.

"It always is," Faith said. "I don't know what I would do without Meredith."

Charlotte smoothed a wrinkle in her dress, a simple blue gown that Faith loaned her. With her expanding belly, Faith couldn't wear most of her old clothes anyway. She wondered if she would ever look as beautiful wearing them again.

"It must be nice," Charlotte said.

"What is nice?"

"Having someone by your side that you can depend on. Stephen has servants and cooks but they come and go. I don't think anyone in his house has been there more than six months."

Faith didn't know what to say in reply, so she just nodded and looked down at Precious. The cat purred in her lap and squinted with each stroke of her hand.

"Do you think he knows I'm here?" Charlotte asked.

"Stephen? I don't think so. Why would he?"

Charlotte shrugged and stared at the fire. "He has a sense about things."

"It's pouring rain outside. I don't think he's storming through town trying to find you."

A strange light danced in Charlotte's eyes. "Though it would be kind of romantic if he were out there trying to find me, wouldn't it?"

"Of course not!" Faith exclaimed. "That's not love; that's obsession. That's madness."

Charlotte blushed. "I suppose. But still...you can't deny that there's a certain charm in a man's obsession, can you?"

Faith's mouth hung open. She was speechless again.

Meredith poked her head into the room and cleared her throat.

"Begging your pardon, mesdames. The cellar has flooded and it's starting to come into the kitchen. I've stopped the door with rags but I'm afraid I won't be able to hold back the water much longer. You might have to go upstairs to keep your feet dry."

"Oh for goodness sakes." Faith clutched Precious in her arms and got to her feet. Then she gasped and dropped the cat onto the chair.

"What is it?" Charlotte and Meredith asked together.

Faith's eyes grew wide as a smile spread across her face. "I felt him kick! He's a strong little fellow!"

Charlotte rushed forward and put her hands on Faith's belly. A few moments later, she yelped.

"I felt it too!"

Meredith clasped her hands together. "Oh, I remember these days so well."

"You never told us you had a child!" Faith said.

A shadow darkened Meredith's smile. "Well, I did...for a while. The poor lass died when she was but a wee one, just two months old. Bringing her into the world did quite a number on my internals so she would be the last one I would ever bear anyway."

Faith walked over to her and gave her a gentle hug. "Meredith, I had no idea. I never even thought to ask."

"It's all right," Meredith said, her eyes shimmering. "I've just been so happy watching you carry your own child with such joy and love."

"What about your husband?" Charlotte asked.

223

Meredith lowered her eyes. "There was no husband, though I wished he would have been." She heaved a sigh and squared her jaw. "A lot of things in my life didn't turn out as I'd planned, but then I wouldn't be here in this lovely house with you lovely ladies. Being a part of the Shelton household has been the pride of my life."

Faith couldn't hold back the tears as she embraced her. She wiped her eyes and pointed a finger in Meredith's face.

"I'll want to hear all about it sometime," she commanded.

Meredith grinned. "Yes'm. But first, I need to hold back Noah's flood. You two run along upstairs. I'll find a way to hold the water back from the hardwoods and carpets."

"We will do no such thing," Faith declared. "Charlotte, let's move this furniture against the wall and roll up the rug."

"But madam," Meredith interjected, "what about – "

"The baby? With the way he kicks, he's liable to jump right out and give us a hand."

Meredith chuckled, though her face was still clouded with worry. "Well, all right then. But don't exert yourself."

"Don't worry," Charlotte grunted as she shoved a table to the side. "I'll do most of the heavy work."

After Meredith hurried back to the kitchen, Faith and Charlotte set about pushing the furniture as far against the walls as they could. They rolled up the rugs and lifted them up onto the sofa, and they also removed the books from the lower shelves and stacked them up higher. Despite her bravado, Faith was starting to feel exhausted by the time they had prepared their second room. Charlotte noticed her fatigue and took her hand.

"Go upstairs and rest," she said. "I can take care of this down here."

"No, no, I can't let you do it all by yourself."

"Do you want me to go tell Meredith how tired you look?"

Faith smirked. "All right, all right. Don't try to move anything too large. If the water comes in, it won't matter where it is anyway."

Charlotte nodded. "I'll ask Meredith to bring you something to eat."

"Thank you."

She gave Charlotte's hand a squeeze and headed upstairs with Precious following behind her.

It's all right, she breathed as she rubbed her belly. *We'll be all right.*

****

1:35 p.m.
Pittsburgh & Lake Erie Railroad Station
Pittsburgh, Pennsylvania

The whistle shrieked, alerting everyone in the depot that the train would be departing in ten minutes.

Allan groaned as he pulled out his pocketwatch. In good weather, the trip to Johnstown would usually only take two hours, but the rain hadn't stopped pouring for nearly a week and some of the tracks were washed out. He would be lucky to make it home before dinner. Right on cue, his stomach growled with anticipation. He had considered sending a telegram to let Faith know that he would be coming back a day early, but he decided he would show up at the door and give her a nice surprise.

The porter who had taken his bags to the luggage car returned with a ticket.

"Safe travels, sir," he said as he handed the ticket over and went to help more passengers.

Allan tucked the ticket in his coat pocket and started walked towards the Pullman car, but he stopped after two steps.

His father stood on the platform, hands in his pockets, a glum look on his face.

"Hello, son."

Allan inhaled through his nostrils.

"Hello, Father."

Mr. Shelton took off his hat and walked closer.

"You, uh, you left in a hurry this morning. I was still a bit groggy."

"Why didn't you get Jasmine or Geraldine or whatever her name was to fix you some coffee?"

Mr. Shelton pointed a finger in Allan's face.

"Look, *boy,* I don't know where this sudden condescension is coming from, but you best stow it right fast. All of a sudden, you're too good for a night out on the town?"

Allan shifted his feet. "I just...I have a child on the way, Father. I wanted to do things different. Better."

"Did that stop you from rushing into that Romanian girl's arms on your last visit?"

"She's Hungarian."

"And you were hungry too, I suppose."

Allan's eyes fell to the ground for a moment. "Father, I know the world we both live in. And there's nothing wrong with you wanting to enjoy it. But lately, I haven't felt the same enjoyment. Faith is a good woman, and she's going to be a wonderful mother. I see how the wives and children of the gentlemen we keep company with are neglected, and I want better for my family."

"So now you decide to grow a conscience? You finally started reading that Bible she gave you?"

"I don't expect you to understand."

"No, I understand perfectly. You think you're the first man to feel guilty about stepping out? Take it from me – no matter how much guilt or conflict you're feeling now, it will be just a vapor in the wind when your wife is nagging in your ear and your child is screaming in the cradle, and you run off and find peace in a bottle and a warm embrace. But let me tell you something. Your momentary conflict of conscience is jeopardizing everything we've been working for."

The conductor blew his whistle.

"All aboard!"

"Father," Allan said firmly, "I need go. We'll talk about this later."

Mr. Shelton grabbed his arm. "Your feelings about the company we keep is irrelevant. You need to wake up and realize the gift you're squandering. That invitation to the South Fork Fishing and Hunting Club was just the beginning. You're Prometheus and you've got a burning torch from the gods. Are you just going to let it fizzle out?"

Allan pulled his arm away. "No. I'm going home to my family."

He turned and marched towards the car. After he boarded, he took his seat by the window and looked down at the platform.

Mr. Shelton stood as still as a statue, staring at him with a stern expression. But there was also hurt in his eyes.

The conductor blew his whistle once more, answered by the train's whistle. The car lurched as the engine's wheels turned and began pulling the train down the tracks. Allan watched his father disappear in a cloud of steam, and then he closed his eyes and rested his head against the window.

****

Gentle knocking sounded at the bedroom door.

"Come in," Faith called from the bed.

Meredith entered the room, holding a platter of fruit and crackers.

"Oh Meredith," Faith said with a smile, "there's no need – "

"Nonsense." Meredith set the platter on the bed and dutifully folded her hands.

Faith popped a grape into her mouth, savoring the delicious flavor.

"Thank you," she said. After a few bites, she added, "How is it down there? Is Charlotte all right?"

"There's a bit of water in the kitchen," Meredith answered. "The hardwoods are safe for now, but if that water wants to come in, there's nothing we can do."

Faith stared out the rain-streaked window. "Allan won't be happy when he comes home tomorrow."

Meredith stepped forward and touched Faith's belly. "I think he'll have other things on his mind."

Precious hopped up on the bed and wedged itself in between Meredith's hand and Faith's abdomen. Both women laughed and Meredith stroked the cat's fur as it purred.

229

"Do you think he'll be all right?" Faith asked.

"Master Allan? Of course. Nothing can stop those trains."

"Unless the tracks are washed away."

"Then they'll just have wait until the tracks are cleared. But that's a whole day away. The rain could stop and the sun could be shining tomorrow morning."

"I hope so."

Meredith took her hand.

"Proverbs chapter 12 says that worry weighs down the heart."

"What else can I do besides worry?"

"You could not worry at all."

"How?"

Meredith gave her a sympathetic smile, then reached into the drawer next to the bed and pulled out a well-worn Bible. Faith had forgotten it was even in there.

"The Lord is our Shepherd," Meredith said in a quiet voice as she placed the Bible in Faith's hands. "Do not let your heart be troubled, and do not be afraid."

Faith watched her rise to her feet and leave the room. She turned and looked at Precious perched on the corner of the bed. The cat's tail swished back and forth as it stared at her with keen eyes.

Do not let your heart be troubled...

Faith opened the Bible and let her eyes fall on the page. It was the story of Queen Esther. At first, she was disappointed, somehow hoping for a passage that would miraculously speak directly to her situation, but as she read one verse and then another, she found herself captivated by the story of Esther's bravery and faithfulness.

She glanced over at Precious and grinned. The cat was curled up in a ball, asleep. She looked down at the Bible once more and a sense of amazement resonated in her spirit.

"Thank You," she whispered. "Forgive my fears and doubts. My worries are so small compared to what Esther went through. Please give me peace."

A heaviness weighed on her eyelids, accompanied by a slight queasy feeling in her stomach. She felt a little bit guilty, being up here all warm and dry while Meredith and Charlotte battled against the encroaching water downstairs, but she knew she needed sleep. She burrowed under the covers and closed her eyes, sending up one last prayer.

"And please bring Allan home safely tomorrow."

****

3:25 p.m.
Seven miles from Johnstown, Pennsylvania

Allan sputtered in his coffee as the train car lurched, the brakes shrieking almost as loudly as the whistle. After a few moments, the entire train came to a halt, prompting annoyed looks from the passengers. People grumbled and murmured as they stood up and looked out the windows. Allan set his cup down, folded his newspaper, and glanced outside. All he could see was the peaceful, rain-soaked valley of the Conemaugh River.

A porter entered the Pullman car.

"Ladies and gentlemen," he began in a loud voice, his hands raised in supplication, "we apologize for the delay. The rain has washed out the tracks down the line and we have to wait for the other trains to clear the way before we can get moving, which I have been told will be in just a few minutes. In the meantime, we invite you to make yourselves comfortable and enjoy some hors d'oevures."

White-vested servers marched into the Pullman with trays of sandwiches and crepes and began handing them out to the passengers. Allan waved the server away when he approached his seat. He turned to the window and stared out across the Conemaugh Valley. Just over those trees was Johnstown.

So close to home, yet still so far...

Smothering an impatient groan, he crossed his legs and opened his newspaper again.

The minutes ticked by at a snail's pace. Allan pulled out his watch.

3:45.

He stuffed it back in his pocket and his stomach grumbled. He glanced around the car and caught the eye of a server at the far end, who came forward.

"May I help you, sir?" he asked with a pleasant smile.

Allan opened his mouth to speak but he froze. His eyes locked with the server's. They both felt it – a tremor shuddering through the entire car, growing stronger by the second. The empty coffee cup on the table rattled and fell off the edge.

A woman screamed. Allan whipped his head to look out the window. His face turned white.

A roaring torrent of mud-brown water thundered through the valley, bristling with uprooted tree trunks and shattered houses. The monstrous wave seemed to reach out with foaming claws, ripping up the earth and flinging debris high into the air.

Allan leaped to his feet. "Get out of the car!" he shouted to the panic-stricken passengers. "Run up the hillside!"

At that moment, the train jolted forward, its whistle shrieking. Allan gripped the table and clenched his teeth. The conductor was trying to outrun the avalanche of water.

"We need to get off the train!" Allan cried, but it was futile. The train wheels screeched as the locomotive took a hard turn. What would happen when they came to the washed out tracks?

The watery beast churned through the valley with savage fury, rising higher and higher until the torrent seemed to gallop alongside the train. The roar was deafening, overpowering the sound of the en-

233

gine. Allan watched in horror as the wall of water rose high into the air, obscuring the valley, trees, and sky.

He closed his eyes and gripped his seat.

"Faith..." he breathed.

The wave came crashing down, lifting the train off the tracks. Screams filled the car as Allan and the other passengers tumbled end over end.

Everything went black.

Chapter Fifteen

3:52 p.m.
Johnstown, Pennsylvania

LOUD HAMMERING ON THE front door yanked Faith out of her pleasant dream and she bolted up in bed. She looked around the room, disoriented and a little dizzy. She thought she might vomit for a moment, but the pounding on the door downstairs continued and a sudden rush of fear pushed the nausea away.

Precious had been napping at her feet, but the cat was now wide awake and meowed nervously.

"It's okay, sweetheart," Faith said as she flung back the covers and jumped out of bed. She grabbed her silk robe from the back of the chair, cinched it tight around her waist, and hurried out of the room.

Pounding echoed throughout the house. Faith came to the top of the stairs and looked down into the foyer, where Meredith and Charlotte stood and stared at the front door.

"Should I open it, madam?" Meredith asked.

Faith swallowed hard. Several more blows landed on the door, but this time, a voice cried out.

"I'm looking for Charlotte!"

All three women gasped. Charlotte's eyes were as wide as dinner plates.

"It's him!" she whispered.

"Come here," Faith commanded, waving Charlotte towards her as she marched down the steps.

"Should I hide?" Charlotte asked.

"You will do no such thing. You are a free woman and he has no business setting one foot in this house."

Charlotte grabbed her arm. "I'm so sorry," she groaned. "I brought this trouble here."

"Hush now," Faith said. "Stand right there so he can see you."

"What if he's drunk? What if he comes in here?"

Faith kept her head held high. "This is a Shelton house. And Sheltons always stand their ground."

Charlotte didn't look convinced but didn't say anything more. She grabbed the handrail as if the house were going to tip over.

Meredith looked only slightly less afraid. "Are you sure this is a good idea, madam? You're not even properly dressed to receive company."

"Yes, I'm sure," Faith declared with a self-assured nod. "But be ready, just in case."

"Ready for what, madam?"

Faith adjusted her robe. "Just...be ready."

Meredith nodded and took a step back. Faith faced the door, flinching at the heavy blows landing on the stout wood. Meredith was right – under normal circumstances, she would never dream of opening the door to anyone, man or woman, dressed in just a sleeping gown and silk robe. But she hoped that her unexpected appearance would disarm and possibly even embarrass Stephen Baldwick and shame him into turning away.

She hoped.

Her hand trembled as she gripped the lock. She breathed deep, gave it a turn, and yanked the door open.

"Mr. Baldwick!"

A bolt of lightning seared the sky. Stephen looked dreadful. He was soaked to the bone and his face was flushed red. A look of fear and shame flashed across his face.

"Mrs. Sh-Shelton," he stammered, trying to look away but not quite succeeding. "Forgive me, I..."

His words trailed off as he looked over Faith's shoulder and saw Charlotte standing on the staircase.

"Charlotte!"

He started to push past Faith into the house but Faith stood firmly in his way.

"Absolutely not!" she growled. "You will control yourself this instant and tell me what is the meaning of this ruckus!"

Stephen winced like a child being scolded by his mother. Then he stood up straight and ran his hand through his stringy hair.

"My apologies, Mrs. Shelton. I have forgotten my manners."

"In a bottle?"

Stephen's face turned even more red. "Perhaps. I feel awful coming over here like this but – "

"You should!" Charlotte cried out, storming down the steps to stand behind Faith. "What sort of man runs after a woman in the rain like a raving lunatic?"

"You must come with me!" Stephen shouted, reaching out for her. "Please!"

Faith blocked the door. "She's not going anywhere!"

"No, you don't understand! We must all flee!"

"Why?"

Stephen took a moment to find the breath to speak. "The dam..." he croaked. "It's going to burst!"

Charlotte pursed her lips. "Those rumors fly every time we have a downpour. Shame on you for being taken like a fool."

Faith folded her arms. "If there were any real danger, someone would have ridden through town sounding an alarm."

"But someone did raise an alarm, on the north side of town!"

"What did they say?"

"What I'm telling you now, that the dam is in danger of collapsing! Please, let us all get to higher ground. If I'm wrong, you can remind me of my mistake for the rest of my life. But heaven forbid this time it is actually true, and – "

The ground shuddered. Faith grabbed Charlotte's hand. Stephen looked behind him and his red face turned pale.

"Run!"

Faith turned to flee upstairs, but not before she glanced out one of the windows. Her heart froze in her chest.

A massive wave of foaming brown water came barreling down the street, obliterating trees and houses. The three women shrieked and hurried up the stairs. Stephen abandoned all gentlemanly manners and pushed hard against their bottoms, urging them forward.

"Go, go!" he cried.

Halfway up the stairs, he stopped and turned. The wall of water slammed against the house with terrifying force, blasting through the first floor windows and doors. Stephen and Meredith threw up their hands and screamed as the torrent carried them away, shattering the staircase right below Charlotte's feet.

"Faith!" Charlotte cried, diving forward.

Faith grabbed her hand and pulled her up the stairs and they fled down the hall to the bedroom. The house shuddered and shook, and Faith could hear the walls crumbling around them.

She threw open the bedroom door and hurried Charlotte inside.

"On the bed!"

The two women clambered onto the mattress. Precious jumped onto Faith's lap and she held the animal close. Her lips trembled with feverish prayers.

Please Lord, save us! Please!

Water began pouring into the bedroom. With a gasp, Faith realized that that she had unwittingly entombed them by running into an upstairs room. If they had gone out onto the roof or a terrace, they might have had a chance, but with the room flooding, there was nowhere to go except to be drowned or crushed against the ceiling.

Despite her peril, sadness gripped Faith's heart as Meredith's dying scream played in her mind over and over. And poor Stephen... He might have been a rogue but he didn't deserve to perish like that. And it was his warning that likely saved her life and Charlotte's.

Lord, have mercy on their souls!

The house emitted a groan like a wounded animal. At that moment, the entire structure leaned forward and the exterior walls collapsed, opening up a huge hole in the roof. A wave of water surged across the floor, carrying the bed up and out of the house.

Faith was stunned. They had made it out alive!

Squinting in the pouring rain, she looked around and felt her soul wither with horror.

Johnstown was a seething cauldron of water and debris. Men, women, and children flailed helplessly in the water, and a number of dead bodies were scattered among the broken boards and uprooted trees.

It looked like a watery hell. Faith glanced back just in time to watch her house get swallowed in an instant and the current carried the bed along at a frightful speed.

"Hang on!" she cried, grabbing one of the bedposts. Charlotte grabbed the other, and Precious burrowed between Faith's legs for shelter.

The noise was unbearable. Faith felt like she was caught in the machinery of a giant locomotive engine. Houses and buildings literally exploded into splinters when hit by the full force of the water, and the structures lucky enough to be protected by less fortunate buildings, as her home had been, died slower deaths, being flooded in their first floors and then lifted off their foundations or simply flattened like boxes.

"Faith!"

Charlotte's cry made her turn her head just in time to see a massive uprooted tree hurtling towards them. The two women crouched down low and Faith felt the branches scrape across her back. Miraculously, the tree swept past them, slamming into a floating house and sending the half dozen people on the roof into the churning waters.

Tears streamed down Faith's cheeks as she clung to Precious.

We're going to die...we're going to die...Oh God, my baby...

Helpless souls clutched at the bed as they drifted past. Faith tried to grab a young girl's outstretched hand, and she brushed her fingertips before the girl was carried off and disappeared into a gurgling swirl of water below a broken roof.

"Faith," Charlotte wailed, "what do we do?"

Faith swallowed hard and raised her hands.

"Pray!"

They both looked up at the sky, eyes wide. Faith tried to block out the shrieks of the dying as she raised her voice to heaven.

"Our Father, Who art in heaven, hallowed be Thy name. Thy kingdom come, Thy will be done – "

"Faith!"

Before she realized what was happening, Faith felt Charlotte's hands press against her back and hurl her off of the bed with startling strength. Faith's arms flailed as she tumbled through the air, over the muddy grave waiting to swallow her whole. But then the water disappeared and she landed on hard wooden planks. Precious leaped from the bed into her arms.

Faith grabbed the cat and looked up. Charlotte was still on the bed spinning in the water. She locked eyes with Faith just before the bed smashed into a brick facade. Charlotte was flung off of the mattress and vanished under the water without a sound.

"No!" Faith cried out as she was pulled back by strong hands. She looked up with tear-filled eyes and saw several terrified faces staring down at her. One of them was the florist whose shop she frequented for fresh flowers.

"Mr. Baumgardner," she sobbed.

"Easy, *bubelah,*" Mr. Baumgardner said as he helped her to her feet. "Are you all right?"

Faith nodded, clutching Precious to her chest. "My friend..."

Mr. Baumgardner held her arms tight. "I saw it. She's gone. I'm sorry. It's a miracle that you survived. She saved your life."

Faith wiped her nose and looked around. She was on the roof of a building that had withstood the torrent thus far, though she could feel the structure tremble.

Precious mewled in her arms. She looked down at the soaked animal.

"Oh my sweetie..."

She nuzzled the cat and then yelped when the building shook under her feet.

"What do we do?" she cried.

Mr. Baumgardner opened his mouth to reply just as the planks under his feet gave way and he disappeared into the water. Faith screamed and scurried away as the boards and bricks fell away like sand being churned by the tide. Several people vanished beneath the waves and those who remained clustered together in the dwindling space. One man in his haste stepped on Faith's foot and she snarled in pain, but he took no notice.

"We have to jump!" an elderly woman declared.

Faith glanced over the edge of the roof at the churning torrent.

243

She knew that she would drown. Her hand instinctively touched her stomach.

Lord, please save me for my baby's sake!

Only a fraction of the building's roof remained. A stout young man tried to jump to the adjoining building, only to be swallowed up by the waves as his fingers barely scraped the brick ledge.

Someone shrieked next to her ear and she flinched with fright. That small action saved her life as a large tree branch whizzed over her head, slamming into the chest of an old woman and launching her into the water. Faith looked behind her and saw an enormous tree grinding against what remained of the building.

She didn't stop to weigh the calculations; she knew she had just moments to act.

"Grab on!" she cried as she climbed into the tangle of branches. She lost her grip on Precious but the cat fell only a couple of feet to the next branch, growling its displeasure.

"Sorry, sweetie," Faith said, reaching down and wincing in pain as the cat's claws dug into her arm. She pulled Precious to her bosom and glanced behind her.

"Hurry!"

Just as the words left her mouth, the building collapsed in a spray of water. Her eyes met those of a frightened man who had just started to reach for the nearest branch, and then he sank like a stone.

Faith blinked away the tears and clung desperately to the biggest branch she could find as the torrent drove her down river. She prayed that the tree wouldn't roll but its great size seemed to be a stabilizing force that helped it stay buoyant, though that also meant it was drawn towards the middle of the flood. A scream burst from Faith's blue lips as the tree slammed into a church steeple, scraping away most of the shingles, but not before she recognized the steeple. It belonged to the church where she and Meredith had attended their first service.

"Hold on, baby!" she called out to Precious, sputtering as foam sprayed into her mouth.

Shouts to her right grabbed her attention. Several people were huddled on a raft that had once been the side of a house. A man reached out towards the tree, even though he was more than thirty feet away. The woman next to him held out her baby, and Faith saw the unspeakable terror in her eyes.

"Take him!" the woman cried out. "Save my baby!"

Faith could only stare in shock. "I...I can't..."

Another volley of screams erupted from the raft as the current carried it straight into the facade of a sturdy brick building. The small craft exploded into fragments and everyone on board fell into the frothing waves. Faith shut her eyes tight.

I can't take this anymore! I can't! Please, just let me die!

The tree shuddered and leaned, and Faith's eyes snapped open. Was the tree going to roll over? She looked around, terrified that she might see her grim fate looming in front of her.

245

But instead of certain death, she saw that she was being carried back towards the center of town. It was as if the flood had turned itself around to churn through the ruined streets again.

What is happening?

She grit her teeth and held on tight as the tree slid to the right and raked through a wooden roof like it was made of paper. Those who had clustered on the roof were thrown into the water. Faith sobbed as she watched them drown, feeling in some way that she was responsible. Perhaps her weight was directing the tree. Perhaps she should just let go...

"Mama!"

The cry came from just behind her and she craned her neck to spot a young boy clinging to a barrel. He was weeping pitifully and Faith wanted to look away, afraid that the water would swallow him up at any moment. But he held on, and the water carried him closer and closer to her tree.

I have to try!

Grabbing a branch with many smaller branches to aid her grip, she leaned out as far as she dared.

"Grab my hand!" she called out.

The boy saw her and his face brightened. "Help me!"

"Don't let go!" Faith commanded. She was afraid he would do something stupid like try to leap into her arms. If she couldn't save him, she wanted him to hold onto his barrel and at least have a chance.

Precious watched her with wide eyes, mewling its warnings. Faith winced as a spray of dirty foam splashed into her face, and when she opened her eyes, the boy was mere inches away.

This was her chance.

Please, God!

She stretched out and grabbed his hand just as she lost her grip on the branch. For one heart-stopping moment, she plummeted towards the merciless water. Then her fingers miraculously closed on another branch that held her weight and the boy's, who had now abandoned his barrel and held onto her arm like a flopping fish.

Faith stared into his panicked eyes. "Do not let go!" Her words were as much for herself as for the boy.

Praying for strength, she hauled the boy closer. He grimaced as small branches scratched at his face but he had the presence of mind not to grab onto the small twigs. His fingers dug into Faith's arm like claws, and despite the mortal danger of the moment, Faith thought of Precious. She turned to see the cat meowing anxiously from a large branch, but safe.

Faith looked back at the boy. "You see that branch near your hand?"

The boy nodded.

"I'm going to give you one big pull and you're going to grab it, okay?"

The boy nodded again. Gathering all of her strength, Faith

247

pulled as hard as she could, dragging the boy a couple of feet closer. He grabbed the branch with both hands and his head sank beneath the water.

"No!" Faith shouted.

Then she saw the boy's white fingers still clinging to the branch, and a moment later, his head popped up again. He sputtered and gagged but he held on.

Faith let out a whimpering laugh. She was so relieved, she couldn't do anything else. Grabbing the boy's belt, she hauled him up higher so that he could get his feet out of the water. He slumped over the branch, vomiting water.

He's alive! You saved him!

Her joy evaporated in an instant.

"Look out!" she shouted to the boy, grabbing her own branch and bracing for impact.

The tumbling wreck of what was once a house seemed to roll across the waves like a boulder down a mountain. Faith squeezed her eyes shut, waiting for wooden planks to impale her shivering body. The wreckage roared like a locomotive as it slammed into the tree. The boy cried out and Faith opened her eyes just as he was tossed into the water. Faith gasped with horror and then again with relief when she spotted him several yards away, clinging to a floating plank.

Lord, save him! her heart pleaded.

The wreckage pushed against the tree, turning it sideways against the current. Fresh terror froze Faith's blood.

The tree was starting to roll.

Chapter Sixteen

FAITH LOOKED BEHIND HER, hoping for anything close by to grab onto. The only floating object nearby was a shattered rooftop, but it was at least fifteen yards away.

Precious meowed pitifully and paced back and forth on its branch. The cat also sensed their imminent peril. Faith reached up and grabbed a higher branch to buy another few moments as the tree continued its turn. She knew she wouldn't be able to keep up with the rotation, and in a few seconds, she was going to be pulled underwater. And she knew if that happened, she wasn't coming back up again.

She turned her eyes towards the heavens and spoke out loud.

"Lord Jesus, I need a miracle!"

Precious suddenly leaped from its branch, sailing past her ear. Faith yelped, turning to watch the cat land softly on the floating rooftop, which had somehow closed the gap and now drifted almost in tandem with the tree.

There was no time for hesitation. Faith let go of the tree and lunged as far as she could. Her fingers scraped against jagged roof shingles, finding nothing to grab hold of. She clawed frantically, shredding the tips of her fingers. Then her grip tightened around an exposed board where the roof shingles had been ripped away.

Water filled her mouth and she gagged violently, struggling to keep her grip on the board and praying that the nails would hold. Precious meowed encouragement, and Faith summoned her last bit of strength to haul herself up out of the water. She sputtered and gasped for breath, flopping on her back. She knew she had only traded one danger for another, but she was still alive.

Precious licked her face with its rough tongue. Faith rolled over and pushed herself to her knees. She touched her belly, fearful for the tiny life inside.

Was there still even a life?

She looked up to survey the flooded valley. The only hope her child had was if she stayed alive herself. Even though the roof on which she sat seemed solid enough, it could be dashed to pieces in an instant. There was one small bit of good news: the water didn't seem to be moving as fast as before. But Faith had no way of turning the raft towards dry land, which was still hundreds of yards away. People were crowded on the hillsides, throwing ropes into the water to try and pull people from the clutches of the current. If she could just find some way to drift closer to them...

A water-choked scream pierced her ears. She turned just in time to see a pale woman being pulled by the current towards the roof at a frightening speed. There was no time to save her – Faith knew what was going to happen. She looked away as the woman's head collided against the timbers with a sickening *thunk!* Faith gasped as flecks of blood spattered on her face.

She looked up at the sky and screamed with all of her might. She screamed for Meredith, for Charlotte, for Stephen, for the woman who had just perished, for everyone she watched die before her eyes.

Just kill me, she wheezed. *Just make it quick...*

Tears streamed down her red-stained cheeks as she thought of Allan. He probably didn't even know what was happening to Johnstown. She pictured him standing in his office, staring at the rain streaming down the windows, oblivious to the fact that his family was about to be snuffed out.

Her gaze dropped for a moment, and then she yelped with surprise. Dry land was several yards closer than it had been just a few moments ago, before the unfortunate woman had collided with the roof and pushed it towards the shore.

There was hope!

Faith exhaled a ragged breath. *Please receive that woman into Your mercy, Lord.*

She searched the water, trying to find a piece of floating debris that she might use as a paddle. Yet all she saw was swirling foam and brown, muddy currents. Her body trembled with chills and she felt

253

despair seeping in.

*No...*she commanded herself. *You can't give up yet. There was hope just a moment ago; there could be hope again.*

She grabbed Precious and held the pitiful animal to her chest. The cat was utterly soaked and shivered along with her. It looked up at her with green eyes that were almost luminous.

Faith held the cat closer and squeezed the tears out of her own eyes.

We have to try...we have to try...

Something dark was in the water up ahead. Faith set Precious down and leaned forward.

It was a tree branch, about three feet above water. And it didn't appear to be moving with the current. That meant it was still rooted to the ground.

A second later, the branch was almost right alongside the roof.

Faith acted on instinct.

Grab it!

Her hand darted out, her fingers raking through the small twigs. She cried out in pain as the skin on her hand was torn away, but she managed to close her fist long enough to grip the branch for a fraction of a second, using her other hand to keep a firm grip on the edge of the roof. It was just enough to cause the broken roof to swing around and send it angling towards the shore.

Warmth flooded through Faith's cold veins. It worked!

In the distance, she could see the outline of the stone bridge that spanned the Conemaugh. Water had nearly reached the top of the bridge, and the arches that normally soared high over the river were clotted with debris. Smoke arose from several wooden piles but no flames were visible.

Suddenly, a massive explosion bellowed across the valley and a volcano of wood, metal, and bodies erupted as if someone had tossed dynamite into the debris. Great gouts of flames spewed in all directions. Faith's eyes widened in horror as she watched the colossal clot of debris piled up against the bridge become engulfed in flames, swallowing helpless souls being carried to a fiery death by the raging current.

Drowning had seemed terrifying enough, but now the jaws of death roared with teeth of flame. And there was nothing she could do to save herself.

"Lord Jesus!" she cried out. "Save me...I beg You!"

Another powerful concussion blasted across the water as more debris exploded, likely a tanker car filled with oil. The water around the debris logjam was on fire, and Faith wept as she heard the screams from those being burned alive.

She looked down at Precious, who stared up at her with flickering eyes.

"I'm sorry, sweetheart," she said.

Precious meowed and pressed against her leg. Faith rubbed her stomach, fighting back a fresh wave of tears.

255

"And I'm sorry too, little Allan. Mommy tried her best. I'll see you in heaven, little one."

She took a deep breath and closed her eyes as her fingers sought out the edge of the roof. Better to drown now than to be incinerated.

Please forgive me, Lord.

A sharp whistle made her eyes snap open. The whistle sounded again and she looked to her left. A group of men were on the shore, waving to her and shouting. One of the men held a large pole in his hand, poised to throw it like a javelin. Faith squinted in confusion, then she cried out.

"Yes! Please, throw it!"

The group of men parted to let the pole-thrower step forward. With a cry that rang out even above the noise of the current and the flames, he hurled the pole with a rope trailing behind it. The pole arced through the air, expertly thrown ahead of Faith's raft on an intercept course.

Before she had time to think about the dangers, she grabbed Precious and leaped off the raft just as the pole impacted the water. She went down beneath the waves, desperately clutching with her free hand. Her fingers grabbed only water.

I'm dead...

Her hand struck something solid and she grabbed on with all of her strength. Her hand slid down the pole and found the knot where the rope was tied, giving her a firm handhold. The current bounced her back to the surface and she gulped a breath of air before her mouth filled with water again, making her gag and sputter. Precious wriggled out of her arms and latched onto her back. Gritting her teeth in pain, Faith reached forward with her other hand and grabbed the rope, summoning every ounce of her remaining strength. Water and foam slammed into her face, blinding her for all but a moment or two, but she was able to glimpse the men on the shore hauling her in.

It seemed like an eternity out there at the end of the rope. Every breath was more water than air and she could barely see anything. The raging torrent clawed at her dress, ripping it into tatters. Despite her mortal danger, she feared that she would be hauled stark naked out of the water.

Her foot struck something hard. A rock? She didn't dare hope. Her house slippers had long since washed away and she felt cautiously with her bare toes.

Yes, it was a rock! She set her foot firmly upon it, relieved to no longer be whipped about. It took considerable effort, but Faith managed to lift her head above water for a few seconds to get her bearings.

Her heart nearly burst out of her chest. The shore was only a few yards away!

Reaching out with her other foot, she was elated to discover more solid ground. She leaned forward against the current and began walking towards the shore, aided by the men pulling the rope. Only moments ago, she was prepared for a watery death, and now she was walking onto dry land.

She was about halfway out of the water when she looked down at her clothes. Everything that ought to be covered was still covered, but just barely. Any embarrassed notions she would normally have felt were shoved aside by the pure joy of being alive.

Faith staggered onto the rocky ground, falling to her knees and vomiting torrents of water. Precious detached its claws from her back and hopped onto the grass, shaking itself dry. Faith looked at the pitiful soaked animal through tear-filled eyes and smiled.

"We made it," she croaked, wiping her mouth. "Oh thank You, Lord Jesus. Thank You."

She didn't have the strength to raise her head but she heard footsteps surround her and strong hands lift her to her feet.

"Thank you, kind sirs," she murmured, too weak to look up see her rescuers. Then a sudden pang of fear gripped her heart.

"My baby..."

One of the men carrying her leaned in close. "Ma'am?"

"My baby!" Faith sobbed. "Is my baby okay?"

The man looked at his companion who held her other arm. "Ma'am, just sit here."

They eased her down on a patch of grass with a couple of other folks who had been pulled from the flood. She watched with admiration as the men gathered up the rope and ran back to the water's edge to try and fish another helpless soul from the watery clutches.

Precious clambered onto her lap, shivering and shaking.

"My sweetheart," Faith said, gathering the poor animal in her arms.

At that moment, the baby kicked and Faith let out a cry. An old woman looked at her with vacant eyes.

"My baby kicked!" Faith exclaimed.

The old woman stared at her for a few moments, then looked out across the flooded valley. Faith felt a twinge of guilt at her outburst. Only one thing could bring that kind of emptiness to a woman's eyes – the loss of her own family.

She reached out and took the woman's hand in hers. Tears ran down the old woman's face as she gripped Faith's hand like her life depended on it. Maybe it did.

Faith also stared out across the water. Screams filled the air and she could only watch as men, women, and children zipped past on the rapid current, many disappearing into the inferno that blazed at the bridge. Their shrieks of terror echoed across the water as loudly as if they were standing on the shore. The men valiantly cast their rope into the water again and again but were not able to draw anyone else from the clutches of death.

Nausea suddenly gripped Faith's senses. She fell back on her elbows, staring up at the gray sky.

"Are you all right?" someone said.

Faith nodded as her vision blurred.

"I'm fi– "

****

A crushing weight pressed on her chest. Faith opened her eyes, only to see nothing. The pressure on her rib cage increased. She tried to move but she was paralyzed.

One thought pierced the terror: *Scream.*

She opened her mouth, only to gag and choke as water poured into her lungs. In her panic, she tried to scream louder, which caused her to inhale more water. Darkness enveloped her like a shroud.

I'm dying! I'm dying!

She awoke with a shout, flailing her arms and legs. Her fingers gripped soft soil and she sat up. It was dark, but not completely dark. She was on land, and she was not drowning. And there was nothing on her chest.

All around her were screams and strange sounds and flickering lights. She rubbed her eyes to remove the crust that half-sealed her eye-lids and she gathered her senses.

Suddenly, the memories slammed into her mind like the wall of water that had obliterated her home.

Charlotte. Meredith. Stephen. Her home. Johnstown.

All gone.

But where was Precious?

Faith called out for her cat again and again, but to no avail. Every muscle in her body ached and she pressed a hand to her belly, begging God for a kick. After a few seconds, she felt a faint movement.

"Thank You," she breathed.

She tottered a few steps and leaned against the tree for support. Her throat was parched and her stomach felt like a gaping hole.

"Precious..." she sobbed, fighting the nausea threatening to topple her again.

Two green eyes appeared in the darkness. Faith fell to her knees.

"Come here, sweetheart!" she cried as she threw her arms wide.

Precious crept forward out of the shadows with something in its mouth. A dead rat.

Faith made a face.

"Put that down!" she said, waving her hand.

Precious crouched low, and for a moment, Faith thought it might lash out at her. Then the cat let the carcass fall to the ground and crawled onto Faith's lap.

Faith stroked its soft fur and shook her head in amazement.

"I can't believe we're still alive," she whispered. "It's a miracle."

Precious purred in agreement.

Faith turned to look at the blaze burning underneath the bridge. From the firelight, she could see that the water had gone down considerably and was just a swollen river by now, but she could also see the debris scattered as far as the light could reach. Shapes moved in the mud like ghosts and chilling screams pierced the cool night air.

It was a scene from the depths of hell. Faith looked up at the sky, hoping to see stars, but the clouds remained.

Did Allan know about the flood? He wasn't due back until tomorrow, but she wondered if word of the town's destruction had reached Pittsburgh. She hoped it hadn't yet, because she knew he would be beside himself with worry.

The air stank of death and rot. Hardly any buildings were still standing, and the despondent shapes moving through the darkness seemed more dead than alive. Many of them screamed at random intervals. Faith suddenly felt fearful of her fellow townsfolk. This tragedy had surely torn many stout minds to shreds.

Precious purred quietly in her lap. The poor thing had gone to sleep.

Faith felt invisible weights tug at her eyelids. Perhaps sleep was the best thing right now. Daylight and several hours' rest would hopefully bring clarity. Her stomach growled but she told her appetite it would have to wait.

Where can I sleep?

She squinted in the darkness. Several yards away was a clump of bushes that looked like they had a bit of hollow space beneath the leaves. Faith got to her feet, holding Precious with gentle hands. She stumbled towards the bushes, a constant stream of prayers on her lips to beg for protection against unseen roots of rocks that would twist her ankle.

In case there were any creatures already taking shelter, she shook the bush and listened for the sound of scurrying feet, but she didn't hear anything. She set the sleepy cat on the ground and crawled under the branches, wincing as they scratched the skin on her back that had been scraped raw from Precious' claws.

She couldn't be mad, though. If the cat didn't have such sharp claws, it would have drowned long ago. A few scratches were a small price to pay for the sweet animal to still be alive. Faith lay herself down on the bed of dry leaves, trying to focus on the cat's heartbeat. Anything to take her mind off of the horrific sights and sounds coming from the ruin that was once a happy and prosperous town.

The last thought to drift through Faith's mind before she fell asleep was that she hoped Allan was sleeping peacefully for one last night before he would learn of the terrible news.

Chapter Seventeen

THE MOMENT SHE AWOKE, even before she opened her eyes, she felt the pain down to her bones.

A violent shudder rippled through her limbs and her eyes snapped open. Her senses flooded with stimuli – cold and clammy skin, gray light stabbing at her eyes, waterlogged ears, parched tongue, and a cavernous, empty stomach. She rolled over and retched hard, vomiting only stringy spittle. A guttural, animal groan creaked in her burning throat and tears stung her eyes.

Pull yourself together.

She didn't appreciate the tone her subconscious took but it was right. Wiping her eyes and mouth, Faith drew in a long, slow breath and crawled out from underneath the bushes. Precious followed, me-owing continuously. The poor thing was just as hungry as she was.

Just as she staggered to her feet and looked around, Faith fell to her knees again.

"Lord, have mercy..."

Johnstown was gone. In its place was a giant field of mud bristling with shattered buildings and uprooted trees. The devastation stretched as far as she could see. Debris still burned against the bridge downriver. The water level seemed to have returned to normal, but the valley itself was now the riverbed. Figures trudging through the mud looked like they were walking on water.

Faith knelt down to take Precious in her arms.

There was only one place to go. The First Methodist Episcopal church. Its grand spire rose defiantly over the ruins, and from this distance, it didn't seem to be damaged at all. Faith could already make out a small crowd of people gathering in its shadow. She didn't know if she would find any help down there, but she knew she couldn't stay on this hillside and die of thirst.

Cradling the cat in one arm and placing her other hand on her belly, she started making her way down the grassy slope. Sometimes she would pass what would look like a bundle of clothes on the ground, but she learned very quickly to keep her eyes up, especially when she heard the din of buzzing flies. When she finally reached the bottom of the hill, it took all of her concentration to keep from vomiting again.

The ground was littered with bodies, human and animal. It was about half a mile to the church, but Faith could hardly stomach taking ten more steps. The stench of death hung heavy in the misty morning air and the buzzing flies seemed to grow louder by the minute.

Just keep walking. Don't look down. Just keep walking.

Faith swallowed hard and took a step forward. Her foot struck something soft and before she could stop herself, her eyes dropped to the ground. Her hand flew to her mouth to stifle her scream.

A dead child stared up at her from the mud, a young girl. The corpse's eyes were wide open and glassy, though their brilliant shade of blue was still apparent. The mouth hung open and flies buzzed in and out. The rest of the body was submerged in the mud.

Faith turned away as sobs wracked her body. Precious nuzzled against her.

Keeping her eyes closed, Faith struggled to grab hold of her mind.

One foot in front of the other. Breathe with every step. Think about the baby.

And pray.

Faith blinked away tears as she started making her way across the muddy expanse.

"Though I walk through the valley of the shadow of death," she whispered, "I will fear no evil, for Thou art with me..."

She recited as many Bible verses as she could remember while trying to avoid obstacles and debris. Some verses just popped into her head, even if she didn't know the reference, though they sounded familiar and comforting. The words would tumble from her lips in barely audible whispers with each cautious footstep. Sometimes she would see something move in the mud but she would just keep walking. There was nothing she could do to help anyone right now, and she was on the verge of death herself. The stench was indescribable and Faith had to continuously force the bile back down into her empty stomach. She also had to resist the temptation to kneel down and take a drink from one of the many puddles around her. With all of the corpses lying around, finding potable water was going to be a miracle.

She stepped on something hard and flat. It was the foundation of a building that had been wiped clean away. Faith glanced around and shivered, trying to process the fact that she was standing in what had once been a busy part of town, but now it was as barren as a desert.

How could water have so much power? Images of the giant wave crashing through her house ripped through her mind and fresh tears fell from her eyes.

"It's all gone," she sobbed. "All gone..."

She started to topple forward but a strong hand caught her arm.

"Miss? Are you all right?"

Faith fought through the dizziness and looked up. A face came into focus, a man's, bearded and weathered. The eyes were kind.

"I'm...I'm all right," Faith stammered, summoning all of her strength to stand up straight. "Just a little overwhelmed."

"Are you looking for someone?"

Faith swallowed hard and shook her head. "Not yet. I'm going to the church."

"I was headed that way myself," the man said. "I reckon I'll help you down there, seeing as you being with child and all."

"Thank you," Faith said, noticing his accent. "I appreciate your kindness. What's your name?"

"Gabriel McMalley."

"Pleasure, Mr. McMalley. I'm Faith Shelton."

Gabriel's eyes widened. "You wouldn't happen to be related to Mr. Allan Shelton?"

"Yes!" Faith exclaimed. "He's my husband. Have you seen him?"

"Sorry ma'am, I haven't."

"It's all right." Faith looked away for a moment. "He wasn't here when the flood hit. He's due back today on the 2:00 train. Probably stranded on the tracks right now."

"If he is, he's probably sick with worry about you."

"Better him than me," Faith said with a mirthless laugh.

Gabriel gestured with his hand. "Let's get a move on."

Faith gripped Gabriel's arm as they navigated their way through the wreckage. It was infinitely more comforting to have someone beside her.

"How do you know my husband?" she asked as she sidestepped the carcass of a large dog.

"Watch out for the nails in the mud there. I work in smelter number seven at the iron works. I had the honor of giving your husband a tour when he first arrived."

"Small world," Faith remarked. "How did he strike you?"

"Mr. Shelton? As a man in charge."

Faith's heart swelled at the compliment. "He's going to run the place some day."

"Well, he'll have his hands full now. The iron works is up river from the town, and it would have gotten the full force of the water."

Faith hesitated a moment before asking, "How did you survive?"

"I wasn't at work today."

Faith thought about pressing him on the reason for his truancy, but she figured that if he had wanted her to know, he would have said something. There was still one more question to ask, though she dreaded speaking the words.

"Do...do you have a family?"

Gabriel nodded. "I do. Back in Ireland. A wife and two sons."

Faith exhaled with relief. "Oh thank God. I was afraid that they were here and something had happened to them."

"No, they just have to deal with bread shortages and constant cold and harassment from the British. Though compared to this, that seems pretty comfortable right about now."

"I agree."

The two shared a short laugh. Faith looked down at the cat asleep in the crook of her arm.

"Do you miss them?"

"Every minute of every day," Gabriel answered. "I was hoping they would come over next year, but I think the Good Lord has thrown a wrench into those plans. I'm more worried about the news reaching them before I can let them know that I'm all right. My poor wife's blood pressure is high enough as it is."

Thoughts of Allan raced through Faith's mind. What if he really was stuck on the tracks somewhere or on a station platform, wringing his hands with worry?

If he is, that means he is safe, and there's nothing you can do about his state of mind right now. You just need to get to that church.

She stumbled and Gabriel gripped her arm.

"We're almost there," he said. "Almost to the Lord's house."

Faith tried to keep her eyes on the steeple rising high into the gray sky, but her gaze would sometimes fall and her breath would catch in her throat. She was walking through what had been busy streets just yesterday, and now were wiped clean as a chalkboard. Occasionally she spotted jumbled debris, as if a giant broom had swept through the town and deposited the rubbish in piles. One house was almost fully intact but was resting on its side. The windows weren't even broken.

More heartbreaking than the damage was the sight of shocked survivors wandering around, searching for loved ones or simply trying to process the tragedy. Orphaned children stood in ankle-deep mud, bawling and clinging to dirty toys. Screams would break out when survivors would discover the bodies of friends or loved ones. Some folks were walking towards the church, but others were heading in the opposite direction, as if drawn to the fire still blazing at the bridge.

When Faith and Gabriel reached the church, a small crowd was gathered. It seemed like nearly everyone was crying, men, women, and children. At least half of the group were young men, those most likely to survive a disaster like this. Their bodies seemed fine but the pain on their faces broke Faith's heart afresh.

She looked up at the building, amazed that it had withstood the raging torrent with hardly a scratch. It had been gutted, of course, and every window was blown out, but the structure itself looked as sturdy as when she had first seen it.

"Wait here," Gabriel said before walking over to a pile of debris.

Faith spotted a little girl in a tattered dress standing by herself, clutching a ragged doll. She knelt down and beckoned the child, but the girl shook her head. Faith held out Precious. The girl stared at the cat for a moment, then turned and walked away.

"I'm sorry," Faith whispered to no one in particular. She stood up and hung her head.

This is what the end of the world feels like.

She spotted Gabriel walking towards her with a wooden chair that was apparently undamaged.

"Where did you find that?" she exclaimed.

"Over yonder. Have a seat."

Faith sat down and sighed. In her home, she had exquisite velvet chairs and overstuffed sofas, but this was the most comfortable chair she had ever sat in.

"Thank you," she said.

Gabriel tipped his nonexistent hat. "Are you all right here for a while? I'm going to go find some water."

Faith nodded. "Thank you again. I don't know what I'd have done if you hadn't come by."

"We all got to look out for each other now, don't we? Just take a minute to catch your breath. I'll be back soon."

He walked alongside the church before disappearing around the corner. Faith thought she would see him reappear on the other side of the building but he seemed to have vanished into thin air. She started to get up to see if she could catch a glimpse of him again when an elderly woman hobbled up to her and wrapped her in a hug.

"Mrs. Walscott!" Faith cried.

The old woman looked at her with shimmering eyes. "Oh my dear Faith, I'm so happy to see you! I...I can't believe this..."

She looked around at the devastation and started to falter. Faith held onto her arm.

"Here, sit," she said, getting up from the chair.

"I'm all right," Mrs. Walscott insisted. "You're the one who should be off your feet."

"I'm fine. Please, sit a moment."

273

Mrs. Walscott gave her a grateful smile and eased into the chair. Her relief was immediately apparent.

"Thank you, dear," the old woman said. Then she hung her head and burst into tears.

Faith knelt down, put her arms around her neck, and wept with her. Their tears fell onto the mud caked on their feet.

After what could have been just a few seconds or several minutes, the tears ran out. Mrs. Walscott looked up at Faith with red, puffy eyes.

"Oh my dear," she whimpered, "what are we going to do?"

"Where is your husband?" Faith asked, bracing for the answer.

Mrs. Walscott closed her eyes. "He's in Philadelphia, praise the Lord. Helping our eldest with a commercial purchase. I loathe that city in spite of its 'brotherly love' so I stayed behind to start the planning committee for the Independence Day celebrations. We were going to meet at the library but I was running late because my French poodle ran his dirty paws all over my dress and I had to change."

Her head bowed low again.

"My driver tried to outrun the wave but the horse got spooked and bolted, overturning the carriage. The poor man must have broken his neck because he wasn't moving when I climbed out. As luck would have it, we crashed right here at the church and I ran up the steeple until the stairs ran out. I held on for dear life with a number of other people, Germans if I understood them correctly. Dreadful attire, but I remember the determination in their faces, and it made me feel safe with them. Somehow we all slept on those awful wooden stairs. When the water finally went down, we came out to this."

Faith squeezed the old woman's hands. "The Lord was certainly looking out for you today. And I hope He welcomes your driver into heaven with open arms."

"I hope so too." Mrs. Walscott wiped her eyes and assumed a more dignified sitting posture. "My house and all my possessions are gone. I looked down 7th Street when I was in the church steeple and all I could see was mud and wooden planks. I couldn't even tell where my house had been."

Then she gasped.

"Oh my! Faith, I am so sorry! Here I am blabbering about my troubles when I haven't even asked about you. Where is Mr. Shelton? Please tell me he is away on business too."

Faith nodded. "He's been in Pittsburgh for the last several days but he was due back on the 2 o'clock this afternoon."

"That's welcome news. He's probably on his way here now, though I imagine it will be a while with the station gone and the lower tracks washed out."

"I think you're right. By the way, a man who says he met my husband helped me down here."

Mrs. Walscott looked around. "Where is he?"

Faith scanned the muddy wasteland but Gabriel was nowhere in sight.

"He was just here," she said with a frown. "I don't know where he could have – "

A handheld bell clanged loudly.

"Folks!" a shaky male voice called out. "Can I have your attention, please?"

Faith helped Mrs. Walscott to her feet and the two women moved closer with the small crowd.

A young man stood on the steps of the church. He was a bit disheveled but looked like he had made an effort to clean himself up, though he was bleeding from a cut on the side of his head. Faith recognized him as the minister's eldest son, Rupert. She also knew that the minister had to be dead, or else he would be here himself.

Rupert cleared his throat and threaded his fingers together.

"Folks," he began, his voice cracking. "Friends. I hardly know what to say. I can't believe what my eyes see, and what I saw yesterday. I watched my father get carried off by the water, and my mother, and my elder sister. I fear they are gone, but I have joy knowing that they are with our Father in heaven. You also have lost friends, families, homes, but for some reason, the Good Lord spared you. I don't know what's coming next, but we survived for a reason, and the most important task right now is staying alive. We need to organize. We need to find food, water, and bedding. Help will arrive, though who knows when it will come. Right now, it's just God and us. First, is anyone sick or injured?"

Several people hobbled forward or raised their hands.

"Go on," Mrs. Walscott whispered to Faith. "Raise your hand!"

"I'm pregnant," Faith retorted. "That's not an illness."

Mrs. Walscott pursed her lips. "All I'm saying is that you need special treatment."

Rupert looked over the crowd and nodded.

"Now are there any folks that feel sturdy enough to help me clear out a space in the church?"

After some mumbling and murmuring, about a dozen people raised their hands.

"All right," Rupert said. "Half of you come inside with me, along with the sick and wounded. The other half, your job is find food and water. Anything you can find, as long as you don't steal it from folks that already have it, unless you can convince them to share. Don't be greedy yourselves, neither. We got people here counting on you. May the Lord bless you."

A large man with a bright red beard spoke with a loud voice.

"You men there, and any women who feel up to the task, come with me. I know some places we can look."

"Thank you, brother Paul," Rupert said. "Anyone feeling weak or faint, come inside too. It's not too pretty in there but at least it's dry. Well, drier than out here, anyway."

Faith tugged on Mrs. Walscott's arm. "Let's go inside," she said.

Mrs. Walscott nodded and her eyes closed for a moment. Faith was worried she might faint but the old woman stayed on her feet. They headed inside the church along with the rest who didn't join the food search party.

The moment she stepped into the church, Faith wrinkled her nose. Mrs. Walscott also made a face.

"Lord Almighty, what is that stench?"

Faith looked around the gutted sanctuary. Mud and debris covered the floor and was piled high against the walls. The pews were gone, either swept out the door or dashed to pieces and mixed with the other refuse. A coating of mud six inches thick covered the floor.

Several people held their noses and gagged. The mud was putrid and smelled like a lake that had been drained, but the air was thick with a different odor.

Faith leaned close to Mrs. Walscott's ear.

"We need to get out of here."

"Why?" Mrs. Walscott asked.

Faith glanced around to make sure no one was close.

"There are dead bodies."

"Oh good heavens! And in a church..."

Faith led her back outside. The smell of mud and death was still noticeable in the open air but not nearly as strong. The two women stood on the steps of the church, staring down river to where the fire blazed beneath the bridge.

"Where can we go?" Mrs. Walscott asked in a fragile voice.

A muffled explosion sounded at the bridge. Faith flinched and watched a seething cloud of black smoke crawl towards the sky.

She turned and looked at Mrs. Walscott.

"We need to pray."

"Pray? Sweetheart, I've already done plenty of that. I don't think the Lord is listening."

Cold fear gripped Faith's heart.

What if she's right?

The voice in her heart was firm.

God is here. Pray.

"I...I think we should pray anyway," Faith said.

Mrs. Walscott nodded and closed her eyes.

Faith closed her eyes as well and said, "Our Father in heaven, please hear our prayer. We are desperate. We don't know what to do or where to go. Please help us. And help these people. We beg You – have mercy. Amen."

Mrs. Walscott looked at her and smiled.

"I never took you for the religious type."

Faith blushed, though she didn't know why.

"I don't know if that's how I take myself, either," she replied. "But there's a world of difference between being religious and being a true believer."

"I suppose you're right. Well, do you think He heard us?"

Faith looked up at the sky, immediately feeling foolish. Something inside her wanted a sign. A dove with an olive branch, like in the story of Noah, or perhaps a sunbeam piercing the clouds and illuminating a safe shelter.

There was nothing except the sights and sounds of devastation and death. Her heart sank but she tried to put on a smile.

"I'm sure He did," she said.

"So what do we do?"

"We walk."

"Where?"

"That way," she said without thinking.

Mrs. Walscott frowned and looked where Faith was pointing. "Oh Faith, it looks a mess. Why that way?"

"Do you have a better idea?"

Mrs. Walscott shook her head.

Faith hitched the hem of her dress up out of the mud. "We can't just stand around and wait for the Good Lord to move our feet. We just have to trust that He'll bless the choices we make."

"Well look at you," Mrs. Walscott remarked with a grin. "You should be up on that pulpit on Sundays."

"Believe me, that's the last place I should be. Let's get moving. And keep an eye out for a bucket or anything that holds water. If we're lucky, the silt will have settled to the bottom by now and the water will be clean enough to drink."

"Lead the way."

The two women held onto each other as they started walking down the muddy street. Faith glanced up again at the sky and prayed.

You haven't abandoned us, have You?

Chapter Eighteen

EVERY STEP THAT BROUGHT them nearer to the heart of Johnstown weighed on Faith's heart. Fresh horrors appeared wherever she looked, and she wished she could just shut her eyes and ears and dissolve like smoke in the wind. Bloated bodies half-buried in the mud, dead children silently screaming at the sky, parents weeping and tearing at their tattered clothes in anguish...it truly felt like hell on Earth.

Yet despite the devastation, there were glimpses of hope. Townsfolk gathered around wrecked homes and dismantled piles of debris to bring out those trapped inside. A burst of cheers erupted from a group surrounding a house as a baby was pulled alive from the rubble. Faith's knees felt weak as she saw the joy on the mother's face when the shrieking child was placed in her arms.

Praise the Lord your child is still safe in your womb. If he had been already born, he would have surely been carried off by the water.

Faith rubbed her belly and felt a comforting kick.

283

"I know that look," Mrs. Walscott remarked.

"What look?"

"That look."

Faith touched her face. She didn't even realize she was smiling. Warmth crept through her cheeks and she looked down at her bulging stomach again.

"I'm just glad he's safe and didn't have to see any of this."

"He?"

"Yes. He."

Mrs. Walscott nodded her head. "I was right about my children too. All nine of them."

"Nine?"

Mrs. Walscott gave her a sly smile. "We lived in Poughkeepsie, New York and it was cold and rainy a good bit of the time, and Mr. Walscott had, shall we say, a 'vigorous appetite', so you can imagine – "

"I'd rather not," Faith interrupted jokingly.

A piercing shriek rang out from a shattered building. Three children were carried out the house, all dead. Their mother threw herself upon the bodies, weeping uncontrollably. A man stood by, stiff as a board, too shocked to react.

"Poor things," Mrs. Walscott whispered. "I can't imagine how that must feel. I've outlived five of my nine children, but none of them were taken from me like this."

Faith started to say something in reply but stopped short when

284

Precious suddenly jumped out of her arms.

"Come back!" she shouted after the cat as it ran in between two broken houses.

She started to give chase but Mrs. Walscott held her arm.

"Is it safe?" the old woman asked.

Faith shrugged out of her grip. "I don't care. I'm going after her."

She hurried down the narrow space between the two toppled buildings, careful to avoid splinters and protruding nails. When she turned the corner, she gasped.

Precious was lapping what appeared to be clean water from a porcelain bowl. There was hardly any silt at the bottom. Faith waited a few moments to let the cat drink its fill and then she lifted the bowl to her own lips. She didn't care that she was drinking after an animal.

Mrs. Walscott appeared from behind one of the houses, panting for breath.

"I hope it was worth it for your – "

Her eyes grew wide.

"Is that...?"

Faith held out the bowl as water ran down her chin. "It's quite clean."

Mrs. Walscott took the bowl and drank gingerly. Small rivulets spilled from both sides of her mouth. When she lowered the bowl, she smiled with embarrassment.

"If only my friends could see me now, drinking from a bowl like a savage."

A cloud passed over her face.

"...I wonder how many friends I have left."

Faith took the bowl from her and set it down.

"Only God knows."

"So what do we do now?"

Faith sat down on a wooden crate and set Precious on the ground. The cat curled up at her feet as if they were at home in the living room.

"Help will come," she said in a quiet voice. "Johnstown is an important place, and people will find out what happened here, and they will send help."

"But what do we do until help gets here?"

Faith drew in a frail breath. She was nauseated with hunger, and she knew her baby was going to need fresh nutrients as well.

"We have to find food," she said. "And we need to avoid groups of people."

"Why?"

"Because right now people are dangerous and unpredictable, especially if help takes a while to get here. There's no law and order anymore. People are going to go mad with hunger and exposure. I say we keep to ourselves until help arrives, or until order is restored."

Mrs. Walscott nodded, and then she grinned.

"You're quite different than the person I thought you were when we first met."

"How did you think about me at first?"

"Ambitious, over-eager, a bit spoiled. You clearly didn't come from money but you wanted to prove to people like me that you belonged in our company."

Faith's mouth fell open. She didn't know whether to be insulted or embarrassed.

"I...I..."

Mrs. Walscott touched her arm in a warm, motherly gesture.

"Don't worry, child. When it comes to a life of privilege, everyone is desperate in one way or another. Desperate to reach the next rung of the ladder or desperate to keep from being knocked down. Despite appearances, no one can relax. And none of that matters now. It's all washed away. But now I see your true strength, and that is much more valuable than knowing the best shops in New York or Paris."

"Thank you," Faith said. "But my so-called strength won't do us any good if we're too weak to find food."

Mrs. Walscott helped her to her feet.

"Then let's find food."

****

Precious meowed hungrily at Faith's feet. Faith broke off a piece of stale bread and held it out. Precious sniffed it, wrinkled its nose, and then ate the morsel.

"Poor thing," Mrs. Walscott remarked, leaning her head against the wood plank wall.

Faith nodded and took a bite of bread herself. "It's a miracle she survived all this."

The sun lay low on the horizon and the last rays of reddish light squeezed through the shattered windows. After hours of wandering through muddy streets and shattered wreckage, the women had found a wooden home that had escaped serious damage, apart from lying on its side. All of the furniture was piled against one wall, which was now the floor. Because of its light construction, it had simply rolled over like a box rather than exploding into fragments when the water hit.

It was also empty, and there were a few edible items to be found in the debris. Faith had discovered some bread in an airtight tin, and Mrs. Walscott had uncovered an unbroken jar of pickled olives. The two women sat quietly in the fading light, eating their food and staring at nothing in particular. They were too tired to make conversation, and a chill was growing in the air.

Faith glanced over at Mrs. Walscott, and the look that passed between them said all that needed to be said. Easing herself to her feet, Faith began searching through the pile of furniture and household items piled up in a corner. After several minutes and just as many splinters, she found what she was looking for: a blanket. It smelled awful and rats scurried away when Faith picked it up, but it was thick and warm.

For a brief moment, she was struck with sadness at how grateful she was to find a soiled blanket that smelled of rat droppings, when just a couple of days ago she was trying to decide on satin curtains for the baby's room. Every comfort had been at her fingertips, and even her lavish home was probably a peasant's hovel compared to the mansion Mrs. Walscott had lived in. Yet here they were, shivering in a tumbled house, eating old food and fearful of every noise and creak.

"You're crying," Mrs. Walscott said.

Faith touched her face to feel wetness on her cheeks.

"I-I miss my home..."

Mrs. Walscott reached out and took her hand. Faith sat down next to her and they huddled together under the blanket with Precious in between them.

****

A whistle shrieked, and shrieked again.

Faith jolted awake, her vision blurry. She winced as the shrill sound stabbed her ears a third time.

What is that?

She rubbed her eyes and stretched her aching neck.

A train... It's a train!

Faith gripped Mrs. Walscott's shoulder and shook hard.

289

"Wake up!" she cried.

Mrs. Walscott murmured some unintelligible words but didn't open her eyes.

Faith scowled and shook her again.

"Mrs. Walscott, wake up! A train has arrived!"

The old woman's eyes flew open and she jumped to her feet.

"Let's go meet it!"

The sun was shining brightly when the two women emerged from the wrecked house. The stench of rot hung in the air but a gentle breeze drifted through the valley and Faith could taste a hint of sweetness coming down from the hills. The valley already seemed to be healing itself.

The train whistle pierced the air. Faith felt the baby kick with excitement and her heart sang. A sliver of hope also squeezed through.

Is he on the train?

Just the thought brought a tear to her eye. He must be worried sick. Has he been stuck on the tracks all this time?

Another whistle jolted her out of her contemplation. Mrs. Walscott took her hand and they made their way through the rubble in front of the tumbled house.

Dozens of people stood with them, staring up at the hills. At the sound of the whistle, hope brightened their faces, even though no one could see the train. Plumes of smoke puffed up from the trees but it was hard to see where the unseen train had come from or where it was heading. The station depot was no more, and Faith wondered how close the train could get to the town.

At least help has arrived.

Her knees suddenly felt weak and she held onto Mrs. Walscott to keep from stumbling. The old woman looked at her with worry.

"That little fellow is drinking you dry," she said. "He's going to get his vittles, whether you eat or not. You need some proper nutrition, and soon."

Faith took a couple of breaths and regained her balance.

"We all do. They must have food on that train."

"So long as you don't faint between now and when it gets here."

"I'm not planning on letting a little fatigue get the best of me after what we just lived through."

Mrs. Walscott grinned. "Amen to that."

"Where should we go?"

"Follow the crowd, I suppose."

Faith thought for a moment. "We should wait for those in charge to set up a relief station. I'd like to think that the people of Johnstown have retained their civility but I don't want to be nearby if I'm wrong."

"Good idea. We should go back to the church. That will be a natural gathering place and a landmark for help."

Faith didn't relish the idea of trekking back across the debris-strewn streets but she knew there was no other choice. The stench of rotting corpses seemed to grow stronger with every step, and roving packs of dogs burrowed under the wreckage to feast on the dead bodies. Faith turned away as she saw two large dogs pulling at what looked like the body of a child.

Lord, help us! her heart cried out as she fought a wave of nausea.

When they came around the corner of a collapsed building, a young man with wild eyes looked up at them as he knelt on the ground. He scampered away quick as a jackrabbit and disappeared.

What was he doing?

Faith's question was answered when she saw a woman's body twisted among the wooden planks, blood seeping from the side of her head. The man with the wild eyes had cut off her ears to steal her earrings.

At that moment, Faith felt terror for her own life. She wore little more than rags and had no items of jewelry, but who knew how depraved men's appetites could become when society broke down? She looked at Precious nestled in her arms. What if someone wanted to make a meal out of her beloved cat?

A quiet voice spoke in her heart.

Fear not.

Faith set her jaw.

All right, she replied. *I will not fear.*

She turned to Mrs. Walscott and pulled her away from the grotesque sight.

"Let's get to the church," she said firmly.

Mrs. Walscott nodded. The old woman was clearly shaken up but she didn't falter.

A number of townspeople soon joined together like a flock of birds, instinctively heading to the church standing tall among the destruction. Faith's skin crawled as she remembered the horrid aroma from inside the sanctuary. She had no reason to believe it was better now and she determined that she was going to wait outside, no matter how long it took for help to reach them.

By the time they returned to the churchyard, dozens had already gathered and more were pouring in from the wreckage. Hardly anyone looked well-nourished, though several people were dressed in unusually fancy attire. Faith's mind immediately went back to the thought of the woman with no ears, and she couldn't help but wonder if these people had pillaged the clothes they now wore.

Yet she knew it wasn't her place to judge. She was responsible for herself and her little child. And Precious. She looked down at the small cat sleeping in her arms. It had to be famished but it seemed content to just sleep and preserve its energy. Faith felt a twinge of jealousy.

After a while, more than a hundred people had gathered at the church but the pastor was nowhere to be found. People milled about aimlessly, quietly sobbing or grumbling to no one in particular. Faith was worried that violence might break out but thankfully no one started any conflicts. Everyone just seemed exhausted, and before long, many people were sitting on the ground, Faith among them. Her head

293

started to swim and dark spots appeared in her vision. Her tongue felt like ash in her mouth and the hunger in her stomach was so deep, every breath was painful.

Mrs. Walscott sat down with her. She patted her lap and Faith laid her head down.

"Close your eyes, child," Mrs. Walscott whispered. "Save your strength."

"What about you?" Faith asked, looking up at the old woman through watery eyes.

"I'll watch over you."

Faith gave her hand a squeeze.

"Thank you."

"No need," Mrs. Walscott said. "Rest now."

Faith could feel the darkness pressing in on her senses. The last thing she saw before she slipped into unconsciousness was Precious stalking a bird perched on the branch of an uprooted tree.

She prayed the cat would catch the bird and eat until its belly was full.

Chapter Nineteen

A GENTLE HAND SHOOK her shoulder.

The fog of sleep slowly dissolved and she squinted up into the sunlight.

"Allan?"

The face hovering over her came into focus, revealing a young man with a confused expression.

"No, ma'am, my name's Private Hector Cartwright with the National Guard of Pennsylvania. Can you sit up?"

Faith grimaced and tried to bury her disappointment. The militiaman eased her up from where she had been lying on the ground. She frowned as she looked around.

"Where is Mrs. Walscott?"

"Who, ma'am?"

Faith clutched Precious to her chest, thankful that at least her cat was still here.

"Mrs. Walscott. The elderly woman I was with. She was right

here when I fell asleep."

"I don't know anyone by that name, ma'am. We've got some food and water over by the church, and I think it would do you good to get some vittles in you."

A mixture of anger and fear welled up in Faith's heart. Why would Mrs. Walscott just leave her sleeping on the ground like this, especially since help had arrived? But what if something had happened to her? What if one of the rogues prowling around had snatched her away?

"Ma'am?"

Faith blinked and looked up at the militiaman again.

"Ma'am," he repeated with a more insistent tone. "Please, come with me. You need some food."

"All right."

Faith got to her feet, almost collapsing but the young man kept a firm grip on her arm.

"Easy, ma'am. Just walk slow."

"I'm fine," she snapped, pulling her arm away. She felt guilty, adding, "I'm sorry. You're right; I need to eat."

"Right over there, ma'am."

A long line of ragged survivors fed into a hastily erected tent where soldiers and volunteers handed out plates of food, cups of water, and blankets. Faith thanked the young man and shuffled over to the back of the line, holding Precious tight.

The smell of food was a welcome change to the stench of death and rot that hung over the ruins. As she stood in line, Faith looked around at the activity bustling around her. She was surprised she hadn't been awakened by the arrival of so many people. Men with dark blue uniforms shouted at groups of other men, some of whom carried weapons and some looked like they had survived the flood themselves. They were going from building to building, house to house, presumably searching for bodies.

But where was Mrs. Walscott?

Faith's thoughts drifted back to the mysterious stranger who had helped her when she had come down the hill yesterday. What was his name?

Gabriel. Could he have been an angel?

Mrs. Walscott had also vanished; was she an angel as well?

Faith had to laugh silently at herself. The notion was preposterous.

Right, Lord?

A gentle breeze stroked her skin. The sensation was strangely comforting, almost warm, despite her threadbare attire. Then she realized how immodest she must appear, especially with all of these smartly-dressed young soldiers walking around. She hoped there would be some blankets left when she reached the front of the line.

After several minutes, she was next for a hot bowl of soup, and she was handed a blanket along with her food. The militiaman informed her that after she had eaten and gotten her strength up, she should make her way across the road to the medical station. He seemed to have noticed her bulging belly but didn't make any mention of it, or gawk at her lack of appropriate clothing. Faith was glad to see that decency still prevailed, especially after witnessing desperate savagery for the past couple of days.

Clutching the blanket and Precious with one hand and holding the bowl of soup with another, Faith walked gingerly to sit down beneath the branches of a massive uprooted tree. Several others were gathered around the fallen tree. As Faith knelt down to take a seat, Precious leaped out of her arms in pursuit of a rat, jarring the bowl of soup from her hands.

"You beast!" she snapped as she watched the broth seep into the ground. She closed her eyes and drew in a weary breath through her nose. Then she looked back at the long line waiting for food.

I could strangle that cat.

"You can have some of mine."

Faith glanced over to her right. Mrs. Walscott held out her bowl.

"Mrs. Walscott!" Faith leaped to her feet and threw her arms around the woman's neck, then immediately stepped back, fearful that she had spilled the soup.

"Oh, forgive me! I'm just so happy to see you."

Mrs. Walscott gave her a gentle smile. "Sorry to leave you for so long. Nature was calling and it is very hard to find a private place around here now. I had to trek all the way past that fallen tree."

Faith didn't know what to say, so she let a polite moment pass and raised the bowl to her lips. She couldn't make out the soup's flavor; all she knew is that it was delicious. She gulped it down rapidly, stifling a sudden belch. Her manners had regressed enough for one day.

"Thank you," she said. "I'm ashamed to say that was the best soup I ever had in my life."

"No shame in that," Mrs. Walscott said. "I can't quite agree with you, but it is certainly among the top of my gourmet soup list."

Faith set the bowl on the ground. Precious showed up a few moments later and licked the remaining drops.

"I'm sorry, sweetheart," Faith said as she took the cat in her arms. "I thought you had caught a meal. I should have saved some for you."

Precious mewled and nuzzled its head against her arm, and Faith felt a strange calmness in her heart. Things were far from hopeful but they seemed less dire than just a few hours before.

So what was the next step?

I need to find Allan if he is here, or at least let him know that I am alive.

She rose to her feet and approached a soldier leaning against the wall of the church.

"Excuse me, sir."

The soldier took off his hat. "Yes'm?"

"Um, we're not sure where we should go. Is there someplace where the townsfolk can send word to their families, or meet people who are looking for them?"

"I reckon your best bet is the train depot, or what's left of it," the soldier replied, scratching his head. "I seen 'em putting up tents and such when we was getting off the train, and there was a bunch of city folks there too. You looking for someone?"

"My husband. He was supposed to be on the afternoon train the day after the flood. He might be here in town right now, looking for me."

The solider slapped his hat back on his head. "The depot would be the place to go, then."

Faith nodded. "Thank you." She paused a moment, and then added, "Could I presume upon your kindness and ask one more favor?"

"What's 'at?"

"Is...is there someone who could take us on horseback? You see, I'm with child, and my friend is weak, and it is a far walk to the depot."

The soldier looked at her belly and narrowed his eyes, as if he were trying to look through her skin and see the baby for himself. Faith instinctively drew the blanket tighter.

"Well." The soldier craned his neck. "Come with me then."

"Thank you," Faith said. She motioned for Mrs. Walscott and they followed him towards the soup tent. Faith stood off to the side as he talked with several of his comrades, and one of them came out to meet her.

The man looked her over with a lingering glare, staring at her belly for several moments.

"You really with child?" he mumbled, spitting out a stream of tobacco.

Faith glared at him.

The soldier shuffled his feet and kicked at a rock. Then he sighed and looked over his shoulder.

"Private!"

The young man whom Faith had approached hurried over.

"Yes sir?"

"I want you to go and fetch a wagon."

"A wagon, sir?"

"You're going to the depot."

The private looked confused. "Why, sir?"

"Are you questioning an order, *private?*"

"No, sir!"

"Good. Now git!"

The private hurried off, and then paused after a few steps.

"Um, sir?"

"Yes, private?"

"Where is the wagon?"

"I don't know, private! Find one! Steal one, if you have to. And if you can't find a horse, you'll have to pull it yourself."

The private's face fell. His look of horror was almost comical and he ran towards the town as fast as he could.

Faith gave the officer a grateful smile. "Thank you, kind sir. But I don't need a wagon just for us."

"It ain't just for you." The officer spat again. "We got a lot of wounded and sick here, and I need 'em out of the way. I hope the private finds a big wagon, because it's going to be crowded."

Now it was Faith's turn to look crestfallen. The officer patted his hat on his head and walked back to his company. Faith looked down at Precious snuggled in her arms.

"It could be worse, I suppose..."

****

An hour later, Faith was being jostled back and forth in a horse-drawn wagon driven by the reluctant private. Several times he had to disembark to move wreckage blocking the way, sometimes enlisting the help of the more able-bodied men in the wagon.

Faith was glad to be leaving the epicenter of rot and death, but she was saddened that Mrs. Walscott was not by her side. Back at the church, the lieutenant had announced that a wagon would be going to the depot, but only the sick and wounded would be taken, along with their immediate family members. Anyone healthy enough to walk or fend for themselves was not allowed.

Despite her age, Mrs. Walscott had insisted she stay behind.

"You need to see a doctor!" Faith argued. "You've hardly eaten or drank anything for days!"

Mrs. Walscott straightened her spine and looked at her with proud eyes. "There are many folks here who need to be on that wagon, you among them. Besides, I'm feeling renewed in my strength. Maybe there is something to those prayers after all."

It pained Faith to be separated from her, but she knew she was right. The space on the wagon was limited and dozens of people who needed urgent attention had gathered around.

The lieutenant had feared a riot and fired a shot into the air to get everyone's attention. He had repeated his commands and those who needed help to make the trip were loaded aboard. Faith considered giving up her spot but the voice of reason inside her heart told her to not be foolish. After a tearful goodbye to Mrs. Walscott and a promise to find her as soon as she could, she climbed up into the wagon and wedged herself in the only space available.

Now as the wagon swayed left and right, it took all of her concentration to keep from throwing up.

"Is it okay?"

Faith looked over at the frail old woman sitting next to her. Her arm was in a sling.

"I'm sorry?" Faith said, swallowing the taste of bile.

The old woman gestured with her other hand. "Is it okay?"

Faith looked down at Precious asleep in her lap.

"Yes, it's fine. Animals are a lot more resilient than people."

The old woman smiled and shook her head. "I meant the baby."

Faith touched her belly.

"Oh, yes. How silly of me. Yes, I believe so. I feel like it's a boy."

The old woman slowly stretched out her hand, an unspoken question in her eyes.

Faith nodded. The woman opened her gnarled fingers and touched Faith's stomach. Faith was amazed at how gentle her touch was. Despite the protruding joints and weathered skin, the old woman's hand felt as soft as cotton.

After a couple of moments, Faith realized that the old woman was saying something, her voice barely a whisper. She wanted to ask what was being said but she stopped when she saw that her eyes were squeezed shut.

She is praying over my child...

Faith closed her eyes and placed her hands over the old woman's, their hearts united in prayer.

When she opened her eyes, she looked at the old woman, who simply smiled back and settled in her seat. No one else in the wagon seemed to notice their shared moment. Even the old woman didn't look back at her again; she just stared off into the distance.

Faith tried to make herself comfortable while holding onto Precious. The wagon bounced over countless potholes and debris, and sometimes the impact seemed a bit softer, as if the obstacle wasn't as hard as wood or stone. Faith didn't look over the side of the wagon to confirm her fears. Perhaps the old woman was wise to keep her gaze raised a bit off the ground.

What will there be at the depot?

Faith tried to warn herself against the dangers of excited expectations, but her heart thrilled at the possibility of finding Allan standing in a crowd of people, desperately searching the faces of survivors.

But what if he's not there?

A gentle voice whispered in the depths of her soul.

I will be there.

Faith knew the voice wasn't speaking about Allan. She looked up at the pale blue sky and prayed.

Thank You for bringing me this far. Please, bring my dear husband back to me.

The baby inside her belly gave a strong kick and she let out a startled laugh. Several people in the wagon looked at her but only the old woman was smiling.

****

By the time the wagon reached the depot, or what was left of it, Faith was nearly faint with hunger and thirst. She could hear the commotion around her and she felt herself being jostled by people getting

305

out of the wagon, but she could barely hold her head up. Her vision rippled and blurred and her heart raced. She might have toppled over backwards out of the wagon if a strong hand hadn't gripped her shoulders and held her up in her seat. She blinked and looked into the old woman's face, amazed that a small person could have such strength.

"Don't forget the little one," she said.

Faith tried to swallow to get some moisture on her tongue. "I won't," she whispered, placing her hand on her belly.

"I meant the kitty."

Precious nuzzled against Faith's other hand.

"Thank you," she said.

The old woman gave her shoulder one last squeeze and then accepted a young soldier's help in getting out of the wagon.

As her head swam and her ears buzzed, Faith heard a voice speak to her.

"Miss?"

Her eyelids drooped lower.

"...Miss...?"

She fell backwards as her vision went black. She didn't hit the ground – she knew that much – but before she could become aware of anything else, darkness closed in on her.

****

The voice was gentle.

Even before she could understand the words, Faith could sense the kindness in the voice, a woman's. She couldn't yet open her eyes, but as she pushed through layers of unconsciousness, she started to understand what was being said.

"...Miss...miss...can you hear me...?"

It took all of the effort Faith could muster to pry her eyelids open. A face came into focus, an expression as gentle as the voice it belonged to. Dark hair was braided smartly on either side of the woman's face, a sharp contrast to her dirty and blood-spattered apron.

"I'm Nurse Clara," the woman said, pressing a warm cloth to Faith's forehead. "What is your name?"

Faith opened her mouth and tried to speak, but no sound came out. Her throat was parched. Nurse Clara motioned for another nurse nearby to bring a cup of water. She held Faith's head up as she helped her drink. Relieved, Faith laid her head back down on a soft pillow. She took a moment to glance around, taking in the sights, sounds, and smells.

She was in a large white tent. Her senses were still fuzzy but she could make out the clatter of tools and bedpans, the din of urgent voices, and the groans and wails of pain and despair.

With a cry, she sat up in the bed, pressing her hand to her stomach. Nurse Clara tried to ease her back down.

"The baby is fine. I heard a strong heartbeat. Please, lie back."

307

Faith obeyed.

"Thank you," she croaked, licking her lips. "My name is Faith Shelton."

Nurse Clara motioned to the nurse at her side to write it down.

"Mrs. Shelton, do you know where you are?"

"Johnstown. There was a flood."

"That's right."

Nurse Clara leaned forward and held Faith's eyelids open, squinting as she stared into each eye in turn. Faith wasn't sure what she was looking for but she didn't resist.

Apparently satisfied, Nurse Clara clasped Faith's hands in hers.

"You're going to be fine, Mrs. Shelton. But you'll need to stay off your feet for a little while and get your strength up, as much for your baby's health as for your own. A nurse will be bringing food around shortly."

"Please!" Faith cried out as Nurse Clara rose to go.

"Yes?"

"Have you seen my husband? Is he looking for me?"

"Who is your husband?"

"Mr. Shelton. Allan Shelton."

Nurse Clara exchanged glances with the nurse by her side.

"I'm sorry, Mrs. Shelton. I haven't come across anyone by that name. But I will have one of my nurses check the names posted outside the depot."

"Names?"

"Yes. Those who are still with us, and those who have passed on and have been identified. Unfortunately, it's going to be a long time before that list is complete."

"No, you don't understand...My husband wasn't in Johnstown. He was supposed to come on the train the day after the flood."

"Mrs. Shelton, the tracks were washed out and the trains are just now starting to arrive in town. It might take your husband a little while to get here, but he will get here."

Tears trickled down Faith's cheeks. "Thank you," she whispered.

Nurse Clara touched her head for a moment and then left to attend to other patients.

Precious hopped up on the bed and Faith brightened.

"I was wondering where you were!" she exclaimed, giving the cat a squeeze. She looked around and wrinkled her nose at all of the sights and smells that accompany a field hospital. Better not to let Precious roam around, licking who knows what off the ground...

Faith lay back down on the pillow, one hand petting the cat, the other on her belly.

Where is your father?

Chapter Twenty

FAITH WAS ABOUT READY to jump out of her skin.

She had been a resident of the makeshift hospital for two days now, and she didn't know how much longer she could stand it. Despite being surrounded by people, she felt very lonely. Mrs. Walscott hadn't stopped by to see her yet. She did have one joyful moment when she caught a glimpse of a familiar face across the tent. It was the boy she had saved from the waters and hoisted into her tree. The last time she had seen him, he was drifting away on a broken piece of wood. At least he was alive, and even though she only saw him for a moment as he was being herded along with several other children – probably all orphans – she thanked God that she had been a part of that miracle.

Nurse Clara would come to her bedside twice a day, as she did with all of her patients. She would take Faith's temperature and check her vital signs and listen to the baby's heartbeat through a stethoscope. Faith would protest that she felt fine, but Nurse Clara would have none of it.

"You've gone through a tremendous trauma," she explained. "We don't know what that experience has done to the baby. Nothing is wrong, as far as I can tell, but we don't want to upset him or her any further."

"But aren't there others who could use this bed? Could I go to more normal accommodations?"

"It's not an issue of room or funds," Nurse Clara said. "The Red Cross has some very generous backers, including some gentlemen whose names I've heard mumbled disagreeably as being at least partially responsible for this tragedy."

Faith frowned. "Who do you mean?"

Nurse Clara looked around and lowered her voice. "Many folks blame the patrons of the South Fork Fishing and Hunting Club. But that's none of my concern. My sole task is making whole what was broken."

"But I don't feel broken. I need to be up and about so that I can find my husband."

"If your husband comes looking for you, he will come here first, and I want him to find you and your baby resting quietly."

Faith swallowed hard and nodded her head. She looked down at Precious, who had been graciously allowed to stay as long as it didn't wander around.

A somber moment passed and Nurse Clara gave her hand a comforting squeeze.

"Be strong, my dear."

"Thank you," Faith said.

Nurse Clara got up from her bedside and Faith laid her head down on the pillow. She stared up at the dirty canvas that stretched overhead and found herself wishing she could see the sky. Her only glimpses would come when she would go to the privy, and she had to ask permission each time. The stench of death lingered in the air, and she could feel her resolve wilting with each passing hour.

I don't care what she says... Tomorrow, I'm leaving.

Precious meowed at her side, seconding her unspoken plot. Faith smiled and stroked its fur.

"Let's be good for one more day," she said. "Rest sounds like a good idea right now."

She rolled over, trying in vain to get comfortable. The baby gave a kick inside her belly, unhappy about being tumbled about. A pang of fear struck Faith's heart.

Maybe Nurse Clara was right. What if the child is born deranged? He must sense the horrors of what we went through. What if he is bitter and hateful?

A quiet voice whispered inside her heart.

Tomorrow will take care of itself. One day at a time. And you are never alone.

An inexplicable peace warmed her heart and she drifted off to sleep.

313

****

A gentle hand stroked her cheek.

Faith slowly opened her eyes. Allan smiled down at her.

"Good morning, darling."

Faith smiled back.

"Good morning, husband."

Allan leaned down and pressed a soft kiss to her lips. Warmth flooded Faith's body and she felt like she was melting into the soft satin bedsheets. Stirrings of desire for this wonderful, loving man gripped her senses and she wrapped her arms around his neck, drawing him closer.

A quiet cooing sound next to her interrupted their passion. Faith looked over at the cherub-cheeked infant wriggling and gurgling on the bed next to her. Allan carefully lifted the baby, his face beaming with pride.

"I think little Allan is hungry."

He laid the baby on Faith's bosom. She looked up at him with a coy smile and drew down the neckline of her nightdress so that the baby could nurse. Allan smiled back and watched with sparkling eyes.

Then little Allan sputtered. His face turned red and he started to cry. Faith tried to hush the baby but his sobs turned to shrieks. Allan recoiled from the bedside as if Faith was suddenly repulsive.

"Make him stop!" he demanded.

"I'm trying!" Faith snapped, trying to get the baby to latch on again. The infant wailed furiously, lashing out with tiny fists.

Something pressed on Faith's stomach. Faith looked down and stared into the blazing eyes of her cat, Precious. The animal opened its mouth, brandishing incredibly sharp teeth, and lunged for Faith's throat.

"No!"

Faith bolted up in the bed, startling the nurse at her side.

"Miss! Are you all right?"

Faith's chest heaved with panicked breaths and her clothes were soaked with sweat.

It was a dream, she told herself. *It was just a dream.*

She took a few gulps of air and nodded her head.

"Yes...I'm fine."

The nurse didn't look convinced. She pressed her hand to Faith's forehead and clicked her tongue.

"You might be feverish," she said. "I'll fetch someone to take your temperature. Can't have an outbreak of typhoid or any such thing."

Faith's eyes widened. "Typhoid?"

The nurse was already out of earshot, hurrying through the clutter of beds and bodies. Faith wanted to lie back down but the thought of settling onto the sweat-soaked sheets made her cringe. Maybe it would be good for her circulation to sit up for a bit...

A hand grabbed her arm. The nurse had returned and was staring at her with wild eyes. Fear gripped Faith's heart.

Oh no, I've got typhoid!

"Your name is Shelton, right?" the nurse asked. "Mrs. Shelton?"

"Yes," she answered cautiously.

The nurse looked like she was about to hyperventilate. "There is a man named Mr. Shelton outside!"

Faith sprang to her feet.

"Where is..."

Her head swam and she collapsed into the nurse's arms.

"Easy there," the nurse said, helping her back into the bed, but Faith pushed her away.

"I have to go out there," she cried, feeling fresh energy flood her limbs. "Help me, please!"

The nurse looked around as if searching for confirmation, then she slipped her arm around Faith's rib cage and held her steady while she found her feet. Faith had done hardly any walking since she had become a resident of the medical tent and she was frustrated that her feet weren't responding as quickly as she wanted them to.

After several agonizing minutes of pushing their way through the crush of people, Faith and the nurse emerged into the daylight. A number of people milled about, some with purpose, others aimlessly. The sounds of shouting and hammers striking nails and saws cutting wood filled the air and several wooden frames were visible above the piles of wreckage. But Faith was only looking for one man, and she didn't see him.

"Where is he?" she groaned, scanning as many faces as she could. She turned to the nurse. "Did you see him?"

The nurse shook her head. "We have runners who go back and forth between tents and the depot. A young man told me that someone named Shelton was here and was looking for Faith Shelton. He ran off before I could ask him anything more."

Faith grit her teeth and stood up as straight as she could. Days of laying in bed had weakened her muscles and she felt like the baby in her belly had doubled in size, but she drew herself to her full height and scanned the faces that surrounded her.

"He's here...he's got to be here!"

The nurse placed a firm hand on her arm. "I'll find him, Mrs. Shelton. You need to go back inside and lie down. He won't be going anywhere."

Faith took a few deep breaths to calm her shredded nerves and nodded. "Okay. Please, find him!"

"I give you my word. Now come."

By the time Faith reached the bed, she was on the verge of fainting. At the same time, she wanted to leap for joy.

Allan was here!

The nurse helped her lie down and promised once more to find her husband. It was hard feeling so helpless but Faith knew the nurse was right. She had to think of the baby.

There was only one thing left to do.

Pray.

She closed her eyes and whispered, "Dear Lord, great and merciful God, please bring my Allan back to me. Bring him back to me..."

****

"He's here."

The words were tinny and distant. Faith couldn't see anything. It took her a moment to realize she had fallen asleep.

"What?" she mumbled, straining to push through the fog in her head.

"He's here. Mr. Shelton."

Clarity seized Faith's mind. Her eyes snapped open and she sprang up in her bed.

Mr. Shelton, her father-in-law, stood at her bedside, a startled expression on his face.

Faith's joy wilted, though not completely.

"Oh...hello...Father."

The nurse next to him frowned. "'Father'?"

Faith swallowed hard and managed a smile. "Yes. He's my father-in-law."

Mr. Shelton stifled a cough. He took out a handkerchief and dabbed his sweating brow.

"How are you, dear child?" he said, his voice heavy with concern. "It's a miracle to find you here."

"Yes...a miracle."

Faith reached out and took his hand. Their eyes met for a moment and a mutual feeling of disappointment passed between them.

Mr. Shelton cleared his throat and looked around at nothing in particular. "Is...is Allan here somewhere?"

Faith's eyes fell and she stroked Precious, who had settled in her lap.

"Not to my knowledge," she answered quietly.

"Was he with you when the flood struck?"

She shook her head. "He was due back the day after the flood. He wasn't with you?"

"No, he left a day early."

Faith's blood turned to ice in her veins.

"He left a day early? When? What train?"

Mr. Shelton's face was as pale as a sheet. His voice was barely a whisper.

"The two o'clock train."

Faith felt like she couldn't breathe. Mr. Shelton turned to the nurse at his side.

"What happened to the two o'clock train?" he demanded.

"I don't know, sir," the nurse answered. "Many trains were overcome by the water."

Mr. Shelton seized the frightened woman by the shoulders. "My son was on that train! How can you just stand there and say, 'I don't know'?"

The nurse wriggled out of Mr. Shelton's grasp.

"I don't know, *sir*. I can say nothing more. Right now, my priority is taking care of this young lady and her child."

Mr. Shelton turned around and looked down at Faith's belly.

"The child. Is it...all right?"

Faith nodded, still struggling to fill her lungs with air. "Yes. He's fine."

Mr. Shelton's lip quivered and he cleared his throat.

"Very good. Glad to hear it. I thank you, miss," he said to the nurse, "for taking care of my daughter-in-law and her child."

The nurse gave a curt nod. "They both need to rest. You can give your information to the orderly outside and he will make sure you stay informed."

"Please...can I have just a moment more?"

"One moment," she said and then left to tend to other patients.

Mr. Shelton cleared his throat again and sat down on the edge of the bed. The frame creaked and groaned but didn't collapse as Faith feared it might. She looked at her father-in-law through shimmering eyes.

"Is Allan..?"

An awful moment of realization hung in the air. Mr. Shelton

stared at the ground, his gaze unfocused.

"I don't know," he said in a small voice.

Faith reached out and took his hand.

"What do we do?"

Mr. Shelton shook his head and exhaled a weary breath.

"I don't know, child." He dabbed his eyes and sat up straight. "But you must rest, and I must seek out accommodation. I shall try to visit again in a couple of days. I have to evaluate the damage at the iron works, and I fear that many of my colleagues have also met an untimely end."

"And you will look for Allan, won't you? Perhaps he's still alive. Perhaps his train escaped the flood."

Mr. Shelton rose to his feet and placed his hat on his head. His eyes avoided meeting hers.

"I will do everything I can to find him."

Without another word, he turned and left the tent.

Chapter Twenty-One

TIME SLOWED TO a crawl. As day faded into night, hopelessness grew deeper and darker in Faith's heart.

If Allan were alive, she told herself, *he would have been here by now.*

Sometimes she would seethe with sudden anger, fuming at Allan, at herself, at Mr. Shelton, at God. Why had he decided to come back a day early? Was she so frail and needy to make him think that he had to hurry back to her bedside? Why didn't his father talk some sense into him and keep him in Pittsburgh as originally planned?

And how could God let this atrocity happen in the first place?

She would wait for a still small voice to whisper the answers from the depths of her heart. There was only silence. A tattered Bible lay next to her bedside but she hardly looked at it. She didn't know what would soothe her restless soul, but she was about ready to jump out of her skin.

Nurse Clara insisted that she remain in bed as much as possible.

She was permitted to get up and walk around for a couple of hours a day, and she yearned for those moments to get out into the fresh air. The weather was remarkably pleasant and it seemed almost impossible that torrential rains had caused a catastrophic flood only a week ago.

Mr. Shelton stopped by two days after his first visit. His stay was short, and Faith got the impression that he felt guilty about having no news of Allan. Their shared grief was a bond but also a barrier between them.

So it was much to her surprise when he came back to the hospital tent the next day. As the sun was going down, he made his way to her bedside and removed his hat.

"I think it's time to go home, young lady," he announced.

"Go home? You mean, to Pittsburgh?"

Mr. Shelton nodded. "This is no place for you to stay. You are likely to catch a fatal infection here among all these invalids."

A passing nurse gave him a stern glare but he turned up his nose.

"And most importantly," he added, "you are a Shelton, and you carry a Shelton. And that child will not be born in a field hospital."

Faith drew in a nervous breath. She was anxious to get out of here, but she knew that if she left, she would never come back, and that meant giving up Allan for good.

He is gone. Don't lose your child or your own life hoping for a miracle that will never come.

"Nurse Barton will have to approve it," she said.

"I don't need her permission to look after my own flesh and blood."

"Oh yes, you do."

Mr. Shelton spun around. Nurse Clara gazed at him with steely eyes.

"This young woman is under my care," she continued, "and she shall remain under my care until I decide she is healthy enough to be released."

Mr. Shelton gestured broadly. "No offense, miss – "

"Nurse."

"My apologies, *nurse*. But look around...this is no place for a woman who is with child!"

"I agree. But it is all we have at the moment while the hospital is being constructed."

"There are plenty of good hospitals just a few hours' train ride away."

Nurse Clara pursed her lips and looked Mr. Shelton right in the eyes.

"I am aware of this, sir, and I would love to send my patients to better accommodations. Soon we shall have the logistics to do so. But as it stands, we have neither the resources nor the capabilities to safely transport our patients, especially those in a delicate situation like this young woman here. Now," she added quickly as Mr. Shelton's temper was visibly staring to flare, "I am pleased with how she is regaining her strength, and I reckon that in a week's time, she will be able to be discharged to another hospital. But until that time, she remains under my watch."

Faith watched her father-in-law simmer for a moment, and then his shoulders slumped.

"That'll be all right, I suppose. One more week couldn't hurt."

"As long as she continues to get stronger. We have the health of two people to consider here."

"I know, I know..."

Mr. Shelton looked down at Faith and offered a defeated smile.

"I have to go back to Pittsburgh tomorrow, which is why I was hoping you could come with me. But if the nurse here insists that you remain, I am afraid I must return without you. The telegraph is working again and I will ask to be notified when you are healthy enough to make the trip, and I can come fetch you."

Faith's eyes met Nurse Clara's for a moment, and she nodded slowly.

"I'm in good hands, Father. We'll be all right."

Mr. Shelton looked uneasy for a moment. He reached out his hand and touched her shoulder.

"God bless you, child."

He turned and hurried out of the tent. Nurse Clara looked down at Faith and took her hands.

"You are one of the lucky ones. Many people here have lost all of the family they have. Plus your father-in-law seems to be a man of means."

"Yes." Faith felt like her own voice was distant to her ears. "I am lucky."

****

From the moment she awoke the next morning, Faith felt a knot twisting in her stomach. Nothing with the baby; just a pang of anxiety that wouldn't go away, no matter how much she tried to console herself. The tent hospital was bustling as usual, though it seemed that Faith's neighbor had passed in the night. The bed was empty, the cot stained with sweat and flecks of blood.

Maybe I should try to escape with Father, Faith wondered. *There's no lawful reason why I must stay here, and if I leave, they wouldn't arrest me or anything.*

Then she caught a glimpse of Nurse Clara's stern countenance as she quarreled with an army doctor about the best way to treat a patient, and she thought it best not to tempt fate.

She went about her morning activity, getting breakfast, taking a walk to get some fresh air. It seemed that every time she stepped out of the confines of the tent, Johnstown was blossoming back to life more and more. The smell of death and water rot was replaced by the aroma of freshly hewn pine lumber and boiling tar and wood smoke and cook pots. Soldiers and militia patrolled the streets, having largely stamped out the epidemic of looting and pillaging. Faith watched some women tend to a large group of children in the shelter of a newly-erected timber frame building. She searched the faces for the boy he had saved but he wasn't among them.

And then there were the continual shrieks of train whistles and bells and the *clank clank* of locomotive machinery coming from the nearby depot. Each train would stop and gush out a stream of volunteers, journalists, entrepreneurs, soldiers, and sightseers. Faith even had her picture taken by a photographer at the tent hospital. The phosphorus flash had made her squint and shield her eyes, and the photographer had hurried off before she could ask him how the photograph might turn out. She only hoped that the image had time to set before she had made her startled face.

There wasn't a clock in the medical tent but Faith had learned to get a fairly accurate sense of time by the routine of people around her. According to her knowledge of the train schedules, Mr. Shelton's train would depart around 4 o'clock, and she found herself feeling fidgety as the time drew closer.

I don't want to be here alone, she finally admitted to herself. Even it meant living with her stone-hearted father-in-law.

She flinched when a nurse touched her arm.

"Begging your pardon, Miss Faith," the nurse said with a bow. "Mr. Shelton is here."

Faith's heart began to race. Should she ask to go with him? What if he refused? Should she –

"Hello, my dear."

She was startled to see Mr. Shelton standing before her, as if he had materialized out of thin air.

"H-hello, Father," she said, holding her cat close.

Mr. Shelton cleared his throat and looked at the nurse hovering around him.

"I'm going to leave now. Train to catch. But I will be back for you and, uh, the child, quite soon. Plus I hear they are building a new hospital across the road there, so you can get out of this ghastly tent."

He gave the nurse another leer before adding, "I have deposited some funds to the hospital on your behalf, which should get you some better care and accommodations."

Faith didn't realize how tightly she was gripping Precious until the animal growled and ran out of her arms.

"Father..." she said, suddenly feeling short of breath. She glanced to her right and saw Nurse Clara tending to another patient. Faith then looked up at her father-in-law and sat up straight.

"Father," she repeated, her voice stronger this time.

A train whistle blew. Mr. Shelton heaved a sigh and took out his pocketwatch.

"Out with it, child. I have a train to catch."

Faith's words hung on the tip of her tongue for a moment and

329

then she swallowed them back. She reached out for his hand.

"Please be careful. You are all the family I have now."

Mr. Shelton gave her an uncomfortable smile and pulled his hand back.

"Yes, I suppose that is our situation now. Well, I must be off. Take care, my dear. Look after the little one."

He practically sprinted away when the train whistle blew again. Faith looked down at Precious crouched on the ground. She opened her arms and after a moment's hesitation, the cat jumped back into her lap and nuzzled against her belly.

"Maybe we should go to California..." she mumbled.

Nurse Clara appeared at her side. Faith noticed her odd expression.

"Is everything all right?" she asked.

Nurse Clara took a moment to compose herself.

"Miss Faith, Mr. Shelton is here."

"Yes, I know. He just left. He had to catch his train."

"No." Nurse Clara gripped her shoulders with both hands. "Mr. Shelton, your husband."

Faith blinked. Then she blinked again.

"My...my *husband?*"

"Yes!" Nurse Clara beamed. "He's alive! He's here!"

Faith clung to the nurse like she was drowning.

"Please do not toy with me," she whimpered.

"I wouldn't dream of it," Nurse Clara snapped. "Now pull yourself together and let's go see him."

Faith leaned on her for support as she gathered up Precious with her other arm and the two women pushed their way through the crowded tent. Just over the heads of the doctors and nurses and patients, Faith spotted her father-in-law's top hat several yards ahead. She grabbed a passing orderly's arm.

"Do you see that large man?"

The orderly craned his neck and nodded.

"Bring him back here," Faith said.

"Yes'm," the orderly replied and rushed off.

Faith looked at Nurse Clara.

"Which way?"

Nurse Clara pointed to her right and they made their way to a side exit. Faith couldn't remember the tent ever being this crowded. She felt a heaviness pressing against her chest, squeezing the air from her lungs. Even the hard-packed dirt floor seemed soft and muddy, and each footstep took tremendous effort. Precious hissed and the baby kicked. Faith yelped, doubling over with pain, but Nurse Clara kept a strong grip on her shoulders and practically propelled her through the tent flap out into the bright sunshine.

Faith raised her hand to shield her eyes.

Then a voice spoke.

"Hello, my darling."

She turned and her vision came into focus. A man sat in a rickety wheelchair. His right arm was in a sling and he was missing both legs below the knee.

And he had the most beautiful eyes she had ever seen.

"Allan!" she cried, dropping the cat and flinging herself onto him. Luckily there was an orderly behind the wheelchair to hold it steady or else the two of them would have tumbled to the ground.

Tears poured down Faith's cheeks as she kissed his face, moved back to look at him, and then kissed him again.

"You're alive! Oh thank the Lord, you're alive!"

"My dear Faith," Allan wept, embracing her with his good arm. "I'm so sorry. I should never have left you."

"It's all right," Faith said with a trembling voice. "None of that matters. I can't believe you're alive!"

Allan smiled at her, his face just as wet as hers. His hand reached down to touch her bulging belly.

Faith smiled back. "He's healthy and strong."

Allan burst into sobs, hiding his face as his shoulders trembled. Faith wrapped her arms around him and held him close. She looked over at Nurse Clara, who wiped away tears of her own.

Faith closed her eyes and turned her face towards heaven.

"Thank You, God. Thank You for bringing my husband back to me."

"Allan!"

Mr. Shelton's voice boomed like a cannon and Faith watched her portly father-in-law come running down the road. Faith was afraid he would crash into them but he drew to a halt just in front of the wheelchair.

Allan looked up at him with shimmering eyes.

"Father..."

Now it was Mr. Shelton's turn to weep.

"My boy!"

He leaned down and embraced his son, wailing powerful sobs. He pulled Faith into the embrace and the three of them laughed and cried together. After a few minutes, they came up for air and looked at one another with beaming smiles and tear-streaked faces.

"It's a miracle," Mr. Shelton exclaimed, shaking his head in disbelief. Then he put on an exaggerated frown. "Where on earth have you been?"

Allan gestured to his amputated legs. "That's quite a long story, Father. And I'm afraid that not all of me made it back."

He looked up at Faith with pleading eyes. She saw the question in them: *Could you still love me like this?*

She knelt down to look right at him.

"You did make it back. God bless us, you did make it back. But I have to agree with your father: where have you been?"

Allan shrugged innocently. "Oh, you know, here and there."

Faith gave him a stern look paired with an amused smile.

"Look here, mister, I could have you wheeled right back where you came from."

Allan laughed. "I'll tell you everything I remember. But first, I'm dying for a taste of whiskey."

Mr. Shelton started to reach inside his coat but Nurse Clara placed a firm hand on his arm.

"Tea," she declared, fixing Allan with her eyes. "Tea would be in order."

Allan exhaled and shrugged again. "Tea would be wonderful."

Chapter Twenty-Two

FAITH ABSENTLY STROKED Precious as she lay on her side. It was the only comfortable position for her, especially since the baby had decided to kick twice as hard and twice as often. She figured it was because the child knew his father had returned to them.

Nurse Clara had arranged for Allan to sleep in a fresh cot next to hers, which the orderlies were setting up now. Mr. Shelton was indignant that his son would spend the night in such a place but Nurse Clara was adamant that she wanted to keep him for observation for at least one night. Mr. Shelton countered that one night was all he would allow and declared that he was taking his family back to Pittsburgh the next day. Faith was ready to leave this place, especially since her family was back together again.

Her eyes came to rest on the bandaged stumps of Allan's legs as two orderlies hoisted him out of his chair and laid him on the cot, facing away from her. She suddenly realized how dependent he was now. Thank the Lord her husband was alive and by her side, but everything was going to be different...

A tear fell from her eye as she watched the orderlies pull the blanket over him and tuck it underneath his shoulder like he was a child. The man who had taken her in to his home and into his family, the man who had been so strong and indomitable in her adoring eyes, now looked small and frail, helpless to even get in and out of bed.

Why didn't he turn around to look at her?

Then she saw why. His shoulders trembled and she heard a faint whimper, quickly stifled.

He needs you.

Faith eased Precious to the side and climbed out of her bed. She walked around to the other side of Allan's cot and knelt down, stroking his sweaty hair. He couldn't bring himself to look at her but he reached out and grasped her hand with desperate strength.

"Please," he sobbed into his pillow. "Don't leave me."

"I would never leave you," Faith whispered, unable to hold back her own tears. She kissed his hand and rested her head on the cot. "Do you hear me? I will never, ever leave you."

Allan sniffled and managed a faltering smile. "I don't know what kind of man I can be for you. What kind of husband...what kind of father."

"Your legs are gone, but not your heart. Not your soul, not who you are inside. We are a family. Nothing can change that."

Allan wiped his eyes. He reached down to feel the baby move.

"He gets his strong legs from his father," he quipped.

Faith snorted a sharp laugh and she covered her mouth with embarrassment. She looked into his eyes and leaned forward to kiss him.

"I love you, Allan Shelton."

"And I love you, Faith Shelton."

She laid her head on his hands and searched his eyes. "What happened?"

Allan was silent for several moments. Then he drew in a shaky breath.

"I remember seeing the water in the valley. It was moving alongside the train, like it was trying to keep pace with it. I could only think of you and pray to God that you weren't at home, or that you were up in the hills somewhere. I didn't really think about my own safety, because I didn't realize the danger. Not until the train turned towards the waves. And I knew that I was going to die. I can't say what I felt at that moment, because I didn't really have time to process what was happening. It wasn't fear or acceptance or denial. It was just...a fact. I was going to die. And the water hit the car, I fell back, and I don't remember anything else."

"How on earth did you survive?"

"I don't know. It is truly a miracle."

"Well, who found you? Where did they find you?"

"I don't know that, either. I just woke up in a hospital tent days later without my legs. No one told me what had happened or how I'd gotten there."

"Did the doctors tell you why they had to cut off your legs?"

Allan paused for a moment before whispering, "My legs were already gone when they brought me in."

Faith gasped. "Oh my goodness..."

"The doctors told me that I shouldn't have come in alive in the first place, and they had to amputate further to to remove the mangled flesh and bone. They were shocked that I pulled through."

"Were you clear-headed during this time? Did you know where you were?"

"They kept me full of morphine for several days. I barely remember anything; it's all hazy and dim. Sometimes I would wake up in searing pain and someone would come and prick me with a needle and I would fade away again. I couldn't tell you how long that went on."

"They didn't ask you your name or where your home was?"

"Perhaps they did but I had no recollection. I don't even remember when I was clear-headed enough to finally tell them who I was. I just remember a doctor sitting on my bed with a very serious look on his face. 'Are you Allan Shelton, Jr.?' he asked. It seemed like years since I had heard my name. I remember crying and saying yes, I was Allan Shelton, Jr. I never thought to ask how he knew my name; I was just so happy to hear someone say it.

"And then everything rushed back into my mind. The train, the flood, the terror... I told them about you, about my father, about Johnstown. When they told me that Johnstown had been destroyed, I felt hopeless. I tried to get out of bed, to somehow run to you, but I fell on the ground. The pain knocked me out again. When I came to, I felt such sadness. Thinking that I had lost you, and losing my ability to walk...I am ashamed to admit this, but if there had been a knife or a scalpel within arm's reach, I would have cut my own throat right then and there."

"Oh, Allan." Faith cradled his head, running her fingers gently along his neck.

Allan took a few ragged breaths and nodded that he was okay.

"For a few days," he continued, "I languished in that dark place. I thought, 'What kind of life awaits me now?' I knew that my father still lived and I had a home to go back to in Pittsburgh, but the thought of him seeing me like this crushed me with shame. Even now, I fear what he truly thinks of me."

"Shhh...hush talk like that. You are still the man you were before all of this."

His eyes shimmered.

"Am I, though? I fear you are just trying to comfort me."

"I am trying to comfort you, but with words of truth. You are my husband, for better or worse. And I know you don't put much stock in religion, but I have been doing a lot of praying these past days.

Despite the horrors and tragedies, the Lord shows His mercy in the most unexpected ways. When we have lost everything, we must look to Him, because He was there all along."

Allan touched her cheek. "You know, I did some praying myself. And I'm starting to think there might be someone watching over us after all."

Faith leaned in and kissed him.

"I am sure of it, Allan Shelton, Jr. You are living proof."

****

A gentle hand shook Faith awake. She rubbed her eyes and looked up to see Nurse Clara smiling down at her.

"Mrs. Shelton, it's time to go home."

Faith drowsily worked the stale saliva in her mouth, then she bolted upright.

"Where is my husband?" she cried, staring at his empty bed.

"Right here, darling."

She turned and saw him in his wheelchair, crouching over a basin of water and running a razor down his lathered face. He looked much stronger than he had last night.

"My apologies," she murmured to the nurse.

"No need, dear. We all get a fright now and then."

Faith stretched her aching back. Nurse Clara placed her hand on her stomach and fixed her with her eyes.

"Take care of the menfolk in your life," she commanded. "They'll need your strength."

Faith was at a loss for words for a moment. "I-I'll try," she stammered.

"I know you'll do more than try."

Faith looked over the nurse's shoulder and saw Mr. Shelton standing off to one side, hat in hand. The nurse noticed him and gave a polite nod.

"They are in your care, sir."

Mr. Shelton returned the nod. "Thank you, nurse. Truly."

Nurse Clara gave Faith a knowing wink and went off to tend to other patients. Allan washed the last bits of lather from his face and looked up at his father.

"You didn't have to come back out here, Father. We could have met you at the depot."

Mr. Shelton took a hesitant step forward.

"You're right, we could have arranged that. But you're my son."

Nothing more needed to be said. Mr. Shelton lowered his eyes as a tear trickled down his cheek. Faith looked over at her husband and saw his eyes glisten as well. She touched her belly as Nurse Clara's words echoed in her mind.

"Take care of your menfolk. They'll need your strength."

She rose to her feet, fighting off the brief spell of dizziness that threatened to topple her balance.

"I don't want anymore blubbering from you fellows," she said with exaggerated sternness. "We are all going to walk out of her with our heads held high."

Mr. Shelton wiped his eyes and slapped his hat back on his head.

"My sentiments exactly. We are Sheltons," he said as he nodded towards Faith, "and Sheltons persevere no matter the odds."

Allan grunted as he struggled to turn his chair around. "I will persevere as soon as I can unlock these blasted wheels."

His father chuckled and went over to help him. Faith summoned a nurse's assistant to help her to the privy and changing area. She came back with her hair brushed and wearing fresh clothes, and when she saw elder and younger Shelton side by side, a prayer arose in her heart.

Thank You for Your mercy, O Lord. I still fear this is a dream, because I cannot believe how lucky I am. Let me never forget Your goodness and Your grace, and keep my faith strong, for the menfolk and for myself.

"I don't know about you two," she said with a grin, "but I could do with a change of scenery."

Allan nodded his agreement. "The dirty skies of Pittsburgh will be a welcome change after staring up at a white canvas tent for days and days."

"You've had it easy," Mr. Shelton snorted. "I couldn't stay another day in that ramshackle hovel they call an inn. The cockroaches were the size of mice!"

"No different than Pittsburgh," Allan replied with a shrug.

Mr. Shelton tried to hold a straight face but he couldn't keep from cracking a smile.

"I suppose you're right, son. Well, let's get a move on. Don't want to keep the mice waiting!"

It took a bit of logistical creativity to get all three of them with Allan's wheelchair and Mr. Shelton's luggage to the train station. After summoning a carriage, Mr. Shelton and the driver had to hoist Allan up into his seat. Faith saw the look of embarrassment on his face, having to be picked up and carried like a child. And she had to silence the faint but nagging voice in her head that complained about how difficult life would be from now on. She retorted with the affirmation that God in His mercy had brought her husband back to him, and she wasn't going to waste that miracle by running away, not when he needed her most.

As the carriage jostled down the street, Faith reached out and took Allan's hand and gave it a squeeze. No words were said as they looked into each other's eyes. That simple touch said everything.

Mr. Shelton dispelled the gentle moment with a loud snort.

"By the devil's beard! There's a boiler from the iron works in the middle of that church."

Faith didn't look. She kept her eyes on Allan. She had seen enough destruction and death to last her an eternity. Her attention was on the man in front of her and the child in her womb. And most importantly, on the God that had brought all three of them together.

I promise, no matter what floods may come again, I will never lose faith.

THE END

A WORD FROM MICHAEL

I hope you liked this book. It was fun to write and there are more on the way. I would greatly appreciate it if you would leave a review on Amazon, Goodreads, social media, and anywhere you might tell everyone how you felt about *Faith in the Floodwaters.* And if you want to let me know what you thought or just want to say "Howdy," you can send me an email at michaelwinstellbooks@gmail.com and I'll get back to you lickety-split.

God bless and happy reading!

AVAILABLE NOW!

HE CALLS ME BY NAME

The Complete Series

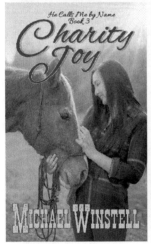
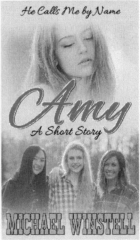

AVAILABLE NOW

DESTINY IN THE DUST STORMS

My Name Will Never Fade, Book 1

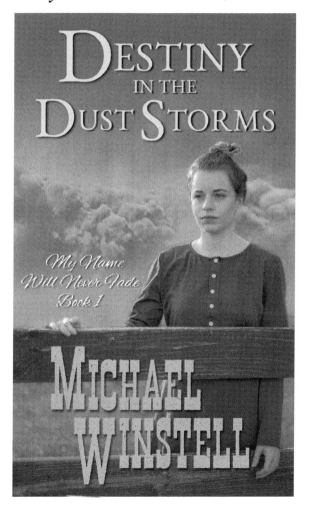

MICHAEL WINSTELL lives in north Georgia.

You can find him online at:

www.michaelwinstell.com

www.facebook.com/michaelwinstell